Michael Denneny, General Editor

Stonewall Inn Editions

ALSO BY LARRY DUPLECHAN:

Eight Days a Week
Blackbird
Tangled Up in Blue

a novel by
**LARRY
DUPLECHAN**

St. Martin's Press

NEW YORK

TANGLED UP IN BLUE. Copyright © 1989 by Larry Duplechan. All rights reserved. Printed in the United States of America. No part of this book may be used or reproduced in any manner whatsoever without written permission except in the case of brief quotations embodied in critical articles or reviews. For information, address St. Martin's Press, 175 Fifth Avenue, New York, N.Y. 10010.

Library of Congress Cataloging-in-Publication Data

Duplechan, Larry.
    Tangled up in blue / Larry Duplechan.
       p.   cm. — (Stonewall Inn editions ;)
    ISBN 0-312-05167-0
    I. Title. II. Series.
PS3554.U55T36   1990
813'.54—dc20   90-37342
                                                   CIP

First Paperback Edition: November 1990
10 9 8 7 6 5 4 3 2 1

For Sweet Genevieve

Sincere thanks to Michael
Denneny, Allen Esrock, Laura
Halliday, Wef Fleischman, Chris
Myers, and Isabel Loriente
Jungwirth for their help and
advice concerning this book.

MAGGIE SULLIVAN WAS NOT A well woman. She clutched the rim of the bowl with both hands and hung on tight, eyes squeezed shut, like a little girl on a roller coaster. A voice in her head said Oh no oh no oh no oh no, and she sucked in two or three quick, anxious breaths, punctuated by a just audible "no—no—no" like some desperate mantra.

Her eyes widened suddenly, and she gasped aloud, as if she'd been goosed; then bowed low from her already prayer-like position and unquestioningly relinquished her breakfast.

"Jesus," Maggie whispered as she pulled the handle down, before falling back against the vanity cabinets, limp as an old Raggedy Ann doll, and feeling as if she'd just run a four-minute mile. She tugged a length of Aurora tissue off the roller and blotted her sweat-beaded lips and forehead. The powdery sweet floral scent of the tissue made her stomach lurch. She touched one knee gingerly, winced, sucked in a breath through her teeth. Both knees were rosy and sore from the flying knee-drop she'd recently performed in front of the toilet. Within a few hours, she was certain, the black-and-blue effect was going to be something to behold.

"Jesus H. Tapdancing Christ," she said.

Maggie Sullivan almost never took the name of the Lord in vain. Not that she considered herself particularly religious—

she did not; still, except for a few months of knee-jerk rebellion her first semester of college, Maggie had simply never been much of a swearer. The chances were better than good that she'd picked up "Jesus H. Tapdancing Christ" from Crockett, who prided himself on his gift for creative profanity, and who'd once informed Maggie that she just wasn't the "swearing type." "Darling," he'd said, "when you say 'Shit' you might as well be saying 'More pancakes, anybody?' Which was just as well, since Maggie Sullivan almost never swore.

Then again, Maggie Sullivan almost never threw up.

Maggie attempted to rise from the floor, but her knees overruled her, and she sat down hard against the cold tile. She drew her legs up to her chest, resting her chin gently on those all-too-tender knees. What, she wondered, what on earth might she have eaten that had declared open season on her digestive tract? Certainly not her usual nonfat strawberry yogurt and toasted whole-wheat English muffin breakfast—the yogurt had looked and tasted fine. Last night's dinner maybe? Granted, Maggie was no Julia Child, but she refused to believe that even her first attempt at fettuccine primavera could have been poisonous. Daniel had polished off his portion of pasta (and part of Maggie's), plus three glasses of sauvignon blanc. Was he doubled over in a sixteenth-floor Century City men's room giving up his breakfast?

Maybe there was some kind of bug going around, Maggie thought. Except she almost never caught bugs going around.

Maggie waited it out for a few minutes, breathing deeply, quietly mourning the sudden and unexpected loss of her breakfast, while the fifty-foot wave of nausea slowly subsided. She leaned forward onto her hands and managed to push herself (with an uncharacteristic lack of grace) into an upright position. Leaning against the sink, she rinsed her mouth and splashed her face with cold water. The woman staring back at her in the vanity mirror was pale as mayonnaise. Her just-dried bangs lay limply damp against her forehead. Her terry-cloth robe was cold at the small of her back, and there were soggy semicircles under her arms.

"Happy anniversary, baby," Maggie said to the mirror Maggie, who returned her bitter little smile.

It had been twelve fast-forward months to the day since Margaret Elizabeth Taylor had become Margaret Taylor Sullivan, and Daniel Christopher Sullivan—to Maggie's pride and delight, and to the unabashed surprise of family and friends both his and hers—had changed his legal name to Daniel Taylor Sullivan. (That Maggie not only take Daniel's name, but that he take hers as well, had been Daniel's idea, suggested one Saturday afternoon as he helped address the wedding invitations.)

The anniversary festivities had already begun with a slice of sweet first-thing-in-the-morning lovemaking. "You'll be late for work," Maggie'd managed to whisper while Daniel kissed her nipples good morning. "I set the clock a half-hour early," Daniel informed Maggie's left breast—which was by that point quite beyond caring if Daniel ever went to work again. The celebration would continue come evening with, among other things, dinner for two at Guido's, the West Side restaurant where Maggie and Daniel first met. Where Maggie, like the heroine of one of Crockett's romances, like some improbably dewey-eyed, impossibly buxom Evelyn, Bambi, or Laurette, fell in love with Daniel Sullivan at first sight. Where one week later Daniel reached across the table for Maggie's hand, and upset a snifter of Armagnac, depositing its contents across the table and onto Maggie's brand new Liz Claiborne. Where six months later Daniel slipped his mother's engagement ring, white gold with infinitesimal diamond chips, onto Maggie's finger; and where Maggie said Yes before Daniel even finished asking. Guido's was Maggie and Daniel's "our place." That her anniversary evening might be ruined by some gastric glitch did not sit well with Maggie.

She poked a slightly discolored tongue at her disheveled double, who poked an identical looking-glass tongue back at her. Both blondes were visibly disgusted at each other's appearance, as well as at their collective bad luck. Maybe this thing, whatever it was, would pass before the evening. "Oh please please please," Maggie wished out loud.

She peeled off her soggy robe, toweled her armpits, chest, and throat, and tried to decide whether to pull her act together and go into work, or if the better part of valor might not be to call in sick and crawl back into bed with a cup of chamomile tea and the latest *Self.* She was leaning decidedly toward Plan B, when the phone rang.

"Hi, sweetheart." Daniel. "I'm glad you're still there. I didn't want to have to bug you at work. Anyway, I just wanted to let you know I might be a little late getting home tonight. I didn't want you to worry." And she would have worried. Had Daniel not called to warn her, and actually been as much as half an hour late getting home from work, Maggie would have worried herself into a full-fledged dither, as her mother might put it, beginning with a case of miffed annoyance during the first ten minutes of tardiness, followed quickly by a gut-level intuitive certainty of her husband's violent demise in a high-speed metal-lacerating catastrophe involving a minimum of five vehicles. The half-hour mark would find Maggie weeping audibly into a dish towel, her imagination having shifted into overdrive, her head filled with visions of herself in basic black and oversized sunglasses, accepting condolences and covered casseroles from sympathetic friends and neighbors. Maggie was a worrier. After a year as Maggie's husband, Daniel knew enough to call.

"What? Me worry? Just because I had the police drag the

5

river that one little old time." She heard Daniel chuckle: she liked to make him laugh. "Try not to be too *terribly* late."

"I promise. Have a good day, sweetheart."

"Daniel?"

"Yeah?"

"Are you feeling okay?"

"Sure. How do you mean?"

"I mean, is your stomach all right?"

"Sure, fine. Why?"

"Oh, nothing. I was just feeling a little bit queasy; I thought maybe it was something we ate last night."

"Poor baby," Daniel said. Maggie smiled; that familiar warmth started just south of her belly button. How could any man sound so sexy just saying "Poor baby"? "How are you feeling now?" he asked.

"Iffy."

"Maybe you should stay home."

"Actually, I was giving that some serious thought."

"Well, just take care of yourself. I'll call you a little later, check up, okay?"

"Okay."

"I love you, sweetheart."

"I love you, too."

By the time she hung up the phone, Maggie felt about eighty-five percent better. Close enough, she thought. She repaired her fallen makeup and hair, dressed, and packed her gym bag. She was turning her key in the front-door deadbolt when it hit again. She couldn't imagine what could be left, but whatever it was, it was coming up, pronto. She flung the door open, sprinted to the bathroom, and just made it.

"California Fitness Santa Monica, please hold." Maggie hated being put on hold by her own place of employment. You crawl from your bed of pain to call in sick and they put you on hold.

The voice on the telephone was male, which meant it was probably Earl, the assistant manager of California Fitness, and Maggie's immediate supervisor. She'd really hoped a woman would answer, maybe Theo, who'd say something like "Don't sweat it, girl: just stay home and get yourself better." Earl was more likely to ask her how sick was she *really*: was it just one of those woman things? Argue that it was all in her head, whine about how there'd be nobody available to take over Maggie's classes, and generally do his level best to make her feel so guilty she'd come in and lead six straight hours of advanced aerobics, even if she were flat on her back in a full body cast. Maggie hoped she wouldn't have to talk to Earl.

"California Fitness may I help you?"

It was Earl. "Good morning, Earl. This is Maggie."

"Tell me you're not calling in sick, Maggie. You are *not* calling in sick. Betty's already called in sick and Theo's got car trouble. I'm up to my ass in old ladies and fat chicks in leg warmers and I'm down to two instructors, so tell me you're not calling in sick, Maggie."

"I'm calling in sick, Earl."

"That's not funny, Maggie. Not funny at all."

"I'm not being funny, Earl. I'm being sick."

"How sick, Maggie? Is this one of those woman things?"

"No, Earl, this is not one of those woman things." She gripped the receiver hard, imagining it was Earl's neck. "This is one of those throwing-up-all-morning things. Okay?"

"Why do you chicks all have to get sick at the same time?"

"It's a conspiracy, Earl."

"Funny, Maggie. You're a funny lady."

"Earl, I'm going back to bed now, and if I feel better later on, I'll come in, okay?"

"You're too kind, Maggie."

"Yes, I know."

"Maggie—"

"Good-bye, Earl."

By ten-thirty or so, Maggie was cross-legged on the TV-room couch, polishing off her second container of nonfat yogurt and was better than halfway through a box of seasoned Rykrisp—all this throwing up had left her perfectly ravenous. She was eating like a health-conscious lumberjack with one hand, and with the other she thumbed the buttons on the television remote, ping-ponging between an "I Love Lucy" rerun and a game show she'd never seen before, involving a huge spinning wheel and many thousands of dollars in cash and prizes.

Maggie could never really enjoy sick days home from work: if she hadn't actually planned to stay home, she found it rather disorienting to be alone in the house with no clear game plan. If she wasn't sick enough to be confined to bed, semiconscious on Comtrex and spiked herb tea, she'd tend either to putter aimlessly (straightening half a closet, washing a load of lingerie and leaving it to mildew in the machine) or succumb to an uncharacteristic lethargy involving snack foods and bad television.

Maggie poked at the remote control a couple more times (*click*—"Lucy, wha' happen?!?"—*click*—"And now, for a zillion dollars and all the tea in China—") and decided to risk going to work. Even throwing up seemed better than this.

She arrived just in time for her eleven o'clock class. She wrestled the heavy glass front doors open and hurried past the registration desk, head down, Ray-Bans on, but couldn't move fast enough to escape an opening zinger from Earl.

"Speedy recovery, Mrs. Sullivan?" he called just a bit louder than necessary as Maggie headed for the employee locker room. Theo met her just as she emerged from the locker room, straightening the straps on her leotard and quietly hoping she was up to the next several hours of nonstop perspiration.

"Girl, I am *so* glad you're here," Theo said with a roll of the eyes and a flip of the hands. "Earl's got his drawers in a wad 'cause I was late and you and Betty were gone. We better shake it."

Maggie followed Theo down the hall toward the aerobics rooms, watching Theo's hard-muscled rear end with an admiration bordering on awe. Theodosia Davis had the most beautiful body Maggie had ever seen on a woman. Legs so long she always seemed to be wearing high heels, even when barefoot, that incredible behind, and the undisputed best breasts on the California Fitness staff; breasts that defied the law of gravity, with or without a bra, in a leotard or in the showers, standing so firm and high that the first time Maggie saw Theo in the showers, she was caught staring in jealous disbelief. Surely, she thought, these *had* to be silicone implants. As if reading her thoughts, Theo said suddenly, "No, honey: they're real." Maggie stammered something unintelligible, but Theo quickly let her off the hook: "That's okay, honey," she said. "Everybody wonders."

Theo admitted to forty-six years old, but seemed to have hijacked the skin of a woman twenty years younger. "One of very few advantages to being black," she declared. "The skin just doesn't age as fast." Theo's eyes were the deepest brown Maggie had ever seen, with a decidedly Egyptian slant; her skin had a color and sheen that reminded Maggie of hot fudge sauce. Theo's looks made Maggie feel pale in every sense. She knew Theo was divorced and had a son at UCLA. And that was really all Maggie knew about Theo. They did not see one another socially, unless you could count the occasional break for a quick Perrier and a bit of small talk between classes. Still, Maggie considered Theo a friend of sorts, and she assumed—she hoped—Theo felt the same about her.

"You feeling better?" Theo asked.

"Much. Fine, really. I was sick to my stomach this morning, but now it's gone."

"Something you ate?" Theo asked.

"I don't know. I don't think so."

"You tie one on last night?"

"Hardly. One glass of wine."

"You pregnant?"

Maggie was taken slightly aback. "Of course not," she said. "What made you say that?"

"Only time I was ever sick at my stomach in the morning was when I was pregnant with Walter, Junior."

"On second thought," Maggie said, "I'm pretty sure it was something I ate."

"If you say so," Theo conceded with a quick one-shoulder shrug. "It's your stomach." Theo opened the door of one of the rooms, where her low-impact aerobics class awaited, stuffed into tights and leotards and leg warmers, and sprawled about the mat-covered floor like Spandex sea lions. "All right," Theo shouted, clapping her hands loudly, "Up, up, up, y'all! Let's go, let's do it!" Theo jogged her way to the front of the room and popped a cassette into the player.

"Pregnant?" Maggie snorted to herself as she crossed the hall toward the room where her own class sprawled. Through the door behind her, she could hear the sounds of women lifting themselves from a padded floor with varying degrees of enthusiasm and difficulty, and the black soul man on the tape asking the musical question, "Chakachakachakachaka-chaka Chaka Khan?"

CHAPTER
2

"BET IT IS," ONE WHISPERED.

"Bet it isn't," whispered the other.

Daniel heard them; he assumed the women were discussing him, but chose for the moment not to acknowledge. He concentrated on his tuna salad on whole wheat and the *Times* Calendar section. Daniel usually ate lunch at his desk; he'd have Wanda fetch a sandwich from Fast and Natural and he'd choke it down between phone calls. But the day he'd seen through the window behind his desk that morning was just too good to pass up—warm and sunny and uncharacteristically clear. He'd forgotten the sky ever got that blue in L.A. The usual Century City wind-tunnel effect—those mischievous gusts that whipped through the cluster of major department stores, specialty shops, food outlets, boutiques, and office buildings, sweeping small women off their high-heeled shoes and onto their smartly dressed behinds—seemed considerably less gusty and more breezy than usual. It was a day tailor-made for lying on the beach in little more than your shades and a coat of Coppertone, risking both sunburn and skin cancer and loving every sizzling second of it. Daniel, who worked for a living, decided to opt for the next best thing: slipping on his shades, loosening his tie, and eating lunch outdoors, sitting on a splintery wooden bench on the plaza just outside the ABC

Entertainment Center, one block and some sixteen stories from his office.

"Why don't you ask him?" Daniel heard one of the women say. Then he heard the two sets of shoes clippety-clippety against the marble, then saw (just over the upper edge of the newspaper) a pair of feet mashed into high-heeled shoes.

"Excuse me," one of the women said, somewhat timidly.

Daniel looked up. A secretary, he thought. Fortyish blonde, nicely (if conservatively) dressed, well groomed. A tiny smudge of what looked like Liquid Paper on the front of her skirt, a tiny floral-print paper lunch bag and a romance novel (maybe one of Crockett's—Daniel could never remember Crockett's pen name) clutched in one hand. A little too much White Shoulders, the same cologne Wanda wore. Nice legs for an older girl. Generally nice, for an older girl. Her friend, standing maybe a yard behind her, was a shorter, dumpier version of the same idea.

"Yes?" Daniel had a pretty good idea what the woman wanted.

"I'm sorry to bother you," the woman continued, with a little smile (part embarrassment, part flirtation), "but aren't you—?" She formed a question mark with one plucked eyebrow.

"No." Daniel's reply was quiet but final. "I'm afraid not." The woman shifted her weight, tilted her head to one side. The fact that she'd managed to speak to this stranger at all seemed to make her bold. Her smile broadened—Daniel could see where this one had probably been quite a babe ten, fifteen years ago. He couldn't stifle a smile of his own.

"Are you sure?" the woman said.

"I'm sure," Daniel said. He pulled his Wayfarers halfway down his nose and looked up into the woman's face. Her expression suddenly showed disappointment, maybe a bit of annoyance.

"Oh. You're right." Daniel pushed his shades back up, smiled. "Sorry to have bothered you," the woman said, turning quickly away. Daniel watched the two secretaries walk away, clippety-clippety; pretty nice ass on the blonde, kind of a wide load on the other one. Daniel took a bite of his sandwich. He was used to this, being approached by strangers, usually women. He had taken a certain amount of feminine attention for granted since he was a boy, when people began saying—sometimes to his face, often to one another, but loud enough for him to hear—that Daniel was handsome enough to be a movie star.

Now, at thirty, Daniel Sullivan was still handsome enough to be a movie star. But more than that, Daniel Sullivan looked like a particular movie star. He looked like Superman.

Before 1978, if Daniel was said to look like anyone, it was usually his father, George—a common enough observation concerning a father and son, and there *was* a resemblance, especially before George Sullivan began to succumb to baldness and middle-aged spread. Post-1978, following the premiere of *Superman—The Movie,* and the celebrity of Christopher Reeve, the star of that wide-screen special-effects extravaganza, Daniel suddenly found himself a celebrity, of sorts. Young boys whizzed by on skateboards, pointed, and called "Hey, Superman!" Restaurant patrons murmured and gestured behind their menus and pretended not to stare. Secretarial types tiptoed up to him and said, "Excuse me, but aren't you—?"

All of which might have been a small annoyance at worst, had Daniel Sullivan been, say, a bricklayer, or a high-school English Comp teacher, or an attorney—which, in fact, seven years and two *Superman* sequels later, Daniel was. But in 1978, Daniel Sullivan had been an actor. And like ninety-five percent of all the hundreds of people running around Los Angeles calling themselves actors, Daniel was a *struggling* actor. Meaning he did not make his living at his craft. Not even close. In fact, in 1978 Daniel was known to describe himself as a professional auditioner. Daniel auditioned for Equity waiver theater and little theater and children's theater and soap operas. If there was a cattle call for the Los Angeles company of a Broadway musical or a commercial for hemorrhoidal suppositories, Daniel would be there. He came within a hair's breadth of understudying "Che" in *Evita* at the Schubert; he was almost the second lead in a soap called "Redondo Beach" (which lasted less than a season anyway, but it would have been nice). The roles Daniel won were most often in ambitious but meagerly budgeted productions of Shakespeare or some other warhorse safely within the public domain, or in experimental new plays presented in minuscule storefront theaters out in deepest, darkest Hollywood, with fifty folding chairs and no stage; and in which Daniel was most often called upon to represent concepts, abstractions (he'd played "Goodness" in two different plays within one year), or the younger son.

Post-*Superman,* Daniel's acting career, which at its pre-*Superman* best might have optimistically been termed promising, took a peculiar, if unmistakable, downward slant. Once, twice, then again he'd been called back for parts (one of them quite good), only to be told that his striking resemblance to a suddenly world-famous movie actor would so distract from the show that, while he was good (and Daniel was a good actor), it was not worth the risk of casting him. By the time a director felt led to advise Daniel that walking around wearing Superman's face might make the acting profession—a tough steak to cut for just about anyone—particularly tough for Daniel, it already had.

When, however, Daniel's agent suggested that Daniel consider "getting into some celebrity impersonation gigs—just as a side thing," something snapped inside Daniel Sullivan. He made a decision. He would *not* go into celebrity impersonation. He would go to law school.

Even law students go to the movies (they do in Los Angeles, anyway), and so at Loyola Law School classmates and faculty alike pointed out Daniel's resemblance to Superman—which, in all fairness to those who pointed, both within Loyola Law School and without, was uncanny, notwithstanding Daniel's repeated protestations to the contrary. The only obvious flaw in Daniel Sullivan's resemblance to Superman was that while Christopher Reeve's eyes, as any number of wide-screen close-ups could attest, were bluer than any L.A. sky in anybody's recent memory, Daniel Sullivan's eyes—as Daniel himself was quick to point out, and as the blond secretary with the pretty nice ass and the clippety-clippety shoes discovered when Daniel lowered his Wayfarers—Daniel Sullivan's eyes were brown.

As the man with Superman's face, Daniel soon became one of the celebrities of his law school class, along with the son of a prime-time soap opera star and a recent USC graduate able to fart his school fight song. Attempts at camouflage proved fruitless: the horn-rimmed glasses Daniel affected for a while were not only superfluous (Daniel's vision was perfect), but wholly ineffective—they only served to make him look like Clark Kent. It required precious little wit to nickname Daniel "Superman," a moniker which, predictably, followed Daniel for his entire three years of school.

Superman Sullivan departed Loyola with a juris doctorate at the age of twenty-seven, in the top five of his class (never a particularly gifted student, Daniel had long ago mastered the application of hard work where natural aptitude failed), and was accepted as an associate at Rosen and Silverman before the ink was dry on his degree, and a full six months before passing the California bar. This was partially, though by no means entirely, due to the recommendation of Harold Benjamin, another ex-actor who had chosen to forgo the thespian's life for the barrister's almost two years before Daniel. Harold was barrel-chested and balding even then, but handsome in a hawk-nosed Semitic sort of way. He was vocally envious of Daniel's classic good looks, of what he called Daniel's "goyish leading-man kisser." Harold himself was a born character actor, eternally forty and unmistakably Jewish. Daniel and Harold had worked together in three plays during their relatively brief careers (the first being a small reader's theater production of *Long Day's Journey Into Night,* in which Harold portrayed the drunken older brother, and Daniel the consumptive younger). It was during that production that Harold confessed his desire for Daniel over a postrehearsal espresso at the Cafe Figaro, and accepted Daniel's characteristically gentle refusal with a good-natured shrug and his trademark grin, a smile somewhat overfull of long white teeth.

Rosen and Silverman, a small but prestigious firm specializing in entertainment law (their client roster read like the guest list for a party at Michael Jackson's), kept Daniel about as close to show business as a lawyer could get without having a stand-up routine on the side, and, for the most part, Daniel was happy in his work. He liked the vast majority of his co-workers and his clients (the former included Harold Benjamin, with whom he shared several old acquaintances, many amusing anecdotes, and the occasional poker game; the latter included a recent Supporting Actor Oscar nominee and a contender for the Best New Artist Grammy award). Besides, nearly three years of steady, substantial income had caused Daniel to realize that, although he'd survived without money for several years, both as a student and as a seldom-employed actor, he generally enjoyed life with money considerably more than he'd enjoyed life without it.

One of Century City's trademark gusts of wind was playing
with a sheet of newspaper, shoving it along the relatively
smooth marble pavement with a sound like secretaries whispering office gossip around the coffee machine. In Daniel's
experience, litter was something of a rare occurrence in Century City—strangely, one seldom saw anyone sweeping or
picking up stray paper, yet the place always seemed almost
unnaturally clean. It was one of the ways in which Century
City reminded Daniel of Disneyland. Daniel watched the
sheet of paper scoot along toward his bench, watched it out
of the corner of his eye (as if the paper were somehow aware
of him, could see him or smell him), like a cat toying with a
lizard before slapping it dead. Just as the paper would have
skittered past, Daniel stamped on it with his black-Italian-
loafered right foot. The end of the line for one piece of litter.

Daniel picked up the paper from beneath his shoe. It was
the front page of a tabloid, one of the less expensive and more
garish publications to be found at the supermarket checkout,
along with the *Enquirer,* the *Star,* razor blades, and Life Savers.
Daniel glanced at the cover page just long enough for his
brain to take in the garishly colored head shot of Rock Hudson (his face drawn and wrinkled, literally old before his
time), and its accompanying headline: "Rock's Last Plea—
Forgive Me, Linda" (followed by three exclamation points).
A little grunt of displeasure erupted from Daniel's throat as
he crumpled the paper tightly in his fist. He hook-shot the
little paper ball into the trash can at one end of the bench he
sat on. He started to take a bite of his sandwich but found he
wasn't hungry anymore.

Why do they do that? he wondered. Why can't they just
leave him alone? In the weeks since Rock Hudson's illness had
been made public, Daniel had quickly grown uncomfortable
with the bizarre circus of publicity that had immediately
sprung up around both Hudson and his illness, like toadstools

on a lawn. Rock Hudson had AIDS. That gay disease was suddenly Rock Hudson's disease, and anybody who didn't know about it just wasn't looking, wasn't listening, must have been living in a cave. More and more it seemed that 1985 was destined to go down as the year America Found Out—about AIDS and about Rock. A strange distinction for the year following 1984, with its done-to-death Orwell allusions; the hyped-up overexcitement of Olympic Games held in Daniel's backyard for the first time in his lifetime; the anticlimax of the Presidential election (how could mere politics compare with Ueberroth's flying saucer?); and the dulling sameness promised by another four years of Reagan. (Daniel was a registered, voting Democrat—the sole bumper sticker on the back of his Volvo read, DON'T BLAME ME: I DIDN'T VOTE FOR HIM.)

Now Ronnie's pal Rock was at least as newsworthy as the President himself; indeed, Hudson's photographic image was as ubiquitous as Reagan's. His ever more emaciated face and body seemed to be everywhere—television, newspapers, every conceivable magazine. You couldn't miss those pictures—and Daniel tried. He'd pass the newsstand in a corner of the nearby mall quickly, avoiding the sight of Hudson's skeletal face on so many magazine covers on shelf after shelf, a morbid multiplicity of mortal illness that nearly turned Daniel's stomach.

But there seemed to be no escape, no hiding place from the horror. Rock Hudson was dying everywhere you turned—hundreds of brave, weary smiles, thousands of dull, red-rimmed eyes. Suddenly, it was all anybody wanted to talk about. The talk was almost as hard to escape as the pictures, talk at least as concerned with Rock's sexuality as with Rock's illness. To discuss one issue was to discuss the other. The disease that seemed to be melting the mammoth movie star from the inside out had also kicked Hudson's closet door to splinters and tossed him outside, like it or not. Rock Hudson's homosexuality—for decades an open secret within the film and television industries of which Daniel Sullivan was still, if peripherally, a part, now suddenly common knowledge from Paris to Peoria—had become the subject of newspaper editorials, letters to the editor, coffee-break conversations, and bad jokes.

Why does Rock Hudson want to be buried face down? So all his friends will recognize him.

Didja hear about Rock Hudson's new movie? It's called *Rambutt*!

Hey—know what GAY stands for? "Got AIDS yet?"

Daniel heard the jokes, heard them and reheard them (those who told them always seemed to think them worth repetition); but he did not find them funny in the least, and he never laughed at them. But neither did he ever tell the jokesters off, tell them he found the jokes cruel and beyond tasteless, or use words like "flaming asshole." He'd wanted to. Every time he'd found himself within hearing distance of one of those jokes, or overheard someone say (with no joke intended) that maybe this AIDS thing wasn't so bad if it got rid of a few of *them*, or maybe it was just God's punishment on *them*, Daniel wanted to speak up, speak out, say something; and sometimes he got so damned close. But then he didn't. He'd shrug it off; walk away; think about something else. Any resemblance to movie heroes notwithstanding, Daniel Sullivan was nobody's hero—never claimed to be.

Which in no way dulled the guilt. The guilt Daniel Sullivan felt every time the opportunity to say, "Listen, anus-breath: some of my closest friends happen to be gay, so I'd appreciate it if you'd take your ignorance elsewhere," came and went. And make no mistake, Daniel felt very guilty. Despite the fact that one of those friends—Harold Benjamin—was still in the closet ("semicloseted," Harold himself termed it, meaning he'd never actually *told* anybody at Rosen and Silverman, although just about everyone at the firm knew or at least suspected that Harold was homosexual). Even despite the fact that, on two separate occasions, Harold and Daniel had both been present when someone felt led to tell a Rock Hudson joke, and Harold himself had kept silent—Daniel and Harold simply glanced at one another, their eyes relaying their respective and shared guilt back and forth between them. Harold liked to say, "Blacks got rhythm—Jews got guilt." Daniel knew the Jews had no monopoly on it.

Daniel worried about Harold. And Crockett. Not that either of them was the kind of person Daniel would ever expect to come down with AIDS. From what Maggie had told him—he couldn't bring himself to read very much on the subject, couldn't seem to get past the photographs of emaciated, blotchy-faced victims, but Maggie read every magazine article, every newspaper story—the men who were dying of the disease were admitting to hundreds of different sex partners per year. Daniel was sure neither Harold nor Crockett was like that. Still, Daniel worried. Gay men were dropping like flies from a disease that looked like something out of a cheap horror flick, a disease nobody could even *talk* about curing, and two of Daniel's closest friends were gay men. What kind of fool wouldn't be worried?

A fast, ugly image splattered against Daniel's mind, like a big bug against a windshield: a picture of an AIDS victim glimpsed in some magazine, a young man with thin blond hair, his face skeletal and disfigured with illness, a face very like Crockett's face. Daniel shook the picture from his head.

"Jesus," he said to himself. Pretty morbid thinking for a man's anniversary, especially for a man stone crazy about his wife. Daniel laughed a little at himself. He dug a hand into his pants pocket and pulled out the tiny box he'd been carrying with him everywhere for the better part of a week. He flipped the box open and looked at the ring again. For the past couple of days, he'd gotten into the habit of sneaking a peek at it every few hours, not so much because he found the half-carat square-cut diamond flanked by small emeralds so fascinating in and of itself (as he'd freely admitted to the lady behind the counter at Zale's, he knew diddly about diamonds and cared less), but because the ever-recurring thought of giving the ring to Maggie made him feel like a six-year-old on Christmas Eve, giddy with the anticipation of watching Maggie's reaction to her anniversary present winking flirtatiously up at her from its little red velveteen settee. Daniel imagined her big green eyes widening, the wordless parting of her lips, the little squeal in her voice as she said "Oh, Daniel!" and finally the smile. The smile that won him. That little-girl grin of Maggie's that never failed to melt him, make him go all gooey like a caramel in the summertime, that nine times out of ten made Daniel want nothing so much as to make love to her, then and there, wherever they were. The fleeting thought of loving Maggie made Daniel's dick stir in his boxers. Daniel flipped the ring box shut and dropped his hands into his lap. "Jeez," Daniel thought. Thirty years old, with a dick that thinks it's seventeen.

Daniel returned the box to his pocket, careful not to nudge his easily encouraged penis in the process. A delivery boy in a khaki coverall hurried past Daniel's bench, carrying a monumental floral arrangement, inciting Daniel to wonder, for perhaps the fourteenth time since breakfast, if he shouldn't buy some flowers for Maggie.

He'd put in a call to Crockett shortly before lunch. Crockett's hello seemed particularly low and husky.

"Crocker? It's Daniel. Did I wake you?"

"Of course not," Crockett said. "I've been up for hours. Getting a lot of work done."

"Well, good. You just sounded a little down."

"Oh, no; just busy, is all." Crockett's voice raised slightly in pitch.

"Well, I won't keep you, then. I just need a little advice. You know today's our anniversary—Maggie and me."

"Of course I know. Happy anniversary, kiddo."

"Thanks, buddy. Anyway, it's about Maggie's present. See, I bought her a ring. Half-carat square-cut diamond surrounded with small emeralds. Emeralds to match her eyes."

Crockett whistled long and low. "Well, good for her," he said.

"So do you think that'll be enough?"

"It'd work for me."

"No, really. Do you think maybe some flowers or something? I mean, it *is* our anniversary."

"Shit a meat ax, buddy—just give her the ring, then drag the wench into the bedroom and fuck her brains out."

"Jesus, Crockett . . ." The man could really border on the rude sometimes.

"It'd work for me!"

"Sometimes I don't know if I'm romantic enough, you know?" Daniel heard Crockett chuckle.

"I'm sure you do just fine."

"Thanks, bud."

Daniel appreciated Crockett's assurance that the ring would be more than sufficient; and he was sure Maggie would love it. Still, he somehow didn't quite *feel* like it was enough.

Daniel's love for Maggie was so unlike anything he'd ever felt for anyone before that even now, after a year of marriage, he often found himself feeling as if he were still adjusting to it, to the awful deep-and-wide reality of it, like a poor man who's won the Irish Sweepstakes must have to adjust to sudden wealth. He sometimes doubted if he was quite up to the challenge of such a love, if he was capable of expressing it properly to Maggie. He could slay her no dragons, wage her no wars, quest her no Holy Grail. Unlike Crockett, he was no whiz with words: attempts at love poetry made early in his courtship had proved as clumsy as a ballerina with her foot in a cast, and he'd burned each one before the ink had fully dried. And in the face of a passion such as Daniel carried in his heart, the words I Love You Maggie seemed almost laughably inadequate, like saying the ocean is deep, the universe is out there, God is big. He had it bad for the former Maggie Taylor, and if there were diamonds bright enough, roses red enough, kisses deep enough, fucking sweet enough to give her some idea just how bad he had it, he'd give them to her if it took his last dime, or his final breath.

"Yes, it is," Daniel heard a voice say. It was little-old-Jewish-woman voice.

"No, it isn't," replied what sounded to Daniel like a male version of the same voice. Daniel smiled to himself, but pretended not to hear.

Daniel looked at his watch. He still had about fifteen minutes. Just enough time to run to the florist.

CHAPTER 3

"YOU REALLY LIKE IT," SHE SAID, almost a question, not quite a statement.

Daniel didn't seem to hear. He was seated on the edge of the unmade king-sized bed, tugging on a blue and gray argyle sock. He didn't answer, didn't even look up. Maggie stood in front of one of the full-length mirrors that covered the sliding doors of the bedroom closet and turned her head slowly from side to side, stretching her eyes until they nearly began to water. She briefly considered pulling a compact out of her purse for a view of the back, but thought better of it. She reached up as if to touch her hair, but then didn't.

That afternoon, right after work, as a sort of anniversary present to herself and also just because she felt it was time for a change, Maggie had had her hair cut. The shoulder-length golden-blond mane she'd worn since loosening her pigtails in the fifth grade was now boyishly short and moussed flat on the sides and back, left a little longer and permed fluffy and full on top. It had seemed like such a good idea when Raoul had suggested it, and she'd liked it well enough at first, sitting in the huge throne-like chair while Raoul smiled beneath his mustache and exclaimed, "Darling, it's divine!"

Now, she wasn't so sure. They were due at Guido's in less than an hour for their anniversary dinner. The dozen long-stemmed red rosebuds Daniel had brought home stood in a Baccarat vase full of water on the dining table. Daniel was pulling on his socks. And Maggie just wasn't sure about her hair. She was reminded of an old television commercial—she couldn't remember what it was for—where a woman looks into her vanity mirror and says, "Why did I cut my hair? I look like a squirrel."

"I look like a squirrel," Maggie said to herself, her lips barely moving.

"You say something, sweetheart?" Daniel said.

"Do you really like my hair?" She studied her reflection again, first from one side, then the other.

"Sweetheart," Daniel said, rising from the bed, "I love your hair." Maggie watched him in the mirror, both sexy and a little ridiculous in only his undershirt, boxers, and argyles. He approached her from behind, slowly slid his arms around her waist, and pulled her close. He inclined his head down toward her ear and whispered, "I love it." Maggie snuggled back against her husband's chest. She could feel him at the small of her back, beginning to grow hard.

"Do you love my dress?" Maggie said, a little smile curling her lips. Daniel stroked up the sides of her waist with his big hands, and down to her hips, then back up again, moving the fabric softly against her skin. The dress was a black cotton knit, soft as cashmere, with long sleeves and just a bit of padding at the shoulders. It tapered at the waist and fell about four inches above the knee, flattering Maggie's slim-waisted, long-legged figure. Daniel kissed the shell of her ear and said, "I love your dress."

Maggie giggled and arched away from Daniel's lips. Her ears were both ticklish and erogenous by turns, and at the moment her left ear had decided to be ticklish. "How about the shoes?" she said, still giggling. "Do you love my shoes?" Daniel released Maggie's waist, and fell to his knees. Maggie looked down to find her husband looking up at her, his face a comic exaggeration of lust, tongue lapping against his lips. "I love your shoes," he said in a husky, breathy voice. He lowered his face to her feet and kissed her black spike-heeled pumps—first the left one, then the right—moans and smacking sounds emanating from his lips.

"Daniel!" Maggie squealed, lifting one foot from the carpeted floor. Daniel looked up, his eyes full of innocence. "Yes?" he said. Maggie swallowed, felt her knees give a bit. She was surprised just how good her husband looked kneeling at her feet in his underwear. She took a deep breath to collect herself and said, "Do you love the stockings?"

"Are they the kind with the lace at the top?" Daniel asked, the beginnings of a smile on his lips. Maggie nodded. Her hose were very sheer black with just the subtlest hint of a gold shimmer. They ended at the upper thigh with wide elastic obscured by black lace. "You vixen," Daniel said, smiling.

Maggie felt a shiver skitter up her spine as Daniel stroked
slowly up the backs of her legs. She herself thought her legs
thickish, but she knew Daniel liked them. Daniel moved his
hands around to the fronts of Maggie's legs and caressed his
way up, finally lifting the hem of her dress, exposing her
thighs, the lacy tops of her stockings, and finally her French-
cut black-lace panties. She'd worn them especially for him, but
she hadn't expected him to see them quite so early in the
evening.

"I see England," Daniel said, almost sang, "I see France."

"Daniel," Maggie said as Daniel raised up on his knees and
raised his arms even higher, lifting her dress up past her hips.
He wrapped his long fingers around Maggie's waist and began
nuzzling her between the thighs, humming low in his throat.
"Daniel!" she repeated, her voice squeaking like a toddler's
rubber bath buddy, as she felt her knees turn to pudding
beneath her. She leaned back against the mirrored closet door.
"Daniel," she said weakly, "the dress. You'll wrinkle . . ." She
felt Daniel's fingers lowering her panties. "We'll be late for
dinner," Maggie ventured. "Shouldn't we call . . ." Maggie's
breath caught suddenly.

"Daniel?" she said softly.

"Hmm?" came a muffled reply from somewhere between
Maggie's navel and her kneecaps.

"Never mind," she said.

They had met less than one year before they married—on a
double date. Daniel was dating Eileen Roth, a tall (five-ten,
barefoot) half Jewish blonde with an excellent nose job (she'd
told Daniel it was a nose job, or he'd never have known), legs
to spare, and a marked weakness for vodka martinis and greasy
hamburgers, sometimes at the same meal. Eileen was an aspiring actress with a dynamite portfolio, a reputable commercial
agent, and two television spots for Virginia Slims to her credit.

Daniel did not hold this against her: since his departure from the acting profession, he had discovered that most physically attractive women in Los Angeles between the ages of eighteen and thirty-five were aspiring actresses. He'd met her at California Fitness, where Eileen conducted Daniel's introductory tour, at the end of which Eileen handed Daniel an aerobics class schedule with her name and home phone number scrawled in the corner. They'd been out together three times—once dancing, dinner-and-a-movie twice—and they'd stayed in together once, when Eileen suggested they double some evening with a buddy of hers from work.

It was only Maggie's second date with Mark. One thing and another, Maggie could not bring herself to remember Mark's last name; possibly because the very thought of him still gave her guilt, almost two years after the fact, and despite her near certainty that Mark whatever-his-name-is had forgotten her completely. Mark was an actor—one with no agent and no commercials as yet (though within two years he would play the romantic male lead on a popular daytime soap opera). She'd met Mark at work, too. She'd admired Mark's physique as he worked the Nautilus circuit along the perimeter of the co-ed weight room, looking thoroughly, if somewhat calculatedly, sexual in Spandex shorts and what was probably once a T-shirt; and when one slowish afternoon he decided to engage her in what passed for conversation at California Fitness—"That's a real pretty leotard"—while she worked the front desk, Maggie certainly saw no harm in a little small talk. And when he got around to asking her if they might "get together sometime, y'know, for drinks or something," Maggie paused just momentarily—she might have preferred someone just a bit more articulate—before scribbling her name and number on a handy aerobics class schedule and handing it to Mark. Articulate is all well and good, but Maggie didn't mind a really good set of deltoids, either.

They converged upon Guido's on a Monday evening. Daniel and Eileen were waiting at the bar when Mark and Maggie arrived. Mark was in the middle of asking the host if the other members of their party had yet arrived, when Maggie spotted Eileen and called out. Eileen turned, as did the man seated next to her at the bar. Daniel saw Maggie. Maggie saw Daniel.

The attraction was immediate and mutual. What *is* it about this girl, Daniel wondered. Certainly she was nice to look at, with that firmly packed little body and those incredible green eyes. But it wasn't as if she were *beautiful,* not in the way Eileen Roth or any number of other women in Los Angeles were beautiful. This girl was . . . cute. Still, even as the Sullivan party followed the host to a corner table, Daniel found himself wondering just how close a friend Eileen's friend was, just how close a friend she was to this guy she was with, how he might get her phone number before the evening was over, and how she might look without her clothes.

The moment she met Daniel Sullivan, all Maggie wanted was to spend the entire evening in his arms. She wasn't sure why. That the man standing at Guido's bar with her buddy Eileen, who shook Maggie's hand in an almost businesslike manner while melting her kneecaps with his smile, was strikingly handsome should have counted for relatively little. Mark was flawlessly handsome, and with an absolutely perfect physique in the bargain. Maggie saw any number of beautiful men in the course of a given workday. Much as she liked the man's looks, there was something else, something more, something about Daniel Sullivan that made her feel warm and comfortable, that elicited in her the rather disturbing desire to climb into his lap and kiss the palms of his hands.

All of which helped make for quite an evening at Guido's. It was a double date to go down in infamy. The Sullivan party—table for four—had hardly been seated and the menus delivered before Daniel and Maggie were eye to eye, grin to toothy grin diagonally across the table, engaged in lively conversation. The subject was Bugs Bunny. "Wabbit season!" said Maggie. "Duck season!" countered Daniel. "Wabbit season!" insisted Maggie, before leaning in closer to Daniel's grin and whispering "You're . . . dith-picable." They fell back into their chairs, convulsed in giggles. Their respective dates were not amused.

"I swear," Maggie said, dabbing at her watering eyes, spotting her napkin with mascara, "I could watch Elmer shoot Daffy's beak upside down every day of my life, and laugh every time."

"I know, I know," Daniel concurred through a couple of sniffy, hiccuppy laughs.

"All right"—Maggie wagged a finger at him—"I'm assuming you've seen 'What's Opera Doc.' " And they burst into the melody of "Ride of the Valkyries," loudly and in two different keys: "Kill the wab-bit, Kill the wab-bit."

"I have it on video," Daniel said.

"You're kidding! When do I come over?"

"Anytime."

By this point, the waiter had returned to their table. Daniel and Maggie did not notice. Eileen ordered a double vodka martini, straight up, no olive, no twist. Mark said Make it two. Hors d'oeuvres time found Maggie and Daniel sitting directly across the table from each other, sharing an order of escargots and comparing their favorite Beatle—for Maggie, it was Paul, hands down; Daniel had never considered the question before, but thought it was probably Ringo. Eileen was about to mention that she thought the group was pretty much overrated and that she personally preferred the Stones, when Daniel changed the subject to the American musical theater.

"Are you kidding?" Maggie gesticulated with garlic-buttery fingers. "I adore *Damn Yankees*!"

"Really?" Daniel smiled. "I played Joe Hardy in summer stock in Sacramento a few years back."

"You're kidding!" Maggie leaned in even closer.

It was on the tip of Mark's tongue to point out that he'd seen *All That Jazz* and liked everything but the heart surgery part and Ben Vereen, but Maggie was wondering aloud whether she should have ordered the fettuccine primavera instead of the veal scallopine, and then Daniel was saying "Want to share mine?" Mark wondered aloud who you might have to fuck to get another drink around here; Eileen was already signaling for the waiter. Some time between the appetizers and entrees, Mark and Eileen had fallen through a black hole and been sucked clean out of the universe as Maggie and Daniel then knew it. For about half an hour there, they just plain disappeared.

By the time it occurred to Maggie or Daniel that their behavior toward their respective dates constituted what in simpler times might have been called a dirty double cross, it was too late. As a busboy wearing what struck Maggie as an awful lot of cologne refilled her water glass, bending close over her shoulder and distracting her attention ever so briefly from Daniel Sullivan, Maggie finally noticed Eileen, a woman she would likely see at work the following morning, a woman finishing her third vodka martini, a woman wearing the unmistakable facial expression of someone who desires nothing so much as to dislocate your right arm at the shoulder. She then turned to see Mark, matching Eileen glass for glass, and looking not so much angry as stung, rather as if Maggie had spent the evening making denigrating remarks concerning the size of his genitals. Maggie looked back at Daniel. He looked like she felt. And she felt pretty bad.

The remainder of the evening was strained, to say the least. Dinner conversation, what there was, was enunciated through clenched teeth, with Maggie and Daniel attempting to bail out the already sunken evening with forced cheer, their lips stretched into tight smiles, while Mark and Eileen remained understandably uncommunicative:

DANIEL: How's your fettuccine, Eileen?

EILEEN: It's fine.

MAGGIE: Mark, isn't this a lovely wine?

MARK: Sure.

They got through it. It wasn't pretty, but they got through it. As they waited in the parking lot for the return of their respective cars, four people standing a cautious three feet apart, Daniel flipped his brain inside out trying to think up a way to leave Guido's with Maggie Taylor's home phone number and without further antagonizing Mark (he had nothing against the man, after all) or Eileen, whom, unless she refused—preferring to take a cab, the bus, or walk—he would be driving home, before it finally occurred to him to call Maggie at work. Maggie quietly hoped Mark would not drive her out to some particularly unsavory part of town and order her from the car; she hoped Eileen would not brain her with a seven-pound dumbbell; she hoped Daniel would call her at work.

Daniel and Maggie said their good nights without so much as a handshake. They kept a good three feet of empty air between them as they said their abbreviated good-byes: "Very nice meeting you," Daniel said. Maggie simply answered, "Yes." Words were unnecessary: they were on the same wavelength.

The silence in Mark's Pinto had icicles hanging from it. Still, Mark was nothing if not a gentleman: much as he might have wanted to call Maggie every conceivable variety of bitch, he kept it to himself. He parked the car in front of Maggie's apartment building, got out and opened her door, and walked her wordlessly to the security entrance. He turned to go with-

out touching her hand or looking at her face, and was halfway
back to the car before Maggie managed to call out:

"Mark." He stopped, but didn't face her. "Mark, I'm
sorry."

Slowly he turned. Step by step. Inch by inch. He kept the
now-traditional three feet between them as he said, "Fuck
you, lady. Just fuck you, okay?" He turned heel and started
back to the Pinto.

"Mark," Maggie called again. Mark did not stop this time,
but hard-stepped his way back to the car, slid into the driver's
seat, closing the car door just a bit harder than necessary, and
burned rubber in all four gears getting out of there. As Maggie never saw or heard from Mark again, not off screen, anyway, she could never be sure whether or not he'd heard her
say, "If it makes you feel any better, I think I'm going to marry
the guy."

It was anything but quiet in Daniel's Volvo, where Eileen
set records for the repeated use of the term "sonofabitch,"
every inch of the way back to her apartment. Daniel accepted the abuse with the long-suffering patience of a Chris-
tian martyr in a quattrocento painting. What else could he
do? As he'd be the first to admit later, he'd *been* a sonofabitch. Eileen had her car door open before Daniel had come
to a complete stop.

"Eileen," Daniel called, "I'll walk you to your door."

"Go home, Daniel," she said, slowly and evenly, without
turning around. "Don't make me have to kill you."

"Eileen, I'm sorry." Daniel approached Eileen's door,
where she was frantically attempting to push her car ignition
key into the lock. "I know there's no excuse for my behavior."

"Damn right," Eileen agreed wholeheartedly, finally
managing to find the proper key and unlock her door. "Now
would you please just leave me alone."

"Eileen," Daniel said just as Eileen slammed the door so

hard behind her it sounded like a rifle shot. "I'm going to marry that girl," Daniel said. The door made no comment.

There was a small scene in the women's employee locker room at California Fitness the next morning, which Maggie later described thus: "Let it suffice to say that the 'C-word' was used." Much as she preferred not to have the "C-word" pitched at her repeatedly in a public place, Maggie felt she had little recourse but to allow Eileen to speak her piece, such as it was, and once the smoke had sufficiently cleared, to offer a heartfelt if utterly lame apology. Eileen, in turn, offered to introduce Maggie's apology to an orifice where very few objects had gone before. Eileen never again said so much as hello to Maggie. "Well, who could blame her?" Maggie said.

All that morning as she worked the front desk, Maggie's heart bounded up into her throat every time the telephone rang. She was just hanging up her second wrong number of the morning and it wasn't yet eleven o'clock, when Theo said, "Line three's for you." Maggie's heart pounded against her eardrums as she squeaked a hello.

"Maggie Taylor?" said a masculine voice.

"Yes."

"This is Daniel Sullivan. We . . . we met last night."

CHAPTER 4

THEY COULD HEAR SPRINGSTEEN from a full block away. Maggie smiled; she could practically see Crockett bopping around the kitchen, his fist around a mixing spoon microphone, singing "Señorita, come sit by my fire" at full vocal capacity and blissfully off-key. By the time they reached Crockett's apartment building, it sounded like third encore at the Sports Arena. The building itself was utterly undistinguished, just one of countless big whitewashed houses—single-family dwellings built in the Thirties, sectioned off into apartments decades later—that lined the streets branching off of Santa Monica Boulevard in West Hollywood. Still, there was no mistaking the sound of Crockett's music, or the sight of Crockett's car.

Daniel pulled into the driveway behind Crockett's VW Thing—Daniel's candidate for the ugliest car ever created—and said, "Diss muss be d'plaize."

Bryan greeted them, holding the screen door open with his left hand, a very nearly empty martini glass in his right.

"Evening, folks," he called over the combined decibels of Springsteen, the E Street Band, and Crockett, who came dancing out from the kitchen, clapping his hands over his head and singing, "Papa says he knows that I don't have any money!"

"Might we turn that down just a tad?" Bryan yelled over his shoulder.

"Yes, dear," Crockett called.

"Not *too* low," Maggie called as Crockett bounded across the sparsely decorated living area to the stereo receiver; and with the twist of a knob, the hardwood floor no longer vibrated underfoot, and conversation became a viable option.

"It's a wonder he's not completely deaf," Bryan said, rolling his eyes toward the ceiling. He leaned down and grazed Maggie's cheek with his own and kissed the air in the general vicinity of her right ear. Maggie tensed just slightly, as she did every time Bryan touched her. Try as she might, Maggie just couldn't quite bring herself to like Bryan Buchanan. And she did try. She really wanted to like Bryan. He was Crockett's steady date, after all, going on six months, and Crockett seemed happy with him. Anyone that special to Crockett had to have something going for him, didn't he? He was certainly Crockett's type—tall, dark, and handsome—which, as a quick glance at her husband would attest, was Maggie's type as well.

So what was it about Bryan that soured him for Maggie? Maggie herself had trouble pinning it down. Maybe it was the way he treated Crockett: ordering him around, forever sighing big sighs and rolling his eyes as if Crockett were some silly child and he the long-suffering parental adult. Maybe it was the fact that she always felt as if Bryan were tolerating, *barely* tolerating their company, hers and Daniel's. For his part, Daniel seemed to like Bryan well enough. "He's all right," was Daniel's assessment, but Maggie couldn't help wondering if that might not be some sort of lawyer solidarity at work in Daniel: Bryan was assistant counsel for a firm in Beverly Hills specializing in real-estate limited partnerships in mobile home parks. "You're just being overly sensitive because it's Crockett," Daniel said. Which was entirely possible, of course. As far as Maggie was concerned, Crockett deserved someone wonderful, a man like Daniel (if, indeed, a duplicate existed). But Crockett seemed contented enough; and, of course, she'd sooner cut off all her hair with a clamshell than risk hurting Crockett by saying anything disparaging about his boyfriend.

Maggie puckered her lips and sent a small kiss into orbit past Bryan's face. Bryan and Daniel shared a firm, brief handclasp, Daniel squeezing Bryan's shoulder. "Get either of you one of these?" Bryan gestured with his martini glass.

"Don't mind if I do," Daniel said.

"Maggie?"

She was about to decline (she thought martinis looked wonderful, very Myrna Loy sophisticated, but tasted like something for disinfecting minor cuts), but then Crockett was back, having boogied his way across the room toward them—it had occurred to Maggie more than once that Crockett Miller always seemed to be dancing, even when standing still.

"Hi, kids, happy day-after-your-anniversary, and remember: the first ten years are the toughest. Mrs. Sullivan"—he stopped in front of Maggie and planted his fists into his hips— "I love what you've done with your hair." He grasped Maggie by the shoulders, surveyed her from several directions. "No doubt about it: you were born for short hair. Your neck is perfectly swan-like. That husband of yours is lucky to have you, and don't ever let him forget it." He kissed Maggie's cheek precisely where Bryan's face had brushed against it.

Maggie smiled so wide she felt her ears shift back. She was still a little unsure about her new hair-do, even though Daniel claimed to like it, even though Theo and Earl and several other California Fitness employees claimed to like it. Maggie knew that if he didn't like it, Crockett, in his own inimitable fashion, would tell her the whole stinking truth. She could practically hear him saying, "My dear, I can only presume there's a lawsuit pending against whatever klutzy queen is responsible for *that!*"

"And the ever-lovely Mr. Sullivan!" Crockett turned to Daniel, rose slightly on tiptoe to deposit a kiss on Daniel's stubbly cheek. (Maggie had begged Daniel to shave, but he was having none of it: "Crockett and Bryan have seen my beard, sweetheart. I'm sure it won't ruin our friendship.")

"You've started working out again, haven't you?" Crockett gave Daniel's upper arm a squeeze.

"Little bit." Daniel's face went rosy around the cheekbones: sometimes he took a compliment like a twelve-year-old boy. Daniel had indeed been managing two or three Nautilus circuits a week for three weeks—following a full year's worth of repeated urgings from Maggie. Maggie wouldn't have thought the results of those workouts would be apparent to anyone but herself.

"It shows," Crockett said. "Looks good, buddy. That wife of yours is lucky to have you"—his voice dropped to a loud stage whisper—"and don't ever let her forget it."

Daniel blushed further. "Crocker . . ."

"Well, kids, my chicken calleth. C'mon, beautiful." Crockett took Maggie's hand and half dragged her toward the kitchen. "Let's you and me have a nice glass of wine and some girl talk." Maggie could just hear Daniel ask, "How about that drink?" and Bryan answer "Comin' up" as she entered the kitchen behind Crockett and was nearly knocked onto her white Calvin Klein–labeled derriere by the combined effect of heat and aroma.

"Something smells like heaven," she said, just as she felt a small wave of nausea come over her, then quickly pass.

"My love, I've been called a lot of things"—Crockett was cajoling the cork from a bottle of sauvignon blanc as Maggie took a deep breath, leaned against a counter, and tried to maintain her equilibrium—"but *never* a slouch in the kitchen." The cork popped. "Or, for that matter, in the bedroom." Crockett wiggled an eyebrow at Maggie as he poured.

"I think it's high time you knew the truth: I hate your guts for being such an incredible cook. Every time we have dinner here, Daniel goes on for half the night about what a wonderful cook you are. 'How about that roast, Maggie!' 'You really should get the recipe for those carrots, Maggie!' If you were a woman, the situation could get quite ugly." She accepted a glass of wine, though she wasn't sure she wanted it. "As it is, I've simply decided that when I grow up I want to be just like you."

"All very flattering, I'm sure; though frankly, I think you'd look funny in my clothes." Crockett raised his glass, clunked it against Maggie's.

"What frightens me is that you'd probably look great in mine." Two blond heads rocked back in laughter. The thought of Crockett in women's clothes seemed the height of improbability, notwithstanding his prowess in the kitchen and penchant for phrases like "girl talk."

Maggie pretended to take a sip of her wine, just allowing it to touch her lips, then set the glass down on the counter. She didn't like this—was it some sort of sequel to throwing up in the morning? she wondered.

"So," she ventured, "I assume you're going to see Bruce."

"At the fuckin' Coliseum?" Crockett said. "No, thank you, please."

"But I thought you were such a big Springsteen fan." Maggie liked Springsteen's music well enough when she heard it, but she'd never bought any of his records—neither had Daniel, who liked it considerably less than Maggie did. Mostly, Maggie liked Bruce's newly muscular arms. Crockett, however, owned every one of Springsteen's albums. He owned at least five different T-shirts from various Springsteen concerts. Maggie knew it was Crockett's habit to attend at least two nights each time Springsteen came to Los Angeles, and that he was not above resorting to ticket agencies or sidewalk scalpers, or sleeping on the ground in front of a Ticketron outlet in Palmdale to get good seats. "Why not the Coliseum?" she asked.

Crockett shot her a look. "Because, my pet, the Coliseum is made for football, the Olympic track and field events, gladiator contests—not for the greatest rock and roll performer of this or any other era. You want to be able to see the man, he's going to look like GI Joe from the stage, and they're gonna have those big, obnoxious video screens up in a lame attempt to make up for the fact that for all most of the audience will be able to see, they may as well have hired a Bruce impersonator. I'd simply rather not."

"Sorry I asked," Maggie said with a bemused smile.

"I should hope so," Crockett said, smiling back. "So make yourself useful and chop up that bacon for me," he said, gesturing toward a paper-towel-covered plate of cooked bacon strips.

"Wait a minute," Maggie said, fists on hips. "I didn't know you were going to make me *work* for my supper."

"Well, now you know," said Crockett. "So hop to it." And he turned toward the sink to run water over a colanderful of spinach. Maggie made a sloppy left-handed salute and said, "Yes, *sir!*" She picked up a large knife from the counter and got to work.

"So, tell me about last night." Crockett's back was turned, but Maggie could practically see his trademark raised eyebrow. "Was it wonderful?"

"Truth?" Maggie looked up from the cutting board, where she was obediently chopping bacon into bits.

"Of course truth."

"It was wonderful. Flowers. Dinner at Guido's, naturally. And this." She stretched her left arm out toward Crockett (the odd bit of bacon clinging to her fingers). Crockett held her fingertips with a wet hand and whistled down the scale.

"Wow! That's one serious piece of cut glass you've got there." Vying for space on Maggie's ring finger with her slender gold wedding ring was a half-carat square-cut diamond, accompanied by six small emeralds, three on each side, like a green entourage. "Emeralds to match your eyes?"

Maggie smiled. "That's just what Daniel said last night." Maggie had literally squeaked with delight upon opening the little box Daniel pushed oh-so-nonchalantly across the table after dinner. Several people turned and looked—Maggie's cry had cut through the roomful of chatter at Guido's. She'd expected nothing like this. It was their first anniversary, after all—their *paper* anniversary. For her part, Maggie had bought Daniel a book: a first edition of the published screenplay for *All About Eve* signed by Joseph Mankiewicz, the writer and director of the film. She had called Crockett on the telephone the day before, suddenly sure her gift was too small, too cheap, just plain not *enough*. Crockett had reassured her as only he could: "Darling," he said, "he'll love it. Of course, he'd love a five-pound bag of kitty litter if it came from you." And Daniel had assured her more than once that he loved the book, and Maggie was confident he did. Still, how could she have even attempted to match a thing like this? "He's going to spoil me rotten if he's not careful," she said.

"And don't you just love it?" Crockett asked with a grin.

"Maybe just a little." Maggie looked at the ring again (as she had done more times in the past twenty-four hours than she'd bothered to count), tilting her hand to watch the jewels glitter in the kitchen's track lighting.

"I trust all this dining and diamonds was the prelude for some serious humpa-humpa in the bedroom?"

"Mister Miller!" Maggie felt the color rise in her cheeks, both because she was still not quite used to the sort of sexual candor that Crockett so reveled in, and because the previous night's lovemaking was still so fresh in her mind and muscles.

"You're so cute when you're embarrassed." Crockett grinned.

"And you're so cute when you think you're being so naughty."

"You haven't answered my question: did the man pork the living bejesus out of you or didn't he?"

"Pork?" Maggie made a sour face. "Pork? You know, if I had to list my ten least favorite vulgarisms for the act of lovemaking, 'porking' would be way, way down there."

"Well, did he?"

She couldn't hold back the grin. "He certainly did."

Maggie laughed, and Crockett said, "Good for you, Sis." Crockett called Maggie "Sis" from time to time, since the night Daniel had pointed out that, with their straw-blond hair, emerald eyes, and small, fine features, Crockett and Maggie could easily pass for brother and sister. Crockett was like the brother Maggie never had; and, in fact, she felt more comfortable with Crockett than with most women she knew. Strange, Maggie thought, that one of her best girlfriends should be a man, especially a man like Crockett, whom Maggie found so physically attractive.

Maggie studied Crockett's clean, square-jawed profile as he dried the spinach leaves on a length of paper towel. His severe flat-top haircut gave him a look somewhere between a marine recruit and an Eagle Scout. Crockett's lean, athletic physique and scrubbed boy-next-door looks somehow kept even his most expansive gestures (and some of them could be quite expansive) from appearing effeminate—only refreshingly androgynous and, to Maggie, at least, strangely sexy. Maggie marveled that a man so unlike her husband, her big, dark Daniel, should be so attractive to her.

"Well well *well* well well." Crockett popped a spinach leaf into Maggie's mouth. "Little wonder you're looking so very flushed and healthy this evening."

"It's all done with makeup," she said. "I was sick as a dog this morning."

"Truly?"

Maggie nodded. "Yesterday, too. Tossed my proverbial cookies."

"You're kidding! But you *never* throw up."

"Never say never." Crockett laughed. "Sure, laugh," Maggie said through a chuckle of her own. "I can't tell you how funny it *wasn't* this morning. I called in sick yesterday—I assumed I'd be flat on my back all day. A couple of hours later, I felt fine. Just like that. Today I just sat down and waited it out. And after it had hit me so *hard*—nausea, cold sweat, shivers—" At which Crockett struck a hard-rock attitude, chopped out a cluster of power chords from his air guitar, and sang, "Shivers in m'knee BONE!"

"Crockett, you are—"

"Shivers in my—"

"You are a lunatic!"

He took her in his arms, a big movie-star clinch. "But, darling, that's why you love me."

"You know," she said through a mouthful of giggles, "I'm afraid you're right." Maggie hugged Crockett's back, running her hands up and down a couple of brisk strokes. Was he thinner than she remembered, his ribs just a bit more apparent than usual beneath his *Born to Run* T-shirt? "Have you lost weight?"

Crockett pulled away quickly. "Little bit." He dumped the spinach into a huge monkey-pod bowl. "I've been working a little too hard lately. Cameo's all over my ass for my next romance, and I'm working double time on my real novel, and there's just not enough hours, you know? Soon as I get *Sweet Seasons* wrapped up, I can slow down a little. Till then . . ."

"Long as you're okay." Maggie ran her fingertips over the ripple of Crockett's triceps—suddenly not sure if he was really as thin as she'd thought at first, or if it was just her imagination. "I worry, you know."

"I know."

"I can't help worrying just a little," Maggie said. "Especially now, what with Rock Hudson and everything." It was as close as she'd ever come to admitting aloud the possibility of Crockett ever coming down with AIDS, though it had crossed her mind more than once. She realized she was holding the large knife motionless in her hand and began chopping again with renewed vigor.

"Yeah," Crockett said without turning. "Funny, isn't it? Thousands of people have already died of AIDS. Thousands. And nobody notices. Nobody seems to give a flying fuck. One fuckin' movie star gets sick, and suddenly America decides to sit up and take notice."

"I don't think it's funny," said Maggie, setting her knife down onto the cutting board with a little more force than necessary. "I think it's a damned shame."

"Now, just watch your mouth there, girlie," Crockett said in a funny little-old-man voice.

"I mean it," Maggie said, turning toward Crockett just as he was turning to face her. "I cannot believe that in 1985, practically the twenty-first century for heaven's sake, somebody can't *do* something about this thing."

"Tell me about it," said Crockett, leaning against the sink and wiping his hands on a dish towel.

Maggie smiled, holding her slightly greasy hands up and slightly away from her body. "Listen to me," she said. "I'm telling *you,* right?"

"Hey, right is right," Crockett said, a sober look on his face. "If this disease were killing off straight guys, there'd be a cure, or a vaccine, or at least a Jerry Lewis telethon by now. And if it takes Rock Hudson coming down with AIDS for something to get done about it, then I'm glad he's got it."

Maggie felt herself cringe. "Oh, Crockett, you don't mean that," she said.

Crockett half smiled, shook his head. "Nah," he said. "I don't mean that."

Bryan and Daniel entered the kitchen together. Maggie and Crockett looked up, both a little bit startled by the two men's sudden appearance. "Wow, it smells fantastic in here," Daniel said, while Bryan went directly to the refrigerator. There was the sound of glass clinking against glass as he rooted around inside.

"Well, don't you two look deadly serious," Daniel said.

"Crockett," said Bryan, his voice a little muffled, "where are the olives?"

"I smell bacon," Daniel said, wrinkling his nose like a bunny and sniffing audibly.

"They're inside the door, on the bottom," said Crockett. "See 'em?"

"No," Bryan said to the further sounds of clinking glass.

"Ah-*ha*!" Daniel sniffed his way toward Maggie, who began giggling at his approach. He took Maggie's right arm by the wrist and brought her hand to his mouth. Making funny animal noises deep in his throat, Daniel began sucking Maggie's bacon-tasty fingertips.

"Daniel!" Maggie squeaked. She glanced toward Crockett, but he wasn't looking at her. He had moved behind Bryan's bent form and was pointing into the refrigerator. "Right there," he said.

"Strange place to hide the olives," Bryan said, straightening up and closing the refrigerator.

"You're right, dear," Crockett said dryly. "Who would have thought to hide them in the refrigerator?"

"Got 'em," Bryan said, heading for the kitchen door and holding up the olive jar toward Daniel, whose back was turned.

"So what were you two talking about in here that's got you looking so serious?" Daniel said to Maggie, who no longer looked very serious at all.

"AIDS," said Maggie at the same time Crockett said, "Rock Hudson."

"Oh," Daniel said, releasing Maggie's hand.

"Two of Crockett's favorite subjects," said Bryan, one foot out the door.

"Excuse me for being aware, Bryan," Crockett said, his voice suddenly weary.

"Aware?" Bryan repeated. "It's the biggest thing in your life." Crockett shot him a hostile glance, which Bryan met with one of his own.

"Damn shame about him," Daniel said to no one in particular, looking somewhere above Maggie's head. "Rock, I mean."

"It's a shame for anybody," Maggie said. Without thinking, she reached up to touch Daniel's belly, then stopped short, remembering the bacon crumbs and grease on her fingers. " 'Scuse me, luv," she said, moving to the sink, gently nudging Crockett out of her way, breaking up the little staring match Crockett and Bryan were having. She lifted the colander out of the sink and onto the counter, and squirted a little liquid Ivory onto her fingers.

Daniel said, "As I'm sure I've mentioned once or twice, I find it particularly difficult to watch Rock Hudson die."

"Why particularly?" Bryan asked, leaning against the kitchen doorjamb.

"Oh, of course, you'd have no way of knowing this—Maggie and Crockett know. Anyway, Rock Hudson's just about my favorite movie actor, ever since I was a little kid. When I was acting, even when I was just dreaming about someday being an actor, he was the kind of actor I dreamed of being." Daniel paused, crossed his arms over his chest. "There was just something about him."

"He was gorgeous," Maggie said. She switched off the water in the sink and shook her hands vigorously a few times.

"No shit," said Crockett, handing her a dish towel.

"Of course he was great looking," Daniel said, "but—" and he leaned back a bit against the oven. "Wow!" He jumped forward. "That's hot." Bryan tried to hold back a smile. Neither Maggie nor Crockett tried.

"Of course, darling," said Maggie. "It's the oven."

"Oh, fine," Daniel said, feigning physical and emotional hurt. "Third-degree burns on my back, and this is all the sympathy I get?"

"Oh," Maggie crooned, her face a silent-movie version of pity, "poor injured baby!" She walked over to Daniel, arms outstretched, moved behind her husband and kissed him on the back. "Better?" she said, stroking up and down Daniel's spine.

"Much better," Daniel said. He glanced down and to one side. "What was I saying? Oh, yeah. Of course Rock was handsome." He moved backward a couple of quick steps— Maggie had him by the belt loop and was pulling him back. Daniel leaned next to her against the counter. "Which of course he was. But he was more than that, you know? I mean, the woods are crawling with tall, handsome actors."

"Really," Crockett said, raising an eyebrow. "Which woods are these?"

Daniel smiled, but chose not to reply. "But Rock," he continued, "Rock was sexy *and* funny. You know? Had that mischievous little gleam in his eye, that . . . that dry, off-to-one-side wit. He made it look easy, and comedy is tough. Not that many great-looking actors can do comedy."

"Cary Grant," Crockett offered.

"Well, yeah," Daniel said, "Cary Grant," and he shrugged as if to say, "But of course Cary Grant is God."

"Chris Reeve," Maggie said, nudging Daniel with her elbow.

"I'm sorry," said Daniel, nudging her in return, "Chris who?"

"Sullivan," Bryan said, leaning toward the door and shaking the olive jar, "martinis."

"Right," said Daniel. He took one step forward, then stopped short. "I saw a picture of him yesterday," he said toward Crockett, but not really *to* him. "Rock." Daniel shook his head slowly. "It's a terrible thing." He shrugged his shoulders a little and followed Bryan out of the kitchen.

Maggie watched him leave, watched the door swing behind him.

"Chicken!" Crockett exclaimed suddenly. Maggie stepped

aside as Crockett rushed to the oven and yanked it open. The scent of the huge roasting chicken intensified and refilled the room as Crockett squirted juices over the bird's deep-brown breast with a baster. The buttery, herb-laden smell seemed to push in against Maggie's stomach, causing an unpleasant woozy sensation that came and passed quickly. "My dear," Crockett said, giving the chicken one last squirt, "this is going to be so good you'll smack your mother!"

He closed the oven door and paused, facing the oven for a brief moment before turning to Maggie. "Anyway," he began, "about what we were talking about before . . ." He made an inconclusive arm motion toward the kitchen door. "I'm okay. Musn't worry your pretty little hair-do about me. I'm just a bit overworked, is all. You're the one who's throwing up all morning long." He suddenly stopped, cocked his head to one side; Maggie watched a thought skitter across his face. "Oh, idea, idea!"

"What?"

"Maybe you're pregnant."

"Pregnant?" Ye gods, she thought. First Theo and now him. You throw up a couple of times and suddenly all your friends have got this pregnancy obsession.

"Pregnant," Crockett replied, Mr. Calm-and-Reasonable. "You know: expecting. In the family way. One in the oven."

"I know what it means, Crockett. I *am* the woman in the room, as you may recall."

"So, Mrs. Woman-in-the-Room, how come it takes the faggot in the room to come up with the notion that you might be—shall we say—with child?"

"Because it's a ridiculous notion, that's why."

"What's so ridiculous about it? You are married, and it is rumored that you have sex on occasion. I admit I'm no expert on heterosexuality, but from what I've read in the papers, that *is* where babies come from."

"Crockett"—Maggie dropped her voice to a hissy whisper—"I use a diaphragm."

"Known to be one hundred percent foolproof."

"Crockett, I am not pregnant," Maggie said quickly and loudly and with just a bit more conviction than she actually felt. That morning, crouched over the toilet, Maggie had allowed herself to wonder if perhaps Theo had been right, that she was pregnant, diaphragm or no diaphragm. She found the idea bothersome: she and Daniel had every intention of starting a family, but not for another year or two. It would be at least that long before the house would be ready, and even at that, Daniel was insistent upon having a tidy nest egg in the bank before having a child. If she were pregnant now, Maggie wondered, how would Daniel feel about it?

By the end of that workday, Maggie had managed to convince herself once again that she was not, repeat *not*, pregnant. Now Crockett had picked up on this pregnancy thing and (in typical Crockett fashion) wasn't about to let up.

"Come on, Maggie," he said, "you're sick in the morning—some might refer to such a phenomenon as morning sickness. Morrrrning sickness, Maggie. When was the last time you had your visitor?"

"My what?"

"Your friend, your monthly, your lady's time."

"About five weeks ago, but—"

"Ah-ha!"

"Ah-ha nothing. My periods have always been irregular." It was not unusual for Maggie to go five or six weeks between periods—the Pill had fixed that for her back in college. "Crockett, I'm not pregnant. Really. Don't you think I'd know?"

"Fine," Crockett conceded too quickly. "You're not pregnant." He tossed Maggie's bacon bits into the bowl of spinach. "But you are. Mark my words. Fairy's intuition. Bring the dressing in, will you, luv?" And he exited, salad in hand, into the dining room, calling "Come and get it" over the Brandenburg Concerto Bryan had slipped onto the stereo while Crockett wasn't looking.

First thing in the morning, as she threw up with the sort of vigor she generally reserved for her advanced aerobics classes, Maggie decided to buy one of those home pregnancy tests.

CHAPTER 5

THE MOUNTAIN OF DIRTY DISHES seemed insurmountable. The thought of rinsing them and loading the dishwasher made Crockett feel incredibly weary. He stood in the middle of the kitchen and stared, as if by sheer concentration he could make the stacks of stoneware disappear. How could I possibly be this tired? he wondered. It wasn't as if he hadn't slept—lately, it seemed he did little else.

He had intended to get up early that morning and get some solid work done on *Sweet Seasons,* by Doralee Johnson (his romance novel *nom de plume*), but instead he'd slept through his alarm and was still in bed at eleven-thirty when his agent called, inquiring as to when *Seasons* might cross her desk. Crockett's last two romance novels had landed in enough shopping carts nationwide to raise his advance from $5,000 for *The Magic Touch* (his first romance) to $60,000 for *Sweet Seasons* (his fourth). Hardly a fortune—a pittance compared to Barbara Cartland's take-home, or Danielle Steel's—but it was enough to enable Crockett to quit word-processing for a living, enough so that Crockett was making a living (not an extravagant living, but a living) as a writer. And enough to make Cameo Romances more than eager to start making its money back— almost as eager as was Roz Shapiro for the shiny new dime she skimmed off the top of every dollar Crockett made.

"So when do I see a manuscript, Doralee?" Roz's voice on the telephone could peel paint at the best of times; at eleven-thirty in the morning, it was even less pleasant than that. "You are now three full weeks past deadline, and counting."

"Soon, Roz."

" 'Soon, Roz'? It's hard to circle 'soon' on the calendar, lovie." Crockett hated it when Roz called him lovie.

"I'm having a bit of trouble with this one, Roz. I know I'm a little bit behind, but I'm nearly finished, I swear."

"A little trouble, hmm? It wouldn't be that we've been writing The Great American Gay Novel on Cameo's time, now would it?"

"No, Roz." In fact, he'd gotten even less work done on *Point Blank,* his first legit novel, than on the romance. The novel, little more than a good outline thus far, was based upon a boy Crockett had known only slightly in high school; a boy who'd been found out as a homosexual in his junior year, and who was found dead by his own hands before the end of the following summer. It had been Crockett's plan, his fervent hope and prayer, that free from the nine-to-five grind he'd be able to make a tidy living as a safely pseudonymous creator of modern-day bodice rippers, and still have time for what he shamelessly referred to as his Real Writing. Instead, he had found himself so achingly tired so much of the time that he'd done precious little writing of any kind for over a month.

"Well, I should hope not," Roz sniffed. "I'd really like to see that manuscript before the first of the month. Is this a can-do?"

"I'll do my best, Roz."

Audible sigh. "So do your best, lovie. I'll be in touch."

"I'm sure you will, Roz."

Crockett had all but given up hope of staring the dirty dishes into the machine when Bryan's voice startled him to attention.

"Why don't you do that in the morning?"

Crockett made a halfhearted attempt at coquetry. "Got something better in mind, have you?"

"You look like you could use some rest."

"Thanks a heap." Much as Crockett was in no mood for hanky-panky in any form (indeed, he felt tired enough to sleep through until Christmas), it did hurt his pride that Bryan wasn't so much as suggesting a tumble in the sheets.

"You're quite bitchy when you're tired," Bryan said evenly. "Like a little baby."

Crockett leaned against Bryan's chest. "I *feel* rather like a little baby at the moment." Crockett waited for Bryan to put his arms around him, hold him. Instead, Bryan took him by the shoulders and moved him gently away.

"Look, I'm gonna go home now, okay?"

"Don't go. Stay."

"Good night, Crockett. You get right to bed."

"Bryan, I want you to stay."

"And I want to go, all right?" Bryan was almost out the kitchen door.

"Why?"

"Because I want to, all right? I want to sleep in my place in my bed tonight. Is that all right with you?"

"Then I'll go with you." He had no intention whatever of going to Bryan's. His own bedroom seemed like a journey. Bryan wheeled around to face him.

"Crockett, I don't want to be with you tonight. I want to be with myself. Why do you make me say things like this?" Crockett stood there without a reply. As a working writer, it especially irked him to be left speechless.

"Fine," he said after a moment. "Go, then. Just get the hell out." The Judy Garlandish tremble that invariably came to his voice and lower lip when he was hurt forestalled any attempt at toughness. Bryan opened his mouth to speak, but didn't. He closed his eyes and made the beginning of a gesture with his hands, before dropping them to his sides.

"I'll call you in the morning," he said as he turned to go.

Crockett stood staring past the kitchen doorjamb, listening to Bryan's footsteps and the cold wood-and-metal sound of the front door closing behind him. As often happened during life's less pleasant moments, Crockett began (only half-consciously) to narrate to himself: the instant interpretation of experience into writing was sometimes just the distancing he needed to keep himself on the safer side of that fine line most people walk every day.

"The sound of his lover's footfalls grew softer," Crockett whispered to himself. "The car door was opened, then slammed, hard and loud. It sounded like finality. It sounded like the end. Tears burned in his eyes, then tumbled silently down his face."

The writer, already embellishing the facts on their way toward art. Crockett wasn't crying. Not that he wasn't hurt, angry, frustrated enough to cry, because he was all of those things. He just didn't seem to have the energy.

It was nearly noon when Bryan called, and Crockett was still in bed. Not asleep—just lying there, covered with two blankets and a comforter, slowly gathering the energy to get out of bed.

"Hi," Bryan said. "Did I wake you?"

"Of course not. I've been up for hours. Getting a lot of work done." Crockett was speaking rather quickly, which he did when he was upset; and he still felt a residual anger at

Bryan for leaving him alone, after he'd done everything but shine Bryan's shoes with his tongue to make him stay.

"Oh," Bryan said. A short stretch of silence, uncomfortable as a pair of too-tight jeans. "Look, Crockett, you know I like you; I like you a lot." Crockett's stomach kinked like a twisted garden hose. He knew what was coming. He had half a mind to say it for Bryan, blurt it out fast and loud and hang up quickly and hard. But he didn't. Why make this any easier for Bryan, he thought; Bryan had already made it pretty easy for Bryan, calling Crockett on the telephone, instead of confronting him face to face, where he might well decide to make a scene. Bryan hated confrontation. Bryan hated scenes.

"I like you, too, Bryan," Crockett said, his voice nearly a whisper. "So you called just to reassure me?"

"Look, Crockett," Bryan began again, "I think it might be time . . . I think it would be best if we backed off a bit."

"Backed off a bit," Crockett parroted. Why don't you just say it? he thought.

"Dammit, you know what I'm saying. I think we should stop seeing each other for a while. I think it would be best."

"That a fact?" Crockett sunk deeper into bed, the telephone receiver wedged between his head and a pillow. "Best for whom, Bryan?"

"Best for me, okay? Look, Crockett—"

"You realize that was your third 'Look, Crockett' so far?"

"Cut it out, Crockett; you're doing it again."

"Am I? And just what am I doing again, Bryan?" Crockett's voice was flat. He wasn't making this easy for Bryan; but he certainly wasn't having a good time.

"You know damn well what. Any time I try to talk to you about something you don't want to hear, you get this Bette Davis attitude going and start correcting my grammar and usage instead of *listening* to me."

"Well, I'm so fucking sorry, Bryan." Crockett was suddenly

shouting, an activity that immediately seemed to require more energy than Crockett could spare. "You're dumping me, first thing in the morning, and on the fucking *telephone,* and here I don't even have the common courtesy to be *nice* to you! Am I ever the shitheel!"

"Crockett, I am not dumping you."

"All right, Mr. Lawyer, tell me what you call it."

"Crockett, I just want some freedom, that's all."

"Freedom. From what, pray tell?"

"From you. I just don't want to be half of an old married couple yet, okay?"

"And I do?" This was utterly rhetorical, argument for its own sake. To be half of an old married couple was exactly what Crockett wanted.

"Of course you do, you know you do. You want to be just like your friends, Daniel and what's-her-name. You want to settle down and buy houses and grow ferns. Well, that's not for me—not right now, anyway. Maybe in ten years, maybe even five, but not now. I want to have some fun while I'm still young."

"In that case, you'd better hurry—tomorrow might be too late." Crockett was talking off the top of his head, just keeping the argument going, keeping Bryan on the phone, not really sure why he wanted to.

"I love you, Bryan," he said.

"No you don't," Bryan said. "You just hope if you *say* you love me enough times, it'll be close enough."

Crockett knew when he'd been nailed. He threw as much bitter sarcasm as he could muster into "Thanks a lot, Bryan."

"Crockett, I don't want to argue. I don't want to fight with you, and I don't want to hurt you."

"Too late," Crockett said, too softly for Bryan to hear.

"I just can't be what you want. You want all my time; you want to know where I am all the time, who I'm with. You want me to be there all the time; not to *do* anything or *go* anywhere; just to sit there and watch the tube or watch you write another one of those books. You want a husband, and I'm just not the marrying kind. I'm sorry, Crockett. I'm just feeling a little bit closed in, you know? Just a little bit smothered."

"My deepest apologies for smothering you, Bryan."

"I didn't mean it that way."

"I'm sure you didn't. Well"—and he was off, talking just a bit too fast, just a bit too loud—"it's been an absolute *picnic* talking with you, Bryan, what say we do this again sometime real soon, okay?"

Another silence, open and ugly as a knife wound.

"I'm sorry," Bryan said, finally.

"That's a song by Brenda Lee." Crockett laughed a loud, percussive, utterly mirthless laugh.

"What?"

"I said fuck you, Bryan. Fuck you." Crockett slammed the phone down hard. He lay back into the pillows and closed his eyes tight, waiting for the pain to hit, waiting for the tears to come. But all he felt was empty, as if his vitals had been quickly, painlessly removed. And there were no tears for Bryan. Perhaps because Bryan had been leaving him for weeks, maybe he'd been leaving all along—he'd just finally made it official.

Crockett drew a long, shaky breath and let it out slowly. Sometimes he felt as if his adult life could be boiled down to a series of men walking into his life, staying awhile, and then walking out again. Johnnie, his jazz singer—a couple of sweet months and he was gone, first on a concert tour to Japan, then to another lover. Daniel. And now Bryan. Crockett wondered how it might feel to be—just once—the one who leaves.

"Alone again," Crockett said to himself. "Naturally." He shoved the covers down to his waist, hoping the cooler air might vitalize him a bit. If he didn't get moving, he could easily lie there all day long. He'd done exactly that more than once: just stayed in bed, falling in and out of sleep, finally getting up around four in the afternoon, groggy and weak, just in time to fortify himself with coffee and start dinner for Bryan.

Before the advance check for *Sweet Seasons* made Crockett a man of modest but independent means, he had as a matter of course worked eight hours a day, five days a week as a word processor, only to go home and work far into the night on one ultimately unsold short story after another. Used to functioning at full capacity on four or five hours of sleep per night, it was quite an unsettling thing for him to find that, suddenly, ten or eleven hours weren't enough.

Crockett was worried. Something was very wrong with him—he was almost sure of it. He'd felt it for a couple of months, even before he'd first been overtaken by the nearly insatiable need for sleep. Crockett's health had always been nearly perfect: once the normal childhood spots and swellings had passed, he'd seldom suffered so much as a head cold. Now, he'd been sniffling for the better part of eight weeks.

He felt he took much too good care of himself for this to be happening to him. He ate good food and took his vitamins. He did three Nautilus workouts per week, and he was at least as strong and flexible at thirty as he'd been as a high-school gymnast, when his floor exercise had been rated the best in three school districts. Crockett consumed alcohol in what he considered moderation: that is, he never threw up or passed out. He enjoyed the occasional hit of dope (though he hated the act of smoking, both for aesthetic reasons—in his opinion nobody but Marlene Dietrich actually looked good smoking—and for its well-documented lung damage), and he'd blow a line of cocaine once in a great while, if it was offered, but he never bought it. Nor was he above sampling the trendy chemical of choice; his most recent pet pill was a little white tablet named MDMA—nicknamed Ecstasy—a drug that possessed Crockett with the desire to dance for six or seven hours at a time, then fuck anything with warm blood. But again, never to excess, and only on weekends: unlike some he knew, Crockett could never write worth a damn when he was drinking or high. As Crockett viewed the situation, he worked pretty hard to keep himself healthy, and that his health should suddenly seem to be failing was an act of ugly betrayal perpetrated on him by his own body.

The slight but insistent swelling of the glands in his throat and under his arms, which he'd noticed almost two months before, had alarmed Crockett even more than the perpetual fatigue. Bryan hadn't seemed to notice it, though it looked and felt to Crockett as if he'd had golf balls implanted beneath his jaw. Nor had Bryan made mention of the weight Crockett had dropped. Maybe he'd actually not noticed (it was only six pounds, after all), but Crockett felt skeletal. His skin had begun to break out in an itchy, reddish rash on his upper arms and under his chin, but Crockett thought it likely that he had worried himself into that.

He had put off seeing the doctor, was still putting it off, half hoping this was something that would pass, that he had been working too hard, that his biorhythms were on a downward slope, that Pluto was crossing his Saturn. Or something. To think otherwise was to allow himself to think the unthinkable.

Crockett touched his throat gingerly: had the swelling diminished somewhat, or was that just wishful thinking? He shook his head from side to side, whispering, "Think of something else think of something else think of something else." He rolled over and punched the clock radio. Bruce was on. He had his guitar, and he knew how to make it talk. Crockett boogied the covers down his body while he made his own air guitar talk. He wiggled out of bed, strumming and strutting his way to the bathroom. He finished the Clarence Clemons sax solo fade-out from under the steaming spray of the shower.

The hot massaging water made Crockett feel a little more alive. He'd make a pot of good, strong coffee and some breakfast, then tackle the kitchen. He'd try to get some work done on *Seasons.* And *fuck* Bryan Buchanan, just *fuck* him and his whole family. One less egg to fry. Crockett stood in the shower until he felt the water growing cool. He wrapped a huge bath sheet around himself like a Dorothy Lamour sarong. He was drying his right leg with a second towel (thinking how thin his calf felt), when he first noticed the spot on his foot. Purple and ugly, like a bruise.

He sat down hard on the toilet seat, his wet legs soaking the rug. This time the tears came. He wept into the towel he was using to dry his legs, crying aloud until his throat hurt, until there were no tears left.

CHAPTER 6

THE GIRL ON THE RADIO WAS walking on sunshine, and so was Maggie. She turned up the volume and sang out loud as she drove, the top down on her Rabbit, the warm wind blowing her hair, oblivious to the amused smile of the occasional passing motorist. She passed a couple of tall, well-shaped young men in matching gym shorts and tank tops, walking shoulder to shoulder along Santa Monica Boulevard. Maggie smiled. As she approached Crockett's street, she briefly considered making a quick right turn and dropping in on him, but changed her mind. She waved in the direction of Crockett's building, smiling and singing. West

Hollywood was a beautiful place. The boys were beautiful. The stores were beautiful. And Maggie Sullivan was pregnant. Officially and happily pregnant.

She hadn't thrown up that morning—about half an hour of overpowering queasiness was the extent of it—but the home pregnancy test she'd bought showed Positive, a rusty-looking ring around the little vial. She called and made an appointment with Susannah Vaccaro, her gynecologist, then called in to work, informing Earl (to his vocal displeasure) that she would be a couple of hours late.

With pregnancy so close to a sure thing, Maggie found that, morning sickness notwithstanding, she liked the idea just fine. She had always wanted children—at least two of them—and so did Daniel. Financial considerations aside, now seemed as good a time as any to start a family. Daniel's career seemed secure and his continued success was practically assured. As for Maggie, she really had no career. Just a job.

Like so many middle-class children of her generation, Maggie had earned a college degree, safe in the assumption that higher education was her due, only to find herself after four years of college with an English/Linguistics degree in her hand, a degree that she soon discovered was of little practical use in the job market—flawless spelling and grammar and the ability to identify a venal nasal stop were obviously at no great premium in the high-tech Eighties. Having entered college with vague notions of becoming a writer, Maggie left behind her a collection of well-researched, well-written, and neatly typed term papers, but as a creative writer she lacked the patience to follow even the briefest attempt at a short story to its conclusion. The best that could be said of what little she did manage to write was that it was clear; but even Maggie realized her writing lacked personality and flair.

Ninety words per minute typing and a working knowledge of the alphabet kept Maggie in mostly temporary secretarial jobs for the first three years following college. She briefly considered, then quickly rejected, the notion of law school—she'd had quite enough of school for a while. At this point she got a job as an instructor at California Fitness. While she'd never considered herself particularly athletic—she had been on the high-school drill team but was never very interested in playing sports herself—Maggie had begun taking regular aerobics classes in college, in the hope of firming her muscle tone. She had never been truly fat, though she had been a plump little girl, and through high school she carried a bit more flesh at the hips and thighs than she considered ideal. By the time she graduated college, Maggie was firm and taut as a twelve-year-old boy, and aerobics instructors began asking if she'd considered teaching.

For the most part, Maggie liked her job. If leading aerobics classes and tours of the California Fitness facilities, assisting the occasional soft-muscled housewife in the proper use of Nautilus equipment, and zapping membership cards with a computer light pen for hours on end hardly constituted personal fulfillment, it was as good a living as she'd made as a temp secretary, and it kept her in better shape. Still, she did not attempt to delude herself that it was a career.

Motherhood, Maggie had reasoned as she sat in the tiny waiting room of Susannah Vaccaro's office, might just be the career she'd been waiting for. Might give her the one thing her life seemed to lack—purpose. An old-fashioned notion by some standards. Anachronistic, even. But so what? If all that liberation didn't allow a woman the freedom to choose to be a mother as well as the freedom to choose to be a Wall Street executive, then as far as Maggie was concerned, bras had been burned in vain.

She'd walked her test vial from Susannah's office to the lab herself, in order to receive her results that day instead of the next. She held the glass tenderly, close to her heart, as if the vial itself, rather than her own flat, hard tummy, contained her daughter—as long as she was trying on the idea of a child, she decided to try on a little girl. Daniel would like a little girl, she thought, handing her little tagged vial to the nurse at the lab.

That afternoon at work, Maggie had had babies on the brain. In the midst of leading a group of intermediates through a fairly challenging abdominal workout, Maggie recalled a magazine ad she'd seen: a picture of a handsome shirtless man holding a tiny baby, wide-eyed and splay-limbed, in his arms. The mental snapshot of Daniel, his big hands cradling the fragile head of their infant daughter, spread a delicious warmth through Maggie, quite separate from the emerging burn of abdominal crunches.

By the time she hit the road back to Dr. Vaccaro's office, Maggie was certifiably schizoid, conducting entire conversations with herself like one of those wild-haired women pushing shopping carts containing all their worldly goods up and down Santa Monica. Only her mode of transportation and her fashion sense set her apart. "Of course I'm not pregnant," she said to the rearview mirror. "Oh God, I bet I am," she answered herself mere seconds later. "I really am. Not." Her mind careened like a Mack truck with no brakes down a San Francisco thoroughfare. When Susannah Vaccaro confirmed Maggie's pregnancy, she could practically hear tires squeal.

"Are you sure?" Maggie, already on the edge of her seat, nearly jumped off the chrome and black leather contraption Susannah referred to as her "Bauhaus chair." It was one of a pair, and matched in both color and style Susannah's chrome and black marble desk.

"I'm sure," said Susannah. "That's my job."

"But I use a diaphragm," Maggie protested rather weakly.

"As far as the medical establishment has managed to ascertain—or anybody else, for that matter—the only completely foolproof method of birth control is abstinence. Whoever comes up with another one will probably win the Nobel Prize and a chance to go for what's behind the curtain where Carol Merrill is standing." Susannah smiled and Maggie smiled in reply. She liked her doctor. Susannah was just a few years older than Maggie, with a cute, almost boyish face framed with neatly bobbed hair, and a sense of humor to rival Crockett's. Having Susannah for a doctor was like being treated by a buddy.

The thought came right on the heels of Susannah's joke: Oh my God, she said to herself, I'm gonna get fat. The lean, solid, can't-pinch-an-inch physique she'd slaved for would of necessity spread and swell. But then again, if anything was worth growing a pair of thunder thighs for, this was it. Despite the residual twinge she felt at the thought of getting fat (or as she thought of it, fat *again*), Maggie was confident she would gladly sacrifice even her hard-won figure to carry and deliver into the world the child of Daniel Taylor Sullivan. Besides, not all women ballooned beyond recognition during pregnancy: maybe she wouldn't put on *too* much weight. And she could always take the weight off after the baby was born.

"And my breasts will get bigger," she thought. She didn't realize she'd spoken aloud until Dr. Vaccaro said, "Excuse me?"

"Nothing," Maggie said, smiling. "Thinking out loud."

"I guess so." Susannah tipped an eyebrow. She looked incongruously small and girlish behind her huge desk.

"So, aside from the breast thing," Susannah said, "how do you feel?"

"Fine," Maggie said. "Great."

I'll have to quit working, she thought, waiting behind five other cars in a left-turn lane. Or change jobs, at least. Even if she hadn't planned on this baby, there was obviously going to be a baby anyway, and Maggie had no desire to run, jump, or abdominal crunch herself into a miscarriage. Maggie's advanced aerobics days were definitely numbered.

She smiled as she noticed the BABY ON BOARD sign in the back window of the BMW in front of her. She could see the top of a baby seat over the backseat of the car. She stretched her neck upward, but she couldn't tell if there actually was a baby on board or not. The BMW moved up a foot or two, and Maggie noticed the license plate: it read MOMNDAD.

Maggie felt her smile broaden. She could hardly wait to tell Daniel.

CHAPTER 7

HE APPROACHED THE YELLOW light going 45 in a 35-mile zone, watched it go red, and felt his heartbeat quicken as he depressed the gas pedal, felt the heady adrenaline rush as he deliberately ran the light, zipping past four lanes of horn-honking cars. He looked back with a strange smile on his face, wondering if he'd be followed by a black-and-white; but there was none. He drove on, his hands bone white on the wheel, his foot trembling against the pedal.

Crockett had never run a red light before in his life. First time for everything, he thought. Run your first red light, contract your first terminal disease. He snorted at his own joke, but it wasn't real laughter: he had a sneaking hunch this was never going to be funny.

As he'd driven the scant few blocks to Dr. Walden's office, he couldn't quite explain to himself why he was bothering to go at all. He'd had no doubt as to diagnosis. Crockett had been reasonably sure what he was up against from the first swelling of his lymph glands. He had recognized the ugly sore on his foot on sight; he knew the story it was bound to tell. Crockett considered himself something of a layman expert on AIDS. He had been working a temporary stat-typist gig at the Kaiser clinic in Culver City back in '82 when he had first read in the *New England Journal of Medicine* about a strange, unpredictable boogeyman of a disease they were calling GRID—Gay-Related Immune Deficiency. He'd run across a copy quite by chance—medical journals were hardly his usual meat—but the word *gay* in large bold-face print on the cover leaped out at him from a waiting-room end table. He spent his lunch break sifting through the Latin, Greek, and other assorted polysyllabic medical rebop to the bad news: young, recently healthy men were dying nasty, bedridden deaths, their bodies' natural immune systems mysteriously shot to hell, their lives snipped short by a plethora of opportunistic diseases—cancers, pneumonias, infections, and parasites that wouldn't get near a healthy person. And almost all these unfortunate young men were homosexuals. He tucked the journal under his arm and took it home.

Then he'd gathered and read every word he could find on GRID, which was relatively little. When the disease was diagnosed in heterosexual hemophiliacs and Haitians, and later renamed AIDS, Crockett surreptitiously tore the relevant pages from the *New England Journal* and tucked them into a manila folder, adding them to the steadily growing file he was keeping on the subject. He watched a mental line graph slope dangerously upward as the diagnosed cases increased from a handful, to hundreds, to thousands.

He read everything, literally *everything,* he could find on AIDS: from the most scholarly to the most absurd; from medical journals he researched at the UCLA med library once his stint at the clinic ended, to the preposterously lurid tabloids whose headlines shouted from the racks as he stood in line at Ralph's market—"Nursing Mom Gives Baby AIDS!" in inch-high letters, in that strange pronoun-less pidgin peculiar to journalism, just above "Dog Dead for Year Pulls Drowning Child From Lake!" Of those headlines dealing with AIDS, and more and more headlines did, the most ridiculous ("World-wide Plot by Homosexual Terrorist Groups to Spread AIDS Virus!") strangely intrigued Crockett, and he clipped and tacked them one by one to the bulletin board above his word processor, slowly assembling a verbal collage the black humor of which only Crockett seemed to find. "Do you really have to pin those things up?" Bryan had demanded more than once.

He spotted a newspaper featuring a full-color cover photo of Rock Hudson and the headline "Rock's Last Plea—Forgive Me, Linda!" on an end table in Dr. Walden's waiting room, but it was one Crockett already had. He sat across from a man who was probably about Crockett's age, but who looked life-times older, so thin his wrist bones stood out and the joints of his fingers looked like tiny knobs. The man was reading a magazine with Rock Hudson's face on the cover. Crockett looked from the man's impossibly thin fingers to the picture of Rock's impossibly thin face, and felt an ache in the pit of his stomach like a boxing glove with a horseshoe in it. Crockett heard his writer's voice, narrating again: "He looked at the picture. He stared into the frightening funhouse mirror of his future." He made a little face at his own second-rate metaphor.

The man with the magazine glanced up from the pages, and Crockett looked quickly down and away, back to the little Formica-topped table next to the uncomfortably hard fiberglass chair he sat in. There, next to a stack of flyers entitled "Safe Sex Guidelines" and "Why Take the Test?" lay yet another magazine with Rock Hudson's picture on it; this one obviously a year or two old—the cheeks were not so sunken, the color in them not so obviously brushed on.

He picked the magazine off the table and was flipping through the pages in search of the Hudson article, when he heard someone call, "Crockett Miller."

Good thing Dr. Walden keeps his office warm, he thought, sitting atop the high paper-covered table, wearing only a length of the same stuff—it reminded him of butcher paper—wrapped like a crisp apron around his waist, and his socks. He experienced a nipple-puckering chill as the doctor's new nurse, a very tall black man with three earrings dangling from his left lobe, applied a stethoscope to his chest. The black man smiled a very white smile and tweaked Crockett's hardened nipple with his long fingers. Crockett quickly palmed his pectoral, but couldn't keep a smile from his lips: the nurse was rather handsome—his high cheekbones and somewhat slanted eyes reminded him of Johnnie.

"Well, it has been a while, hasn't it, Crockett?" said Dr. Walden as he entered the room. The doctor smiled, his teeth small and even as a little boy's. "I won't even ask how you're feeling, 'cause you and I know you never come in unless you think you're fixin' to die." Crockett had not been in to see the doctor for over two years, when he'd experienced a recurring pain in his testicles—diagnosed as "referred pain" from his overly Nautilused lower abdominals. "Sugar, you don't know the *meaning* of the word checkup." Dr. Walden put fist to hip. "I'm beginning to take this personally." Crockett failed to hold back a sheepish grin. Though he didn't see the doctor very often, Crockett considered Dr. Walden his family physician, and loved him in much the way he'd loved old Dr. Mason, the cotton-topped pediatrician who'd given him his childhood vaccinations.

"So," the doctor said, "what seems to be the trouble today?"

"Well"—Crockett hesitated—"I have this swelling in my throat."

Crockett could hear a low, low hum deep in Dr. Walden's throat, and smell the cherry pipe tobacco in the doctor's clothes and blond pompadoured hair as he pressed gently beneath Crockett's jawline with his soft, warm fingers.

"So how's the writing? Deep into your latest romance?"

"Not as deep as I should be," Crockett said. "I've been so tired lately. Like all the time."

"Have you been experiencing any sort of recurring cough?" Crockett shook his head No. "Fevers?"

"No."

"Nightsweats?"

"Nope." The doctor was whispering: he was so close he seemed ready to give Crockett a kiss. He moved his hands to Crockett's armpits. "Just sort of a cold I can't seem to get rid of." "How long?" Dr. Walden asked.

"Couple months maybe."

The doctor stepped back, glanced at the papers on his clipboard. "You've lost some weight since I saw you last. You having any diarrhea?"

"Now and then."

"Often?"

Crockett hesitated. "No. Not real often."

Dr. Walden drew a long breath, blew it out. "Well," he began slowly.

"There's one more thing." Crockett reached down and slid off his right sock.

"Well, that's some nasty bruise." The doctor held Crockett's small, fine-boned foot in his palm, looking as if he might say "this little piggy went to market." He pinched Crockett's big toe before relinquishing his foot.

"What?" Crockett's voice shot up like a siren. "You mean, it isn't Kaposi's?" His heart beat wildly; his stomach fought his Adam's apple for space.

"Kaposi's—" Dr. Walden's eyebrows, so blond they looked like cellophane, jumped on his face. "Good Lord, child! It's a bruise. You probably bonked your foot on something getting up to pee in the middle of the night."

"Jesus H. Buttfucking Christ!" Crockett spun about on the table and stretched out full-length, did a big, stagey scream. "I thought it was a fucking Kaposi's sarcoma lesion. I thought I was a goner." Kaposi's sarcoma, a form of skin cancer most often found in the very old, was one of the more recurrent opportunistic diseases found among AIDS victims.

"Lord, you poor thing. Reading *Newsweek* and diagnosing yourself. Why'd you bother coming to me at all, Dr. Miller? A second opinion?" Crockett smiled, nodded. "Well, I hope you're satisfied." Dr. Walden treated Crockett to a playful but sharp slap on his thigh. "Gave yourself a nice little scare, didn't you?"

Crockett sat up, wrapped his arms around his bent knees. "So I don't have it?"

"Kaposi's sarcoma? Definitely not."

"I mean AIDS."

"Well . . ." Crockett's heart sank like lead. "Between what I can see and what you've told me, I'd say you're looking a lot like ARC. That's AIDS-related complex, which is—"

"Thank you," Crockett said quickly, "I know what it is."

"Well, excuse me for breathing." Dr. Walden raised one eyebrow. "In that case, Doctor, I probably don't have to tell you that ARC may never erupt into full-blown AIDS."

"But it may." Crockett's voice was almost a whisper. The doctor nodded slowly.

"Yes. It may."

"How can you be sure I've got it? Shouldn't I get a blood test?"

"If you want to. But I'd advise against it."

"But why?"

"I'll turn the question around. Why test? Even if you had no symptoms at all, you're a gay man in Los Angeles, and I assume you haven't been celibate for the past ten years. You're almost sure to test positive for AIDS antibodies." He reached out and touched Crockett's shoulder with a big, soft hand. "So would I. And then what do you do? Worry yourself into an early grave? What's the point?"

"Well, fuckin' A, what am I supposed to do?"

"Get on with your life. Write your book."

"But I'm sick."

The doctor smiled a little. "Believe me, Sugar, this is not sick. This is uncomfortable, inconvenient. The past year or so, I've *seen* sick."

"I know." Crockett thought about the man in the waiting room. "It's just that . . . isn't there something I can, I don't know, take? Something I can do?"

"Take care of yourself. I mean *really* take care of yourself. Booze, cut down or cut it out. Same with drugs. Eat good food. Take your vitamins, get your rest."

"That's all you've got?"

"Sugar, we just found *out* about this thing three, four years ago. Right about now, that's all anybody's got. There's research going on, of course—you've probably read. I can see about getting you into some experimental program, if that's what you want. But mostly it's just . . . take care of yourself. And safe sex, you know about that."

"I know." Crockett did know. He had demanded that he and Bryan trade no semen in their lovemaking, a sore point between them from the beginning of their relationship.

"No exchange of bodily fluids—semen, that is."

"I know."

"We think saliva is okay, deep kissing, but we're not sure."

"I know."

"There's evidence that condoms stop the spread of the virus, but again, we're not sure."

"Yes, I know." He saw no reason to mention that, with Bryan gone, he was looking forward to lots of the safest sex—no sex.

"There's a couple of support groups around town you might want to look into. Talk mostly, quite a bit of hugging—a lot of people find them helpful . . ." The doctor's voice trailed off.

"Should I tell people? I mean the men I've . . . made love with."

Dr. Walden paused a moment. "That's up to you. Again, I'd have to ask why. As far as I'm concerned, any gay man who hasn't been completely celibate for the past ten years should be taking damned good care of his body, and having safe sex or none at all. If you know someone who isn't, somebody you've known in the Biblical sense, maybe you'll want to tell him, just so he'll know to be careful. It's up to you."

Making a right turn onto Santa Monica, Crockett realized there weren't an awful lot of people he could tell. Not that there hadn't been men, because there certainly had been. In the dozen years since Crockett's first adult sexual experience—a dance major from UCLA picked up at the Odyssey, a popular over-eighteen dance bar; a boy whose name Crockett could not remember, but whose hard-muscled body he would never forget—there had been lovers, dates, rendezvous, casual quickies, the occasional Erica Jong zipless fuck, and one back-room orgy. The only thing was: even if he remembered most of those men's names (which he did not), even if he had the first clue as to where they lived (which, by and large, he had not), what could he do? Call 411, get a number, dial up, and say, "Hi, you probably don't remember me, but you porked the living daylights out of me once about seven or eight years ago, and whattaya know? I'm carrying AIDS! Some coincidence, huh?"

Of the men he'd spent any real time with, Bryan (who had so recently packed up his freedom not to raise ferns and walked away) had never ingested Crockett's semen, and seemed in little or no danger—from Crockett, anyway. Crockett thought he might tell Bry anyway, if only in the hope he'd get over the notion that AIDS was just a nasty rumor started by the *National Enquirer* to scare gay men away from sex.

He thought he should probably tell Johnnie—who had slurped Crockett's bodily fluids on more than one occasion—provided he could find Johnnie. Crockett had purposely lost touch with him once he'd taken up with that bodybuilder—Kris or Kurt or something—and he no longer knew where Johnnie lived. His telephone number was unlisted: presumably one needed an unlisted number once one had cut an album that found its way into the jazz vocalist bin at Tower Records in Westwood.

Crockett slowed to a stop as the light went yellow. One red light per day seemed to be his limit. He shoved a cassette into the tape deck: the Beach Boys sang "Little Deuce Coupe." Crockett tapped the gas pedal in rhythm. The L.A. sun shone valiantly through the smog and into Crockett's car, warm on his bare arms. A good-looking Mexican boy in a pair of low-hanging Levi's and no shirt pedaled by on an old Schwinn one-speed. Crockett followed the boy with his eyes, watched the muscles rippling beneath his sweat-shiny skin, the sun on his long black hair. Crockett felt something bubble up inside of him, working its way up. He suddenly felt like putting the Thing in park, jumping out, and running after the boy on the bicycle. He felt like ravishing the boy on a bus-stop bench;

finger-combing his hair, kissing his big, brown nipples, licking the sweat off the small of his back. It was a real good feeling. It felt juicy and nasty. It felt like life. Crockett smiled. He didn't feel much like a dying man at the moment.

The atonal blare of car horns: the light had turned green. Startled, Crockett lurched into first gear in a series of midget whiplashes. Easing into second, the thought hit him from out of nowhere, like a careless driver from out of his blind spot. His heart tried something funny, and a chill shot through him, incongruous with the warm day.

He'd have to tell Daniel. He'd have to.

CHAPTER 8

HE COULDN'T GET IT OUT OF HIS head, no matter how he tried. He hummed other songs aloud—"My Country 'Tis of Thee" and "I Want to Hold Your Hand" and "Mention My Name in Sheboygan." He ran his times tables all the way through the twelves. He tried reciting all of Oberon's speeches from *A Midsummer Night's Dream* ("Ill met by moonlight, proud Titania." Her line. "Tarry, rash wanton; am not I thy lord?" Her line), but still it came, slithering in between the heroic couplets, bending the melody of "Down by the Old Mill Stream," slipping through the spaces in the middle of the equal signs: the voice of Paul Anka, singing "Having My Baby." And that woman, whatever her name was, singing the answer part about how she's a woman in love and she loves what's happening to her. He'd never liked that record. Not in 1974, when it was number one on the pop charts and you couldn't seem to escape it no matter where you turned that dial, and certainly not now, eleven years later, as it played nonstop in his mind, over and over like some tape-loop from hell.

"Whatcha mumblin' about, honey?" Maggie slurred, slow and sleepy-lipped as she often became in the snuggly, funky aftermath of particularly good lovemaking. She tugged a rumpled sheet up over her legs, leaned back against Daniel's chest, and hoochie-coochied her firm, sweat-damp fanny against Daniel's crotch. Daniel's penis stirred and stretched, lengthening into the peachfuzzy crease between Maggie's buns.

"I can't get this damned song out of my head." Daniel thumped his head against a pillow, as if he could tap the song through his ear, like an aspirin from its bottle. The Soviets could use this to extract state secrets, he thought. The relentless Paul Anka torture.

"Head?" Maggie was stuck in lovemaking mode. She hoochied her coochie once again.

"I said I've got this song in my head, and I can't get it out. 'Having My Baby' by fucking Paul Anka."

"Fucking who?" Maggie said, sliding her ass up and down the underside of Daniel's dick.

"Paul—forget it." Daniel quickly surmised the futility of any attempts at conversation, and instead strummed a brief impromptu solo on Maggie's left nipple with his thumb. Maggie grew warmer and wetter with every note. She directed her husband's hand due south, where the heat was more than matched by the humidity; she made a noise somewhere between a moan and a sigh as a couple of Daniel's fingers slipped into her and began playing finger games.

After a while, Daniel wrapped his arm around Maggie's waist and maneuvered them both up onto all fours. He plucked Maggie's nipples and stroked her belly (still flat, though not for long); he toyed with her toy and reddened her haunches with the rhythmic slapping of his loins against her upturned butt; while in Daniel's head, Paul Anka sang on and on, a dementedly repetitious soundtrack to Daniel's personal blue movie.

Later, Daniel lay on his back, feeling good all over, listening to the deep, even breathing of the woman lying by his side, just beneath his armpit, her face half in shadow in the dying daylight; this sweet, strange creature who was carrying his baby inside her. He imagined his infant son in his arms in a daydream so vivid he could nearly smell the baby powder, almost feel the dampened diaper. His stomach growled, loudly and long. Maggie had met Daniel at the door with kisses, hugs, and the news of her pregnancy. Daniel, surprised but thoroughly pleased, had practically waltzed his wife into the bedroom, where they spent the following hour and more, and where they'd made a good deal of love, but no dinner.

Daniel's belly rumbled again, followed by a giggle from Maggie's side of the bed.

"You laughing at me?"

"Nope. Just thinking."

"What about?" Daniel raised up on one elbow, the better to see his wife's smiling, if still somewhat flushed face.

"I was just thinking how I can't wait to tell Crockett."

"About the baby?"

"Of course, about the baby," she said. "I mean, he's practically an uncle or something, don't you think?"

"More like a fairy godfather."

"Very cute." Maggie kicked at him with her heel, thumping him on the shin and further rumpling the already well-rumpled sheets.

"Sorry," Daniel said, laughing softly at his own joke. "Couldn't resist. I'm having lunch with the Crockman tomorrow. Can I tell him then?"

Maggie sprung up in bed. "Don't you dare. I want to see the look on that face as much as you do. We'll invite him to dinner and tell him together."

"All right, Mommy," Daniel said, hands up in surrender. "We tell him together."

"Promise?" Maggie sat up forehead to forehead, nose to nose with Daniel. Daniel raised his face, just an inch or so, just enough to allow a soft kiss upon the tip of Maggie's nose. He painted a little stripe with his tongue tip from her nose down to her upper lip, and could think of no good reason not to kiss that, too. His tongue dillydallied with hers for just a bit, and what started out as a kiss to her lower lip turned without warning into a slurpy little sucking sort of a thing.

"I promise," Daniel whispered.

"Promise what?" said Maggie.

CHAPTER 9

THE MOMENT HE SAW CROCKETT, Daniel knew something was wrong. Daniel had arrived at the Old World a few minutes early—easy enough, seeing as it was one brief, fifteen-floor elevator ride and about thirty-five steps from Daniel's office. He was seated at a small table near the back of the long, dimly lit room, raising a martini glass to his lips for that sweet first sip, when he spotted Crockett, a lone Izod in a roomful of pinstripes, striding resolutely toward the table where he sat. When their eyes met from halfway across the restaurant's one long, narrow aisle, Daniel realized the strained stretching of Crockett's lips barely qualified as a smile.

The look reminded Daniel of the last time he and Crockett had lunched together at the Old World—the last time he'd taken lunch with Crockett at all—over eighteen months earlier, shortly after Daniel's proposal of marriage to Maggie Taylor.

He would likely never forget Crockett's expression that afternoon, his brow crimped with earnest concern as he said, "You're sure this is what you want?"

"I'm sure," Daniel said. He'd never been surer of anything in his life.

"Then you're really in love with this woman." Crockett made a couple of absent stabs at his omelette aux fines herbes.

"Very much in love, I'm afraid."

"I'd just hate to see you rush into anything, that's all. Anything you might regret down the road, you know?"

"I know."

Crockett had stared into his plate, harpooned a small piece of food with his fork, then dropped the fork, egg and all, onto the plate, where lay the remains of a lunch not so much eaten as mauled.

"Your happiness is very important to me, you know." He kept his eyes lowered—he seemed to speak as much to his eggs as to Daniel. "I love you, Daniel," he said so softly ice tinkling in a glass of iced tea would have covered it. He looked up into Daniel's face, punctuating his statement with a look deep into Daniel's eyes, a look so naked Daniel had to look away at his half-finished martini before he could say, "I know, kid." He dropped his voice well below ice-cube decibels and added, "I love you, too."

Crockett had given up all pretense of smiling by the time he reached the table. Daniel had been reasonably sure Crockett had something serious to discuss—though he had no idea what—when Crockett called him at the office the previous afternoon. "I need to talk to you," he'd said. "It's important."

He'd supposed at first that Crockett might need some free legal advice, as he did from time to time—and Daniel was only too glad to spend the odd hour looking over some agent's contract or whatever else Crockett might be wrinkling his forehead over. Between the busy workday and Maggie's news—and Daniel knew it would take every bit of willpower he possessed not to spill *that* little bag of beans—he hadn't given the subject of Crockett's summons very much thought until the dismal look on his buddy's face made him wonder if perhaps it might be some trouble with Bryan. He slurped a quick sip of his drink: he hoped it wasn't about Bryan. Daniel didn't like Bryan very much; he only bothered with the man at all because he was Crockett's . . . Crockett's friend. He acknowledged that he had no real right—that nobody really had any right to judge someone else's love relationship. Still, it just didn't seem to Daniel that Bryan loved Crockett. And if anybody needed and, furthermore, deserved to be loved, it was Crockett.

"Hi." Crockett's voice was a husky whisper, his face looked drawn and tired, as if all his features had dropped down a fraction of an inch since the last time Daniel had seen him. Daniel swallowed the last mouthful of his martini and said, "Sit down, buddy."

"How you doing?" As Crockett slouched into a chair, Daniel was sure he could detect Crockett's lips making one last valiant attempt at a smile.

"I'm all right," Daniel said. "How are you?" he asked, half dreading the reply. Crockett opened his mouth to reply, but the waiter had returned to the table, hovering in the immediate vicinity of Crockett's shoulder. "Give me an iced tea," Crockett said without actually looking at the waiter. "He'll have another one of those." Crockett gestured toward Daniel's empty martini glass.

"Oh, no," Daniel protested. "I've got too much work to do this afternoon."

"Trust me, Daniel. You'll want another one." The look on Crockett's face made it clear this was not a suggestion: this was a warning.

"One more," Daniel said to the waiter. "Jesus, Crockett"— Daniel leaned in toward his friend's face—"what is it?"

Crockett took in a long, quavering breath; then let it out slowly. "Do you know what ARC is?"

Daniel suddenly felt cold to the bone. He wasn't exactly sure what the last two letters stood for, but he'd read and remembered enough to know what the first one meant. "That's . . . that's like—" His voice dropped to a whisper: he couldn't quite say it aloud. "AIDS. It's like AIDS, isn't it?"

"Yes," Crockett said with a slow nod of his head, "it's a lot like AIDS."

"Oh, no, Crockett." Daniel sat back slowly, involuntarily, in his chair. "Not you. No way."

"Yes, Daniel," he said with what struck Daniel as a strange calm.

"But you don't look sick," Daniel protested, his voice rapidly rising in pitch. Images from entirely too many magazine photographs, emaciated faces and scarred bodies, began shooting across Daniel's mind. His heart drummed into his temples. "You look fine, you *act* fine. You can't have—that."

"I *am* sick, Daniel," Crockett said. "I don't have AIDS, not full-blown AIDS anyway, not yet. This, this AIDS-related complex, it's like the preliminaries, it's like the overture, it's pre-AIDS. I don't have any of the things that'll kill you, yet, but I am infected with the virus and it's like, chipping away at my immune system. Sometimes I swear I can hear it."

Daniel reached across the table and took Crockett's hand, suddenly noticing just how thin it felt, not even thinking that he was in a public place, well beyond caring who might see. "Oh God, Crockett, not you. No way."

Crockett clutched Daniel's hand in his own. A miserable lump grew in his throat. "There's more, Daniel."

"God, Crockett, I am so fuckin' sorry."

"Yeah. Me, too. Listen, Daniel—"

"How did Bryan take it?"

Crockett paused for a deep, audible breath. "Bryan's gone. He left me before I even found out about . . . about it. The other night, after you went home."

"The hell with him, Crockett. He isn't worthy of you."

Crockett gave him a look just this side of accusation. "Yeah? And who is?"

Self-consciousness swept across Daniel's face in a hot blush, and he had to look away. He addressed the tablecloth.

"Look, Crockett: this should go without saying, but I'm gonna say it anyway. Anything you need, anything—medicine, whatever—you just call me." Daniel was aware of the fact that Crockett, newly self-employed, held no medical insurance.

"Thank you. I appreciate that. Hey, who knows? This could be as bad as it gets for me. They say not everybody who gets ARC will get AIDS. Maybe I'll be lucky."

"You are lucky," Daniel said with an assurance he hardly felt. "You're gonna be all right."

"Daniel, I—" Crockett stopped short, as the waiter returned with their drinks.

"Are you ready to order?" he asked. Daniel removed his hand from Crockett's quickly, like a muscle spasm.

"We'll need a few minutes, please," Crockett said without looking up. Once the waiter had moved out of earshot, he continued, his voice barely a whisper. "Daniel, you have to get tested, for the AIDS virus. Right away."

It took Daniel entirely by surprise. It just hadn't occurred to him. "Really? But that . . . it was years ago."

"Daniel, read the papers, for God's sake. The gestation period for this thing might be five years, it might be ten; they just don't know. Look: you probably aren't infected; but if you *are* infected, you could be infecting Maggie every time you make love to her. Wouldn't you rather be sure?"

"Oh, my God," Daniel whispered. "Maggie." He gulped half his second martini in one swallow. He wondered when he'd be able to get out to a doctor or a clinic or wherever he'd be able to get the test during the day, so Maggie wouldn't have to know.

"Yes, Daniel. Maggie. Besides which, I'm assuming you're planning to have children some day. If Maggie's carrying the virus, your baby could be born with it."

Daniel's entire body quaked. He shook so violently he splashed vodka on the back of his hand. "She's pregnant," he said.

"Now?"

Daniel nodded, his lips pulled tight.

"Then the sooner, the better." Crockett pulled a piece of paper from his hip pocket and pushed it across the table toward Daniel. Daniel rested his fingertips on top of the paper, but didn't pick it up, didn't actually look at it; looking instead into Crockett's eyes as if his life were on fire and he was searching for an emergency exit. "It's the address and phone number of the clinic at the Gay and Lesbian Center. It's absolutely anonymous and confidential. You never give your name or anything." Crockett tapped Daniel's fingers with his own. "Call them."

Daniel felt as if he'd been bludgeoned mercilessly with a large baseball bat, and not allowed to fall down. He felt emptied; split like a side of beef; cored like an apple. Strange, he thought, how life could be. There you sit, in the middle of a perfectly ordinary crazy workday, in the middle of a perfectly ordinary Century City restaurant with your best friend and a martini, thoughts of your newly pregnant wife at the back of your mind; when suddenly some guy in battle fatigues and an old beret storms in with a chip on his shoulder and an Uzi submachine tucked into his armpit and paints the room red; or an 8.5 Richter quake drops twenty-two floors of office building into your lap; or the Russians decide to drop the Big One on Los Angeles and vicinity. Or maybe your friend drops the news that he's infected with the twentieth-century edition of the Black Death. And maybe, hey just maybe you are, too. And that newly pregnant wife of yours, and your unborn firstborn, to boot. Ain't life a bitch?

Life's a bitch, and then you die. Where had he seen that recently? Daniel laughed, little more than a sniff, when he remembered: it was lettered on his secretary's coffee mug.

"Daniel?" Daniel slowly became aware of Crockett's fingers, thin and cool, massaging, wringing his hand. "Daniel, are you all right?"

"Life's a bitch," he said through a weary excuse for a smile. "And then you die." He held Crockett's hand tightly.

"So how's Crockett doing?" Maggie asked, a forkful of chicken enchilada poised between plate and lips. Daniel watched her stare down the morsel of food for a moment before returning the fork to her plate without eating: a corollary to so-called morning sickness, she had found, was a markedly diminished interest in food at any time of the day.

"All right, I guess," Daniel said, poking absently at his dinner. Maggie's chicken enchiladas counted among her better dishes, but Daniel wasn't hungry, either. He had a headache, and the light from the lamp hanging over the dining-room table seemed blindingly bright.

"You guess? Didn't you have lunch with him today?"

"Yes," Daniel said.

"Well?" Maggie was looking searchingly into Daniel's face, as if waiting for him to slip, as if she were an interrogating detective. "What did you talk about?"

Daniel shrugged. "Nothing much."

"Liar," Maggie said. Daniel felt a little adrenaline pump, a sudden surge of fight-or-flight at the utterly irrational thought that Maggie somehow knew what he and Crockett had talked about. Of course she doesn't, he told himself, as his heartbeat slowly returned to normal. "What do you mean?" he said, staring at the border of his placemat instead of Maggie's face.

"You told him, didn't you?" Maggie said. "Daniel, look at me." He looked up to find a playfully scolding expression on his wife's face, her lips pursed and twisted to one side. "You told Crockett about the baby, didn't you?"

"Yeah. I guess I did," he said.

"Daniel." Maggie rolled her eyes toward the ceiling. "And they say women can't keep a secret. Honestly." She wiped her lips with her napkin and got up from the table. "Come on," she said. "Get up."

"What?" Daniel rose from his chair, confused and in no mood for games.

"Just follow me," Maggie called as she walked toward the kitchen. She was dialing the wall phone next to the stove when Daniel realized she must be calling Crockett.

"Hello? It's Maggie." She held the receiver just away from her ear, and gestured Daniel closer to her. He half squatted down toward the receiver.

"Hey, Mags," he barely heard Crockett say. "What's the buzz?"

"The jig is up," Maggie said. "A certain husband of mine"—she poked at Daniel's belly with a finger—"who cannot be trusted with a secret, has already confessed to telling you our big news before we could do it together. So, I've called to give you a chance for a well-deserved I-told-you-so, since you *did* told me so, then I believe congratulations are in order."

There was nothing from the other end for a moment. "Hello?" Maggie brought the receiver back to her ear. "You there?" Maggie smiled and moved the receiver between her head and Daniel's again, by which time Crockett had obviously finished speaking.

"What, no I-told-you-so?" Maggie said. "Heaven knows I deserve it."

"No," came Crockett's voice, "just congratulations. I'm very happy for you both. Just make sure you have enough kids so you can name one of them Crockett."

"We'll try to arrange that," Maggie laughed. "Though frankly"—she made a face at Daniel—"I'm not sure I'm ever letting this man *touch* me again, after the double cross he pulled today."

"Try not to be too tough on him, Mags," Crockett said. "I think he was just a little excited."

"Don't defend him," Maggie said, looking directly into Daniel's eyes. "He's a cad!"

"Uh-oh," Crockett said, "sounds like trouble in paradise."

"Talk to you later, honey," Maggie said, "I have to go beat my husband now." She brought the receiver back to her ear. "You, too." She smiled. "I love you, too. I will. Bye." She hung up the phone and smiled. "Crockett sends his love," she said, and started out of the kitchen. "Well," she said, "at least now I know."

"Know what?" Daniel said.

"That you, Daniel Sullivan, cannot keep a secret."

Daniel leaned against the wall next the phone. He rubbed his face with both palms. "Can't keep a secret," he said to himself.

CHAPTER
10

DURING THE SUMMER OF 1978, Daniel Sullivan played the dual roles of Oberon and Theseus in a low-budget production of *A Midsummer Night's Dream* presented at the Black Orpheus, a small Equity waiver theater on Cahuenga Boulevard West, just off the 101 Freeway in Hollywood. Harold Benjamin was Nick Bottom in that same production, which would be his last stage appearance. It was during rehearsals for *Dream* that Harold came to a major life decision: that, at the age of twenty-nine, he was tired of being a starving actor—he was ready to make a living. While Harold opted almost immediately for law school, Daniel would spend two more years as an actor before giving up, beaten by the acting life and his resemblance to Superman. It was at the open call for that show that Daniel first met Crockett.

As Daniel remembered it, he was none too sure if he liked Crockett at first. He recalled his initial reaction to Crockett as one of vague, barely discernible annoyance, like a fly in the room. Daniel had just entered the Black Orpheus, where auditions were scheduled to begin within the half-hour. There were maybe two hundred people in the room—men, women, and children. The ad in *Dramalogue* had been extremely slender and quite vague, asking for "all ages, all types." Consequently, the group assembled in the Black Orpheus that afternoon ran the gamut of age, shape, and ethnicity, their only common features being universally edgy body language (finger-drumming, leg-recrossing, and spasmodic laughter) and the composites (head shot on the front, résumé on the back) they clutched fiercely to their bosoms.

Daniel scanned the crowd for Harold Benjamin. He had made no actual plan to meet Harold at the Black Orpheus; he had not, in fact, even spoken to Harold in over a week and had no real reason to believe Harold would be at the theater at all, except for the knowledge that, when not currently engaged in some theatrical endeavor, Harold Benjamin (like Daniel himself) auditioned for everything. He spotted Harold sitting near the front of the theater toward stage left, engaged in conversation with a blond-haired guy he didn't think he'd seen before. Daniel hesitated before approaching Harold and Company: he had no way of guessing Harold's relationship with the blond guy, or Harold's hopes for the future of that relationship, and he had no desire to inflict his presence where it might not be appreciated. He had all but decided to move toward the opposite side of the dusty, dimly lit theater, when Harold suddenly turned toward the rear exits and caught sight of Daniel. He smiled and waved, and gestured Daniel over.

"Daniel!" Harold reached over the back of his seat and treated Daniel's hand to a vigorous pumping. "Good to see you, buddy."

"You too, guy." Daniel smiled, relieved that he seemed to be in no danger of interrupting any sort of gay mating ritual, and at the same time pointedly aware of Harold's little friend, who seemed to be staring a hole into him.

"Daniel," Harold said, gesturing toward the blond, "this is Crockett Miller. He's in my Thursday improv workshop. Crockett, this is Daniel Sullivan, the guy I was telling you about." As he shook hands and traded introductory smiles with Crockett, Daniel quickly decided this Crockett guy was cute (not actually handsome, but somehow cute), and wondered what Harold might have told the guy about him. Daniel had barely retrieved his right hand when Crockett lifted a pale eyebrow and said, "So, Harold tells me you're straight." Harold slapped Crockett on the shoulder and said, semiplayfully, "Bitch." Daniel looked at Harold, then at Crockett, unsure whether this guy was mocking him, engaging in some sort of in joke with Harold, or if this was the Crockett Miller version of light conversation. Daniel finally replied, in what he hoped was an even, disinterested tone, "Matter of fact, I am." Daniel watched as Crockett's eyes moved up and down him, taking him in. "Oh, well," Crockett said in that off-to-one-side Mae Westish way so many gays seemed to enjoy using (and which Daniel generally found less than becoming in a man), "it's a dirty job, but I guess someone's got to do it." He punctuated this hardly original jibe with a look, a direct hit smack into Daniel's eyes, accompanied by another eyebrow-raise and a slight pursing of the lips; a look that made Daniel feel as if his privacy had been invaded, as if he'd found this little blond homosexual snapping Polaroids through his bathroom window. Maybe, he thought, this cute little guy is a cute little flaming asshole.

"What I *meant* was," Harold said quickly, "I was telling Crockett how much you look like Christopher Reeve, the guy in *Superman*. Don't you think?" He turned the question over to Crockett, who gave Daniel another slow once-over before saying to Harold, "In a general sort of way, I guess." He turned to Daniel. "You're much better-looking," he said, and smiled what looked like a genuine smile, warm and wide; and Daniel couldn't hold back a smile himself.

The audition process was lengthy, and only intermittently interesting, with two hundred-odd people of varying degrees of talent, ability, training, and knowledge of Shakespearean scansion, all being called upon to read or (in the case of several small children) recite. Daniel read twice; first as Demetrius, with a tall, striking redheaded young woman reading the lovesick Helena; and, after a wait of nearly three hours, he was called upon to read the "Ill met by moonlight" scene as Oberon, with the same redhead reading Titania. The woman's eyes connected with Daniel's just before they began to read, and they exchanged smiles. Pretty, Daniel thought.

Daniel had played Oberon twice before—both in high school and during college—and so found it unnecessary to refer to the script. The redhead didn't need the book, either— not for the Titania scene, anyway—and their reading together was (in Daniel's opinion) better than most he'd seen that day, as their familiarity with the play made it possible for them to *act,* not merely read. There was a healthy smattering of applause after the director halted the scene with a brisk "Thank you." "And thank *you,*" Daniel said to the redhead before they stepped down. "Thank *you,*" she replied. When he returned to his seat, Harold smiled and squeezed Daniel's shoulder. "Nice job, buddy," he whispered.

"Thanks." Daniel, almost before he realized it, turned to Crockett for his reaction.

Crockett leaned over to whisper into Daniel's ear, his breath tickling a little as he said, "You're very good. But you know that." Daniel wasn't quite sure what to make of that last bit: did he come off as conceited, or overly sure of himself? The director's voice from behind them said, "Is there a Crockett Miller here?" Crockett turned, waved his hand toward the rear of the theater. The director, a very large overweight man of perhaps thirty-five, with thick lips and very small eyes, raised up a bit in his seat.

"Mr. Miller," he said, holding up a piece of paper, "is this some kind of joke?"

"No," Crockett said with a big, boyish smile. "No, it's not."

"All right, then: let's hear you. Bottom of page fifty-six, 'Thou speakest aright.' " Crockett scurried past Daniel and

Harold, and up the stairs to the stage. The stage manager (perched on a stool, far stage right) held an open script toward Crockett; Daniel was surprised to see Crockett wave it away. He stood downstage center, legs apart, hands clasped behind his back. "Ready?" he called toward the back of the theater. "Anytime," came the reply. Crockett turned to the stage manager, who fed him the preceding line:

" 'Are not you he?' "

" 'Thou speakest aright,' " Crockett began. " 'I am that merry wanderer of the night. I jest to Oberon and make him smile . . .' " Pretty good, Daniel thought. He obviously wasn't attempting a performance—he stood with his hands behind his back, like a little boy at a spelling bee—but his diction was good, and his scansion. And he obviously knew the speech. Daniel and Harold turned to one another at the same time. Daniel mouthed "Not bad"; Harold nodded, his lower lip pushed forward. Daniel turned back to the stage. There was something about this cute little guy, he thought. He'd probably make a good fuck. Daniel smiled at his own error. A good Puck, that is.

"What?" Harold whispered.

"Nothing."

Crockett finished the speech: " 'But room, fairy! Here comes Oberon.' " A moment of silence; Crockett peered out over the rows of seats. "Okay?" he called. "Thank you," came the reply, and Crockett left the stage. "Was I okay?" Crockett whispered, presumably to Harold, as he sat down, the old threadbare seat creaking beneath him.

"Yes," Harold replied. "You were fine." Crockett turned to Daniel. "Really?" Daniel smiled, flattered that Crockett should solicit his opinion, his approval. "You're good," Daniel said, just above a whisper. "How long have you been working?" he asked.

"Do you suppose we could have it quiet?" came the director's voice from behind, before Crockett could reply, and they slid down in their seats, like schoolboys caught in some mischief.

"So," Harold said, "do we want to go get a bite?" The auditions were finally over, and Harold was hungry. He, Daniel, and Crockett stood in the theater aisle as actors ("all ages, all types") brushed past on their way toward the exits.

"Sounds great by me," said Crockett.

"Daniel?" Daniel was looking over and beyond Harold's head, scanning the room in search of the redhead. "Ground control to Major Sullivan," Harold said, finally catching Daniel's attention.

"What?"

"Lunch. You know? Food?"

"Lunch? Sure. Fine."

"Sure, fine," Harold repeated with a tolerant smile.

"She's already gone," Crockett said.

"Who?" Harold asked.

"He knows who." Crockett gestured toward Daniel. "Soon as the auditions were over, she was out of here like a shot."

"*Who* was out of here like a shot?" Harold asked.

"Forget it," Daniel said, just a little bit testy. He was a little disappointed about not meeting the redhead and at least trying for her phone number; mostly, though, he wasn't sure he appreciated Crockett nosing into his business. Little busybody, he thought.

"Fine, forget it." Harold shrugged.

Daniel took a quick, rather furtive glance around the lobby as they walked through—no redhead. They stopped in their tracks just outside the doors, blinded by sudden sunlight. Both Daniel and Crockett immediately reached for sunglasses.

"Cafe Figaro okay?" Harold asked, shielding his eyes against the glare with his hand.

"Sounds good," Crockett said.

"Fine," Daniel said.

They had hardly settled themselves into three of the cafe's hard wooden chairs (Harold and Crockett on one side of the table, Daniel alone on the other) before Crockett leaned in toward Daniel and said, "Look, I'm sorry about what I said before. I have this bad habit of sticking my nose in where it doesn't belong." Crockett extended his right hand across the table toward Daniel. "I hope you'll accept my apology."

Daniel looked into Crockett's face. Initially, he'd assumed this was some kind of bitchy little joke, but obviously there was no punch line here. Just this little green-eyed guy with his right hand sticking out. He took Crockett's hand, clasped it tight, and watched Crockett's face split into a smile. And just like before, in the theater, Daniel couldn't keep from smiling back.

"Thanks," Crockett said as they unclasped their hands. "The look you gave me, I knew I'd stepped over the line. I was just con*sumed* with guilt, all the way over here."

Daniel shrugged, toyed with the corner of a menu. "It was no biggie."

"You were pissed. You were standing there thinking, 'Who *is* this asshole?' "

Daniel smiled. "Yeah. Guess I was," he admitted.

"What *are* you talking about?" Harold asked.

"Forget it," Daniel said, with a little wave of his hand.

"Forget it? Again?" Harold's voice jumped up in pitch. "Why do I feel like I just fell in from another planet?"

"Trust me, Harold," Daniel said. "It's not important." He looked across the table at Crockett, and the two of them shared a little smile, like two kids with a secret.

"Let me ask you something," Daniel said, after ordering the bacon cheeseburger and handing his menu over to the waiter.

"Ask," said Crockett.

"Just what was that business back at the theater, right before you read?"

"Oh, that. See, I've never done any acting before."

"Never?"

"In my life. So—"

"You just run around memorizing Shakespeare?"

"No. Well, yeah. See, I've got this truly amazing memory, ever since I was a little kid. I mean, I read something or hear it or whatever and I just re*tain,* you know? I've seen *Midsummer Night's* six or seven times—read it more times than that. I've had it memorized for years."

"You mean the part of Puck," Harold said.

"No. The whole play." Crockett lifted a glass of ice water to his lips and downed half of it in a series of quick gulps.

"The whole play?" Daniel and Harold asked in stereo.

"Yeah." Crockett wiped his lips with the palm of his hand. "I saw the play in the sixth grade, on this field trip, and I just fell in love with it. I guess it's my kind of play—all those fairies and fools. So anyway, I decided to try out for this production, right? So I need a headshot and a résumé, right? Well, the picture was easy enough—I've got this friend who's a pretty good photographer. But I didn't have a résumé, obviously, since I've never done any acting. So at first I thought, I'll bullshit, just make up some shit. And then I thought, fuck it—honesty's the best policy. So I typed up my name and address and phone number, and under 'Experience' I wrote 'none.' So I guess the guy thought I must be kidding."

"So why the sudden urge to act?" Daniel asked.

"It's something I've always wanted to try. It looks like fun."

"Fun?" Daniel laughed. "Spoken like a man who's never done any acting."

"Well, anyway," Crockett continued, "I figure, how tough can it be? I mean, you learn your lines, you remember where you're supposed to stand, and the rest is just common sense, right?"

Daniel's posture straightened abruptly. "Is *that* all you think acting is?" Daniel could feel himself bristle, and fought to keep it down.

"Uh-oh." Crockett made a frightened face. "I put my foot in it again, didn't I?"

Harold spoke up before Daniel could. "We've already had the argument you're about to have," he said to Daniel. "What say we not have it now."

"As an abrupt change of subject," Crockett said, leaning in toward Daniel, "can you take a compliment?"

Daniel, brought up short, paused a quick moment before saying, "Sure. I guess so."

"Well, if you don't mind my saying so, you're one of the handsomest men I've ever met." Crockett tilted his head to one side and looked into Daniel's eyes. "Have I stepped out of line again?"

Daniel fought the urge to avert his eyes from Crockett's and said, "No. Of course not." Hoping he looked cooler than he felt, through a wave of embarrassment he would never have expected—this was hardly his first compliment from a man—Daniel managed to say "Thank you."

"Compliments will do you no good," Harold said. "Heaven knows, I've tried." He gave Crockett a playful nudge with his shoulder. "He's determined to waste himself on women."

"Well, lucky for them," Crockett said, looking right at Daniel, smiling that smile again. Daniel made no reply. He smiled, and shifted in his seat, trying to ease the discomfort of his erection.

That night, Daniel dreamed he was making love to the red-headed woman from the auditions. He lay on top of her, thrusting slowly, kissing her deeply. As often happened in his dreams, Daniel (or some part of Daniel) watched as if from outside the dream itself, like a man at the movies. This part of Daniel registered the unusual vividness of the dream; how he could actually feel the woman's body, warm and solid beneath him, her hot wetness wrapped around his penis; how he could taste her mouth, hear her soft, throaty noises. As if he closed his eyes (both Daniel the participant and Daniel the observer), like a slow dissolve in a movie, the dream changed; and when his eyes opened again, he was kissing Crockett, fucking Crockett. Daniel noticed the change, but registered little or no concern. This new kiss seemed as sweet as the other, the body as warm and yielding, the pussy felt as—

"Wait a minute," said the observing Daniel, loud enough for the dreamfucking Daniel to hear. "Guys don't have pussies!"

Daniel sprang up in bed, suddenly wide awake, eyes wide open. "Guys don't have pussies!" he said to his empty bedroom, the words out of his mouth almost before he realized he'd said them. What the fuck? he thought, as his disorientation slowly gave way to total recall of the dream that had awakened him. Shit, he whispered slowly to himself.

He glanced at the clock radio on the upturned crate that doubled as a nightstand. The LED readout shot reddish light across the dark room, projecting rosy ghosts against the opposite wall. It was 3:42 A.M. Daniel felt the familiar throb between his legs. He slid back in bed, and took his cock in both hands. No fantasies, no pictures came to Daniel's mind as he pulled at himself—quickly, vigorously, almost violently, breathing hard, hissing breaths through clenched teeth; but as he came, with a rough, barking sound from his throat, a picture of Crockett's smiling face came through the black and red kaleidoscopics behind Daniel's eyes, and he could almost hear

Crockett's voice, like a snippet of tape, saying "one of the handsomest . . ."

A couple of days later, Daniel got the message on his phone machine: a soft, boyish voice which identified itself as Denny (no last name—just Denny), stage manager and assistant to Gilbert LaTouche, director of *A Midsummer Night's Dream* at the Black Orpheus Theater. "Mr. LaTouche," the voice said, "has decided to forgo call-back auditions and has cast the play. This is to let you know that the dual role of Oberon and Theseus is yours if you want it. Please give me a call at . . ." Daniel smiled as he scribbled down the phone number. He knew this production would hardly be Royal Shakespeare Company or Joe Papp in Central Park; he wouldn't be able to quit waiting tables at the Good Earth natural foods restaurant in Westwood Village; but it would be a stage, however small, a role he enjoyed, a chance to act.

The next message was from Harold: "Hi, kid. This is Harold. Have you heard from Denny? I did. Call me." The bounce in Harold's voice told Daniel his friend had been offered a role, too. He leaned back against the wall and punched Harold's number.

"Lo?" Harold's trademark telephone greeting.

"Lo, yourself," Daniel said.

"Daniel. So nu? We gonna be working together or what?"

"Fraid so," Daniel said. "I got Oberon. You?"

"Nick Bottom."

"Well, hooray for us. So how about your little friend," Daniel said. He hoped to seem very matter of fact, though his heart was beating faster than normal. "Davy, wasn't it?"

"Crockett," Harold said. "His name's Crockett."

"Crockett, right." Daniel had no more forgotten Crockett's name than his own. Over the past couple of days, Daniel had repeated it to himself several times—"Crockett"—just to hear it, just to feel it on his palate, on his tongue tip. He had made the effort to call to his mind everything he could about Crockett Miller: the green of his eyes, his naughty-boy smile, every word he'd spoken to Daniel in the hours he'd spent in Crockett's company. Daniel knew very well what was happening: he was developing a crush on this guy, Crockett Miller. This had never happened to him before, not with a guy, not like this: the dreaming, the thoughts, the recurring image of Crockett's face as it looked just before he said, "Have I stepped out of line again?" This was strange, and a bit disturbing. And it was . . . interesting. Once or twice he'd told himself to stop it, just *stop* it. And then he'd thought, Stop what? He hadn't *done* anything. He hadn't suddenly become someone else, something he didn't want to be. He just seemed to . . . like this guy.

"Have you heard from him?" Daniel asked. "Crockett, I mean."

"Yeah, I have, matter of fact. You won't believe it, but they offered him Puck."

"Really?" Daniel heard his own voice jump in pitch, felt his pulse kick up again. "Cool," he said, immediately wondering where that expression had come from: "cool" was not a usual Daniel Sullivan expression. "If you talk to him, uh, tell him I said congratulations. I mean, you know, remind him who I am, and—" Jesus, he thought. Pull it back, Sullivan.

"I won't have to remind him," Harold said. "He remembers you. He went on for half an hour after we all had lunch, about how *ador*able you are. That's Crockett's word: adorable." Daniel grinned so wide he was sure Harold must have *heard* it. "But I'm sure you're used to that sort of thing by now," Harold continued. "Being adorable must be such a burden." Daniel wasn't used to this bitterly facetious tone from Harold; he wasn't sure what to make of it.

"Oh, gimme a break, Benjamin," he said, joking his way around his discomfort.

"Hey," Harold countered, "give *me* a break. You think it's some kind of picnic hanging around a guy who looks like you?"

"What are you talking about?"

"Forget it," Harold said.

"Harold!" What is *with* this guy? Daniel wondered.

"Look." Harold spoke quickly, as if the words tasted sour in his mouth. "I like the kid: you know? *Like* him. I was hoping maybe we might have something, you know? But all the way home from lunch the other day, all he could talk about was my friend Daniel. 'I really like your friend Daniel. Isn't he handsome? And does he have a girlfriend? And how long have you known him?' When he finds out you got the part, he'll probably come in his fuckin' pants!"

Daniel felt as if he were being pelted with contradictory emotions: the pleasure of knowing Crockett asked about him; sympathy for Harold, wanting Crockett and feeling thwarted by a buddy, a *straight* buddy; guilt feelings for having come between Harold and someone he wanted; and then more guilt for not feeling a little more guilty about it. Daniel liked the idea that Crockett was attracted to him and not to Harold. He liked it a lot. And he felt like a flaming asshole for it.

"Hey, buddy," Daniel said, "I'm sorry."

"It's not your fuckin' fault, and I don't need your fuckin' pity, okay?"

Daniel could think of no good reply. He felt as if Harold had spit on his shoes, and he was none too sure he didn't deserve it. He tapped the back of his head against the wall a few times, just hard enough to hurt. Finally, after what seemed like weeks, Harold said, "Look, I'm sorry, Daniel. That was uncalled for."

"S'all right," Daniel said, despite not feeling very all right. "Hey, you want to go have a beer later?"

"Can't," Harold said. "I have to work tonight."

"Oh." Daniel wondered if Harold really had to work or was just avoiding him.

"Rehearsals start next Tuesday. I'll see you then, anyway."

"Right," Daniel said.

"So I'll talk to you later, okay?"

"Okay." Daniel dropped the receiver down. He sighed from the soles of his feet. He hoped Harold would be all right. He wondered if the redhead would be there on Tuesday.

He spotted her on the way to the Black Orpheus, a scant few yards from the theater. Daniel was behind the wheel, driving slowly along Cahuenga West, looking for a parking place. The redhead was walking toward the theater, a long-striding Katharine Hepburnish walk, her flame-colored hair pulled back in a ponytail. Daniel found a spot, parked hurriedly, and lit out after her. He jogged along on tiptoe until he was a couple of yards away from her, then slowed to a walk. He called out "Hi, there!" She stopped and looked over her shoulder— once, then again as a glimmer of recognition came to her eyes and a pretty smile to her lips.

"Hi there yourself," she said. "I was wondering if I'd see you today." Daniel smiled. She'd thought about him, too. Maybe she'd dreamed about him. He looked her over quickly, hoping it wasn't too obvious. She was a very sexy girl, more so than he'd remembered, even with her hair back, even in the boyish outfit she was wearing—white Izod and khaki pants, penny loafers with no socks. "What part did you get?" she asked. "Oberon?"

"Uh-huh. Titania?"

She shook her head. "Nope. Helena."

"Oh. That's too bad. I mean, I think you'd have made a good Titania." Daniel offered his right hand. "My name's Daniel," he said. "Daniel Sullivan."

She slipped her hand into his: her hand was slender and soft, but her grip was solid. "Carleen Stewart," she said. "We should probably get moving"—she glanced at the tiny tank watch on her left wrist—"or we're gonna be late." As she flipped her wrist to check the time, Daniel noticed the ring.

"You're married," he blurted.

"Yes, I am," Carleen said evenly. "Is that all right?"

Daniel felt a blush burning around this ears. "Fine for you, I guess," he said. "Not so great for me."

"Oh?" The look on her face had just a trace of flirtation to it. A young man and woman hurried past them, heading toward the theater.

"Tell you the truth, I was just gearing up to ask you out," Daniel said.

"Oh." Carleen smiled as if she'd never been complimented by a man before in her life. "Thank you, Daniel. I'm flattered."

"Well, I guess we'd better get going," Daniel said. Well, Daniel thought as they approached the tattered awning over the theater's entrance, that's that. He was disappointed, of course, that he wouldn't have a chance with Carleen. And, in a way, he was also just a little bit relieved—though at that moment, he couldn't have said why.

CHAPTER II

AS FAR AS CROCKETT WAS CONcerned, he just wanted to be the guy's friend. It would never have occurred to him to want anything more. At first, anyway. Daniel Sullivan was Harold's straight buddy, and straight is straight—no use beating your head against *that* wall. On the other hand, this Daniel—big and handsome and deliciously sexy as he was—seemed not the least uncomfortable with gayness as a concept or by gays as friends. Harold was living proof of that. So if Crockett hadn't a Fudgesicle's chance in hell of ever landing Daniel Sullivan as a lover, damned if he wasn't going to do everything in his power to make Daniel his friend.

Circumstances seemed in Crockett's favor from the first rehearsal, when Carleen, the redheaded number Daniel had seemed so hot for, turned out to be married; furthermore, she was not (as Crockett had assumed) cast opposite Daniel's Oberon as Titania, but as Helena. Titania was played by a tall, striking black girl named Charisse, with shoulder-length corn-row braids and a small gold ring piercing one side of her nose. Even if Daniel had wanted to get close to Carleen, Gilbert LaTouche's directing methods worked to keep them apart—and to bring Daniel and Crockett together.

By way of underscoring the relationships in the play, Gilbert instructed the seven actors playing the "rude rustics" (Harold Benjamin among them) to keep to themselves as much as possible, having as little to do with the rest of the cast as they comfortably could. "Think of yourselves as a group," Gilbert said, his considerable body mass testing the strength of the chair he sat in, an omnipresent Virginia Slim smoldering between his fingers. "A club. A gang." Soon those seven actors had marked off in pink chalk the first five rows of the theater, stage right, as their "turf." They called themselves only by their character names and laughed at inside jokes, and by the second week of rehearsal they were wearing T-shirts with their character names lettered on the front and "Rude Rustics" across the back. Gilbert presented the four Athenian lovers (Carleen Stewart among them) with two decks of playing cards and a book entitled *Win at Bridge* and said "play bridge."

Within a week, the foursome were bridge addicts one and all, and inseparable. Gilbert instructed Daniel and Charisse to avoid one another "like the purple plague" when not onstage. "I want *tension* here, cherubs," he said. When addressing his actors singly, Gilbert LaTouche preferred last names—as in "Mr. Sullivan, Miss Stewart"—while insisting his cast and crew call him Gilbert. Speaking to two or more of them at once, he usually referred to them as "cherubs." "Oberon and Titania, Theseus and Hippolyta: these are very tense relationships we're dealing with. I want tension, tension, tension."

"Mr. Miller," Gilbert told Crockett following the first read-through, "I want to see you at Mr. Sullivan's side *con* stantly. I want you right there with him, never more than arm's distance away. He wants his shoulders rubbed, you're there; he wants a cuppa coffee, you fetch. You're his butler, you're his valet, you're his gofer. You're Mr. Sullivan's *boy.* Got it?" Crockett got it, all right. He wanted nothing more than to be Mr. Sullivan's boy.

"And Mr. Sullivan," Gilbert continued, up from his chair and pacing the edge of the stage, smoking deeply and letting the ashes fall where they may, "I want you to *use* Mr. Miller." Crockett smiled and winked at Harold from across the room at that one; but Harold neither smiled or winked in return. "From the moment you enter this theater, Mr. Miller is *yours.*" Crockett tried to catch Harold's eye again, but Harold was looking elsewhere.

Later in that first rehearsal, as Helena pursued Demetrius through the Athenian woods onstage, Crockett sat in the audience, one seat behind Daniel. While Daniel watched the on-stage action, Crockett watched Daniel watch. He's so fuckin' beautiful, Crockett thought. The man has sexy *ears.* Jesus, the nape of his goddamn *neck* is beautiful. Crockett imagined leaning forward in his seat, wrapping his arms around Daniel's neck, and nuzzling his hair. Crockett shook his head vigorously, then quickly switched his attention back to the stage where Demetrius rebuffed Helena yet again. He took in a deep breath, blew it out. No doubt about it: this man made Crockett very warm.

When the idea came to him, it seemed so simple, yet so perfect, it made him smile. Crockett leaned forward against the back of Daniel's seat, his crossed forearms barely touching Daniel's back. "Sir?" he whispered near (though not quite into) Daniel's ear.

"Hmm?" Daniel turned his head just slightly toward Crockett.

"Anything I can do for you, sir?"

"What?" Daniel whispered, turning completely around in his seat.

"You know: a cup of coffee? A shoulder rub, perhaps?" Crockett smiled and lifted an eyebrow. Daniel smiled a smile that made Crockett feel as if his stomach were trying to escape via his mouth. His breath caught in his throat when Daniel leaned in so close his lips just grazed Crockett's ear, and whispered, "Actually, a shoulder rub wouldn't be bad." And he turned his back again.

Crockett smiled and grabbed big handfuls of Daniel's shoulders, massaging deeply into his thick, solid flesh. He closed his eyes, enjoying the sensation of Daniel's muscles beneath his fingers and palms, the sound of the deep, low hum coming from Daniel's throat. He pushed his thumb hard into Daniel's trapezius muscle, and it startled him when Daniel let out a grunt loud enough for the actors on stage to hear. Crockett's hands and forearms were very strong, from his gymnastics days, and he was afraid he hadn't known his own strength. He jumped back in his seat at the sound Daniel made; he tried to look nonchalant when Gilbert bellowed, "Do you suppose we might have it *quiet*?"

When the onstage action resumed, Crockett leaned forward

again and whispered into Daniel's ear, fighting the urge to introduce his tongue to it, "You okay? I didn't hurt you, did I?"

Daniel turned, grinning. "No," he whispered. "It hurt so *good.*"

After that, not a rehearsal went by when Crockett didn't find time to give Daniel's shoulders a long, deep massage. No one else in the cast seemed to think it particularly odd to find Crockett kneading Daniel's shoulders between scenes or at the end of rehearsal while Gilbert gave notes—Gilbert had instructed Daniel to *use* Crockett, after all. As far as Crockett was concerned, he intended to keep rubbing until Daniel said "Enough." It was his chance to touch that big, handsome man's body at least once a day. Besides, nothing gave Crockett more pleasure than making Daniel feel good.

It was almost too easy: he'd wanted to be Daniel Sullivan's buddy, and well within the first two weeks of rehearsal for *Dream,* he seemed to be just that. He'd done everything he knew to make Daniel like him. He'd complimented the color of Daniel's shirt when he really meant to compliment the size and shape of Daniel's chest. He once offered Daniel a bite of the apple he was eating, and took it as a good sign when Daniel didn't bother turning the apple over before biting. He made a habit of sitting next to Daniel in the theater and whispering witty comments, gleaning double entendres from Shakespeare's lines, or poking fun at the other actors or at Gilbert LaTouche. And, lo and behold, Daniel did like him. It wasn't as if he'd actually ever said anything—a guy like Daniel wouldn't do that. And it wasn't any particular thing Daniel did, either, or in the smiles and glances and jokes he shared with Crockett. Mostly, it was just a feeling Crockett got. He was sure Daniel felt it, too. That warm, comfortable feeling of just being with Daniel, sitting in the theater during break, reading—Daniel plowing through *The Brothers Karama-*

zov, Crockett curled up with Gordon Merrick's latest. That feeling of being with somebody you like, and who likes you back—just hangin' out with a buddy.

For Crockett, it was like something from a book or a movie. He had never had many male friends. Even as a boy, he usually formed his close friendships with females—sharing hopscotch and secrets with beribboned little girls in elementary school, developing close bonds based on similar interests, similar attitudes, and a similar sense of loneliness with overweight or homely (and hence boyfriend-less) girls in junior high and high school. Crockett had never felt any real interest in team sports—the concept of shared achievement always seemed hollow for him—and so he had never excelled in them and avoided participation in them as much as possible. Gymastics, which he discovered in high school, was ideally suited to Crockett's strong, compact body and to his disposition: the gymnastics *team* notwithstanding, Crockett was ever mindful of the fact that his victories were his own, his failures personal failures. Through junior high and high school, Crockett's avoidance of any sport that ended in the word *ball* worked to diminish his chances for youthful male bonding of the usual sort, and helped strengthen his ever-growing feelings of being different. Crockett realized by the age of eleven or twelve that he wanted to be with boys in the same way that girls wanted to be with boys. That realization only served to make him less and less comfortable in the company of other boys, and buttressed his status among those same boys as an alien creature—after all, he wasn't on any teams.

Since establishing and accepting his identity as a gay man, it had seemed to Crockett that there was (by and large) very little point in any contact with heterosexual men not necessary for getting through a normal workday. By definition, they made lousy candidates for dating, so even the particularly attractive ones were only of use as decorative objects. Generally, they were not nearly as interesting to talk to as were other gays, and were known to become difficult when in the company of a known homosexual—fashionably mid-Seventies tolerant at best ("So you're gay, so hey that's cool, so different strokes, right . . .") and physically abusive at worst. For the most part, Crockett saw no good reason to bother with straight men at all. With the gay men he knew, practically everybody was either a prospective lover, a current lover, or an ex-lover. If this made for an emotional depth much rarer in relationships between heterosexual men—as some claimed, and which Crockett conceded was possible, though how would he know?—it could also add emotional dimensions to friendships that rendered them uncomfortable or unpleasant almost as often as not.

And now, Daniel Sullivan—this big, handsome het—was his buddy. Daniel knew Crockett was gay, and it didn't seem to faze him in the least. Daniel treated him like a buddy, like a regular guy. And being friends with a regular guy was so wonderfully simple: no wondering who should make the first move, no wondering if they'd ever get to bed together, or if they'd ever want to see one another again afterward. No muss, no fuss. Just a couple of regular guys being buddies. Which would have been just fine. Except, of course, for the fact that Crockett wanted Daniel so bad he could hardly stand it.

It was strange. It just sort of snuck up on him. There seemed to be no precise moment of decision: he certainly couldn't recall ever sitting down and saying to himself, "By golly, I'm going to make *love* with Crockett Miller before I'm through." In fact, by the time Daniel consciously acknowledged that he wanted Crockett, he was already trying to figure out how he could *get* Crockett without becoming the talk of the entire cast, without attracting the attention of Harold Benjamin (who, it seemed to Daniel, was watching Crockett and him very closely from across the theater), and without jeopardizing his public identity as a heterosexual.

Scarcely one week into rehearsals, Daniel realized his feelings for Crockett were qualitatively different from the sort of localized groin-level lusts he'd had for guys before. For one thing, he couldn't seem to get the little guy out of his head. He'd spot a small, slight blond from across the room at the gym, and for a quick moment he could swear it was Crockett— and then the guy would turn, and of course it wasn't Crockett at all. While pushing vegeburgers at the Good Earth, he'd suddenly remember some silly, funny thing Crockett had said during rehearsal, and he'd catch himself grinning like some kind of fool while he worked. In the midst of making love with Jennifer, the woman he was dating semiseriously, off-and-on (an actress and dancer with a nose like Streisand's and wonderful little breasts), Crockett's face popped into Daniel's mind out of nowhere, and he'd come, shouting, with Crockett's picture stuck behind his eyes.

Daniel's earlier homosexual fantasies had almost always consisted of Daniel on the receiving end of a blow job, or Daniel ramming into some guy's behind, with perhaps some repetitive pornographic monologue ("yeah, man . . . take it . . . yeah, you like it, doncha . . ."). His fantasies about Crockett—and Crockett was starring in more and more of Daniel's fantasies—most often involved kissing. He'd lie sprawled across his bed, stroking himself, his lips stretching into an elongated "ooh," as if drinking through a straw, his tongue lapping up empty air, while he imagined kissing Crockett; not only Crockett's mouth, but his eyelids and earlobes and nipples. He'd never even considered kissing men before; and now he could hardly look at Crockett without wanting to scoop the man into his arms, hug and hold and grind up against him, and kiss him hard enough to hurt. What had started out as a perfectly commonplace, perfectly manageable little sexual spasm had quickly taken on all the earmarks of—and Daniel could hardly even think of the term without feeling silly—a crush.

That Crockett wanted him, too, was a foregone conclusion: he'd made his attraction clear from the starting gun. That was the easy part. The tough part was that, notwithstanding his desire for Crockett Miller, Daniel wasn't gay. As far as the world was concerned, he was a straight guy, and he had every intention of keeping it that way. Even if he'd known how one gay man went about pursuing and wooing another—how, he wondered, did these guys ever connect outside of gay bars?—he was sure he didn't want to get involved in any sort of gay courtship. He didn't want to have to take on some sort of bisexual identity. He didn't want Harold to even suspect that anything might be going on between Crockett and himself. He didn't want to become half of a male couple with matching his and his bath towels. He just wanted Crockett.

Not that he had the first clue as to why he should suddenly consider taking a man (any man) to bed, when he'd never felt strongly enough to consider it before, when he had always been perfectly content to keep the occasional homosexual urge safely on the fantasy level. Not that he had formulated a satisfactory answer to the question "Why Crockett Miller?" Though he was definitely a cute little guy, Crockett was hardly the best-looking man Daniel had ever seen, and he was certainly not the first homosexual ever to express an interest in Daniel. Not that he was sure he'd know how to make love to a man properly, provided he ever did get Crockett horizontal. Or if, having accomplished that, he would particularly enjoy sex with a man. There was, in fact, every indication that this was something better left to fantasy.

And yet, he wanted Crockett, wanted him like mad, like a fat man wants his lunch, like he'd never wanted a man before in his life. And he knew if he was ever going to get Crockett, it would have to be done before Gilbert LaTouche's *A Mid-summer Night's Dream* ended its run. In the meantime, Daniel began to notice Crockett testing the boundaries of their relationship; at the same time unknowingly—or maybe not so unknowingly—testing certain boundaries within Daniel. During one of the shoulder rubs that had quickly become a daily ritual, Crockett had reached down and stroked Daniel's chest with his palms—one slow upward motion of his hands across Daniel's pectorals that took him by surprise, tickled his nipples, and caused him to suck in an audible breath. And then Crockett's hands were off him.

"Sorry," Crockett whispered to the nape of Daniel's neck. "I couldn't resist." He paused for a moment, as if waiting for some sort of reaction, maybe even retaliation, before he said, "Do you mind?" They were seated (Crockett directly behind Daniel) in the last two rows of the theater, well out of view of the rest of the cast: it was highly unlikely that anyone saw. Of course, Daniel enjoyed the feeling of Crockett's small, strong hands on him. He had, in fact, during that very shoulder rub imagined taking Crockett by the wrist, bringing Crockett's hand to his lips and kissing his palm. Daniel shrugged and said, "Nah. I don't mind."

Later that same week, Crockett, now sitting next to Daniel, made a sleepy noise down in his throat, slid down in his seat and leaned over to one side, so his head pressed against the side of Daniel's shoulder. "You mind?" Crockett said softly. Daniel glanced over at Crockett—his strange, bent position obviously more concerned with making contact with Daniel's shoulder than with actual comfort. A little smile came to Daniel's lips: he could have so easily reached over and stroked Crockett's practically beardless cheek, his short straw-colored hair. "I don't mind," he said.

During the third week of rehearsals, Crockett arrived over an hour late, dashing down the center aisle like a sprinter nearing the finish line. Daniel was onstage, barefoot and bare-chested, wearing only a pair of Cal State Northridge gym shorts—the costumes designed for Oberon and Puck were very brief, and Gilbert wanted Daniel and Crockett to get used to acting "half naked." Crockett had been rehearsing in a red Speedo swimsuit for over a week. Denny, the stage manager, was also onstage, fully clothed, script in hand, standing in for Crockett. Onstage action halted and every head in the theater turned at Crockett's arrival. Dozens of eyes followed as Crockett ran up the side stairs to the stage. As he approached his stage position, Daniel noticed that Crockett was dripping with sweat—he smelled just slightly ripe, even from arm's distance. His hair was damp and disheveled. He was beautiful.

"Mr. Miller." Gilbert's voice came up from the house seats, his diction clipped, his tone Arctic. "As I'm sure you are aware, you are *extreme*ly tardy this evening. And after passing yourself off as a professional for lo these many days."

"I'm sorry, Gilbert," Crockett said, "but my second bus never showed up, and I just waited and *wait*ed, and finally I had to hitch." He did a nervous little hitchhike pantomime. "Twice."

"Gracious!" Gilbert cried. "My dear, do you mean to tell me you take the *bus*?" He intoned the word "bus" as if it had dog dirt all over it.

"Two buses," Crockett corrected. "From Century City. That's where I work."

"Land sakes," Gilbert said, obviously ready to run through his entire repertoire of quaint old exclamations, "isn't there anyone who can give this poor cherub a ride from Century City?"

"I can," Daniel blurted. Daniel worked in Westwood, and lived in Palms—neither area more than a few miles from Century City. Riding Crockett to rehearsals would present only the smallest inconvenience; it was practically on the way. And for the look on Crockett's face when he turned and said "Really?" Daniel would have carried him piggyback from Century City. "Sure," he said.

"Marvelous!" Gilbert exclaimed with an expansive gesture of his massive arms. "Now, do you suppose I might re*hearse* now?"

"I really appreciate this," Crockett whispered just before action resumed onstage. He said it again as he climbed into the passenger seat of Daniel's '72 Maverick. "I really appreciate this, Daniel," he said. Daniel shrugged it off. "No sweatskies," he said, turning the ignition key. Where am I getting these expressions? he thought to himself. No sweatskies?

There was very little conversation on the way to Crockett's apartment: Crockett gave directions as Daniel drove, and Daniel said, "Mmm-hmm."

"Pull over here," Crockett said, and Daniel stopped in front of an old, rambling apartment building along the northwestern edge of Culver City, in what those who lived there liked to refer to as "the nice part"—muggings, burglaries, and instances of gang warfare were minimal. Consequently, rents were considerably higher than warranted by actual property values. There was a long moment of uninterrupted engine hum (Daniel had put the Maverick in park, but had not cut the engine), before Crockett said, "I really appreciate this."

Daniel smiled. "So I've heard." Crockett's smile shined in the light of the car's headlamps. "I just live a couple miles away," Daniel said. "We're practically neighbors."

"Well, anyway I do . . . you know . . ."

"Appreciate this," they said together, and shared a quick staccato laugh. "Well," Crockett said, as if it were a complete thought. "Good night." He drew an audible breath in, then out, then leaned in close to Daniel and kissed him, very softly, on the cheek. It was so soft Daniel could barely feel Crockett's lips, so quick he hardly had time to register what Crockett was doing before he had already done it, and it was over.

"Do you mind?" Crockett said. Daniel tried to say no, but found he hadn't the breath. He shook his head quickly from side to side.

Crockett smiled, then blew out a breath as if in relief. "I'm glad. Well, good night," he said, opening his car door. "See you tomorrow."

"Right," Daniel said, his voice a bit husky to his own ears. "Bus stop, Santa Monica and Century Park East."

"Right," Crockett said, climbing out of the car backward. "Good night." He closed the car door hard and stood on the curb as if waiting for something. After a moment, Daniel realized Crockett was waiting for him to drive away. He put the car in drive and pulled away, smiling at nobody and nothing, throwing a grin through the windshield and out into the night. He reached up to touch the spot where Crockett's lips had grazed his cheek, as if they might have left some sort of trace, some kind of kiss residue.

Tomorrow night, he decided, he'd be ready. When Crockett kissed him good night, he'd know it was coming, and he'd be ready. He'd feel it, he'd *experience* it. He'd really be there. Shit, he thought, maybe he won't do it again.

The following evening, Crockett wished Daniel good night and kissed him on the cheek, without so much as a Do-you-mind, and Daniel was ready for it. He knew it was coming and he felt it, warm and sweet against his skin. And Daniel smiled most of the way home. Crockett kissed him again the following night. And the next. Until, like the shoulder rubs, it simply became one of those things Crockett did.

As the show moved into dress rehearsals, Crockett was already beginning to anticipate and dread the end. The end of rehearsals, which meant the beginning of the run, which meant the beginning of the *end* of the run. And the end of his friendship (relationship? buddyship? What *was* this thing, anyway?) with Daniel Sullivan. Crockett had a crush on Daniel so strong he could practically smell it on his own skin, like a heavy sweat. He woke up every morning horny and hard from dreams of Daniel. The hours he spent at work, hours of tedious typing, were made more bearable by looking forward to being with Daniel, to working with him onstage, seeing him in costume, little more than a dance belt covered with artificial leaves— Crockett wore a similar one for his role—exposing so much of Daniel's body. He looked forward to rubbing Daniel's shoulders, and to the ride home in Daniel's car, and especially to the good-night kiss Daniel allowed him every night.

Crockett's own behavior surprised him. He was not generally given to unrequited crushes, not since high school. On the contrary, Crockett absolutely required some sense of emotional and physical reciprocity. True, he often found himself in romantic situations in which he seemed to try harder, give more, love more than his half. And yet, in any relationship, even from the most casual trick, he needed to feel confident that he was wanted, desired, and not some worshiper kneeling at a phallic altar. Unlike some he knew, Crockett had never been one to waste time and energy in the pursuit of straight men, either as "trade" or as recipients of unappreciated emotional offerings—there was just no percentage in it. Yet here he was, making a minor spectacle of himself over a heterosexual, albeit an unusually kind and tolerant heterosexual, one understandably used to admiration, and secure enough to allow Crockett what he surely realized was a crush. Crockett often imagined himself looking, not only to Daniel himself but to the entire cast and crew, and possibly to Los Angeles at large, like a clumsy, slobbering puppy, all but humping Daniel's leg.

Even knowing that Daniel's feelings for him were no more than friendly—and Daniel liked him, any fool could see that—

Crockett found the thought of losing Daniel's daily company weighing heavy on his mind. He would likely never see Daniel again once the show was over. After all, they had very little in common outside of the show. Besides, Crockett had by now decided that his first show would be his last: acting, he found, was fun in a way, and interesting, but he could hardly imagine pursuing it as a career. He was no more sure than before what he did want to pursue as a career. So the chances of running into Daniel Sullivan at future auditions, or of working with him in other plays, were slim to nonexistent.

And so it was with decidedly mixed emotions that Crockett faced the official opening night of the Gilbert LaTouche production of Shakespeare's *A Midsummer Night's Dream,* which moved smoothly from two well-received invitation-only previews into its initial five-week run. Everyone connected with the show, Daniel and Crockett included, seemed to think it was good, and Crockett felt confident that his first stage performances would not greatly embarrass either Gilbert LaTouche, Daniel Sullivan, or himself. But, like a schoolboy facing the last few weeks of summer, Crockett could feel his remaining time with Daniel running through his fingers. And much as he lectured himself that advance anxiety was pointless and wasteful, Crockett couldn't seem to keep the taste of melancholy from the back of his throat as he sat next to Daniel in the men's dressing room, stroking pancake makeup onto Daniel's back with a sponge applicator. He felt almost no nervousness or anxiety concerning his own performance on-stage—he had felt none at the previews. He knew his lines, of course, and his blocking, and just about everyone else's, for that matter. He saw no reason to be nervous. Presently, his strongest and most insistent emotion involved the desire to wrap his arms around Daniel's bent-over back and not let go for hours.

The opening-night performance came off almost without

incident—the evening's sole technical hitch came during Act IV, Scene 1, when Crockett encountered some difficulty removing Harold's papier-mâché donkey head. Audience reception was warm, and the ovation swelled perceptibly during Crockett's curtain call. There were delighted squeals and quite a lot of hugging after the final curtain. Crockett was taken entirely by surprise when Daniel caught him up in a big hug, their nearly naked bodies (sticky with sweat and makeup) making a wet slapping sound on impact. "Nice job, buddy," Daniel said, and before Crockett could gather his wits enough to make some sort of reply, Daniel let go of him and turned to hug someone else.

The ride back to Crockett's apartment was strangely quiet, considering the excitement of the evening. Daniel made the occasional attempt at conversation, but Crockett didn't even feel like trying:

"It went real well tonight," Daniel said.

"Uh-huh," said Crockett.

"I heard a theater critic from the *Times* was there, and he was smiling," Daniel said.

"Really?" was the best Crockett could do for a reply. He was knot of emotions, most of them painful. Daniel's after-curtain hug had only served to whet Crockett's desire, make him even more keenly aware of just how much he wanted Daniel. He had allowed himself to fall in love with Daniel Sullivan, when he knew better than to do a thing like that. He felt like a fool. Fucking fool, he thought.

"You say something?" Daniel asked.

"No," Crockett said.

When Daniel pulled over in front of Crockett's apartment building, it didn't occur to Crockett that, unlike other nights, Daniel turned off the engine. Crockett had by this time all but decided not to kiss Daniel good night anymore—what was the point?—but when he turned to bid Daniel a kiss-less good night, he found Daniel turned sideways in the car seat, facing him, a little smile on his face. Waiting to be kissed.

"Good night, Daniel," Crockett mumbled, before leaning over and kissing Daniel's cheek as softly as he could. He started to draw away, but Daniel's hands were on his shoulders, holding him still. And then, so quickly he didn't see it coming, Daniel's mouth was on his, kissing him hard. And just as suddenly, Daniel pulled away. He stared into Crockett's eyes for a brief moment, just long enough for Crockett to suck in a quick breath, just long enough for his mind to register the event. Daniel kissed him again, his fingers tight on Crockett's shoulders. He pushed his tongue between Crockett's teeth; Crockett grabbed the back of Daniel's neck, pushing their faces together even further, sucking Daniel's tongue.

When their mouths parted again, Crockett trembled in the warm night. His penis was hard, and his mind was splitting with questions. Was Daniel gay? And if he was, what had taken him so goddamn *long*? And if he wasn't, why were they smooching in the front seat of a '72 Maverick? Was a few humid kisses in his car all Daniel had in mind? Or did he want to make love? What the fuck was going on here?

"Are you sure you know what you're doing?" he asked.

Daniel took a couple of breaths, shook his head from side to side. "No," he said. "May I come in?"

CHAPTER
12

HIS LIPS WERE SO SOFT: IT CAME
as something of a surprise. Daniel would have thought a man's
kiss would feel hard or rough or something (men have beards,
after all), but Crockett's mouth felt as soft and good as that of
any woman he had ever kissed. He had not decided for certain
to do what he finally did in that car seat, though he had been
considering it for several days, Ping-Ponging back and forth
between yes and no dozens of times within a few moments'
thought. He hadn't even consciously decided to cut the car
engine in front of Crockett's place; but once he had, he knew
the time had come. And once he had kissed Crockett's lips, he
knew there'd be no turning back. Not that night.

Crockett led Daniel by the hand through the security gate
and upstairs to his apartment, now and then looking back at
him as if he half expected Daniel to disappear like a mirage.
Standing outside Crockett's front door, waiting for Crockett
to maneuver each of three keys into each of three locks, Daniel reached over and touched the side of Crockett's neck with
his fingertips, following the curve down to his shoulder and
off. Crockett's spine stiffened, and he dropped his keys onto
the concrete step with a jingle-jangle sound, disproportion-
ately loud in the relative stillness of the night.

"Jesus fuck, Daniel," Crockett said through an audible

breath. "What are you doing to me?" He bent over and retrieved his keys, and finally managed to open the door. They were both inside and the door shut behind them before Daniel answered, "Kissing you." He pulled Crockett to him by the front of his T-shirt, wrapped his arms around Crockett's back, and they kissed again. Crockett slipped his arms around Daniel's waist, dropping his keys again, which clattered to the floor behind Daniel. Daniel parted Crockett's lips with his own and shoved his tongue into Crockett's mouth, twirling it around Crockett's tongue, then drawing it back to scribble across Crockett's gums. He sucked Crockett's lips one after the other, then bit the lower one and worried it between his teeth. He bit Crockett's chin, hard enough to hurt a little, hard enough to make Crockett gasp a little, then kissed it a tiny butterfly baby kiss. He took Crockett's face (puffy-lipped and red-chinned) in both his hands and sprinkled it with little kisses: his lips, his cheeks, forehead, eyelids, his chin again.

He pulled up at the hem of Crockett's shirt, raising it toward his armpits, and Crockett tugged it up over his head. Daniel stroked down the sides of Crockett's shoulders and arms, then slowly down Crockett's front, feeling Crockett's nipples pucker as his fingers brushed them. Crockett's eyelids closed, and his chest expanded with air. "Ah," he sighed, "Daniel . . ." His eyes still closed, Crockett reached for the buttons of Daniel's shirt and began unfastening them. He pulled Daniel's shirt out from his pants and opened the front of it, and began nuzzling Daniel's chest, ruffling the hair with his face, humming softly on one note, like a small engine.

Daniel's breath caught as Crockett began licking his nipples; first one, then the other, then back again.

"Crockett," he said finally, scratching softly at the back of Crockett's neck. Crockett seemed too busy to hear. "Crockett?"

"Hmm?" Crockett said, the sound of his voice muffled against Daniel's chest.

"Where's the bedroom?"

It was strange, yet strangely familiar territory Daniel explored with his hands and mouth and body as he lay naked with Crockett upon the latter's single bed. He had certainly seen Crockett's naked and near-naked body enough times: the stage costumes they both wore left precious little to surprise, and they had showered less than an arm's distance apart every day for over a week, since they'd begun dress rehearsals, since they'd both begun applying makeup to their entire bodies, so he had seen Crockett's hard, compact gymnast's body—all of it. Now he could feel it, all of it, solid and warm underneath him. Daniel liked being on top, rubbing his hard-on up and down the grooves on either side of Crockett's groin, between Crockett's thighs, across Crockett's moist belly.

Crockett locked his heels around Daniel's waist, and they bucked against one another, kissing and rubbing, moving in moist pantomime of what Daniel really wanted. "Yep," Daniel whispered, "if you were a girl, you'd definitely be fucked by now." And Crockett said, "There's some KY under the bed."

It had been so long since he'd been with another male like this, Daniel had all but forgotten how different it felt with a guy: Crockett was so tight and dry compared to any woman, even with the help of the KY jelly, and it had required quite a bit just to enter him. Being inside Crockett, watching the rapturous look on Crockett's face, hearing the sound of Crockett's voice, moaning softly, whispering things so nasty Daniel blushed: all worked to stoke Daniel's excitement. The feeling of Crockett's hands stroking up and down Daniel's back and sides and ass, his fingers tugging at Daniel's nipples, kept him on the edge of orgasm as he rocked his hips forward and back, as slowly as he could.

Daniel felt himself only seconds, fractions of seconds from the point of no return, when suddenly Crockett trembled violently beneath him, spasming and spewing white ribbons across his own chest and belly. Then Daniel exploded, too; his eyes shut tight, his body clenched like a fist. His mouth and throat opened wide, as if to scream, but no sound came. Daniel heard only his own pulse pounding against his temples, and Crockett repeating in a husky whisper, "Oh, Daniel . . . oh my God . . . oh, Daniel . . ."

Crockett awoke early, lying on his left side, his back pressed against the warm, solid front of Daniel's body, his dick already hard. He usually slept on his back, but the size of his bed barely allowed for two grown men to sleep in it together exactly as he and Daniel had slept—on their respective left side, back to front. Daniel was already awake: he had slipped his hard penis between the backs of Crockett's thighs, and was moving in short, slow strokes, massaging the perineal ridge between Crockett's anus and balls. He nuzzled the top of Crockett's head, and whispered "Good morning" into his hair.

Crockett didn't say anything for a moment, and when he finally did, he said, "I had the craziest dream last night."

"Yeah?" Daniel wiggled the tip of his middle finger around the indentation of Crockett's navel.

"Uh-huh. I dreamed I was making love with this straight guy I know. And it was pretty wonderful. And the funny thing is, I'm obviously still asleep, because I'm still dreaming."

"So keep sleeping," Daniel said, wrapping his hand around Crockett's hard-on, giving it a good squeeze. "Would you like me to suck you off?" And Daniel crawled down toward the foot of the bed, taking the covers with him.

"Not just at the moment, okay?" Crockett pushed himself up to a seated position against the headboard.

"No? How come?"

"Daniel." Crockett hugged a pillow tight against his chest.

"Yeah?" Daniel sat up on his haunches, his erection swinging like a pendulum.

"Have you slept with men before?"

"No. Why? Wasn't it good?" His penis began to droop just a bit. "You looked like you were having a good time."

"No, it was fine. Great. Never?"

"No," Daniel said. "I mean, I messed around a little when I was a kid—eleven, twelve years old—but not with men, no. You're my first actual *man*. And you know something?" he said with a mischievous one-sided grin. "You're good."

"You were having sex at eleven years old?" Crockett asked, his voice rising in pitch and volume.

"Well, yeah," Daniel admitted with a smile halfway between proud and sheepish. "I was kind of an early bloomer. That's how my mom likes to put it. The summer before I turned eleven, I had this major growth spurt, and by the time I started the sixth grade, I was full grown. All over."

"You were that big—tall—at eleven?"

Daniel smiled, reached out and stroked the top of Crockett's foot. "Yep," he said, grabbing Crockett's big toe. "This tall *and* this big."

Crockett snatched his foot away, clutched the pillow closer against him. "And having sex? With who? Whom?"

"With Vinnie DiFilippo," Daniel replied.

"Of course," said Crockett, utterly deadpan.

"He lived down the street from us in Phoenix, where I grew up. Vinnie was a couple years older than me. His little brother Robert and I used to have sleepovers a lot."

"Sleepovers?"

"Yeah," Daniel said. "Didn't you ever sleep over at a friend's house?"

Crockett shook his head. "No."

"What a waste," said Daniel. "Anyway . . ." Daniel stretched out on his belly next to Crockett. Crockett started to reach out and touch Daniel's back, but then pulled away. They were getting way off the subject. "Anyway, I was sleeping over with Robert DiFillipo one night, and he and I were sitting around in our pj's, and I was showing him my dick. I had just had this growth spurt, you know, and mine was about three times the size of Robert's, and he was really into it. Just touching it, you know, we didn't know what the fuck *else* to do with your dick."

Daniel turned on his side, facing Crockett. Crockett noticed Daniel was hard again. "So suddenly Vinnie walks in. And there we are, me and Robert with our wienies hanging out, and of course we're both scared shitless, I mean we're in deep shit trouble now. He's gonna tell Mom, he's gonna tell Dad, they're gonna call *my* folks." Daniel chuckled. "Know what Vinnie does?" Crockett shook his head. "Vinnie closes the bedroom door, props the door shut with a chair. He sits down on the bed with us, opens up his pants, pulls out *his* dick, and teaches us both how to masturbate. God bless him."

"So that's all you did with these kids?" Crockett said. "Just jerked off?"

"Oh, no," Daniel said, rolling over on his back, hands behind his head, making his biceps bulge. Crockett fought the urge to bury his face in Daniel's armpit. "Well, with Robert, yes. But Vinnie? That kid was something else. Snuck into Robert's room one night while Robert was asleep—gave me my first blow job. Came in another night with this little jar of Vaseline and says, 'You wanna put it in me?' I didn't know what he was talking about. But he showed me what he was talking about pretty quick. That Vinnie," Daniel said with a little laugh. "Couldn't get enough. At thirteen years old, mind you. Thirteen." Daniel let out a little whistle.

"So you're sucking and fucking your little brains out at eleven," Crockett said.

"Yep," said Daniel. "That lasted about six months. Then we moved here, and that was the end of that. I didn't make it with anybody but *these* guys"—Daniel held up his right hand and wiggled his fingers—"until my junior year in high school, when Terri Lynn Dailey let me go all the way, quote unquote, on her rumpus room sofa." Daniel smiled and added, "God bless her."

"Well, are you gay, or what? Are you, like, seriously closeted or something? Was last night like your coming out party?"

"No," Daniel said. "I'm not. Gay. I like women. I mean, I really like women. I intend to marry one. And, I also like you. I'd never really wanted to with a man before—not enough to *do* it, anyway. But with you I did. Want to. Zat okay? Hey," he said, falling down onto all fours and switching subjects in one smooth motion, "do you think we could go to my place tonight? My bed's a lot bigger."

"Okay." Crockett fought back a smile. Daniel had obviously taken it for granted that they'd be together again that night, that Crockett either had no plans for the evening—a Friday evening, at that—or that he'd drop any plans he might have had so as to spend the evening with Daniel. And he was right.

"Holy shit!" Daniel said, glancing at the small windup alarm clock next to Crockett's bed. "I gotta get home, shower, and change. I gotta go to work." He bounded out of bed and began poking through the motley collection of cast-off clothing on the bedroom floor. "Where the hell did I throw my pants?"

"Daniel!" Crockett shouted. Daniel snapped to attention; his penis bobbed back and forth with a life of its own.

"What?"

There were so many things Crockett wanted to say, things he wanted to ask. He wanted to say, "So what is this? What am I to you? Your experiment in adult bisexuality?" He wanted to say, "So how long do you suppose you'll feel like kissing and hugging and fucking the living daylights out of me? And what happens when you've had enough? What happens to me? Hey, dude—what happens to my fuckin' *heart*, goddammit?" He wanted to say, "I think it's only fair to warn you that I could very well be in love with you." That's what Crockett wanted to say. What he said was, "They're over there."

"What?" Daniel repeated.

"Your pants." Crockett pointed across the room. "Over in the corner." Daniel bent to pick up his pants, and Crockett watched Daniel's genitals swinging between his legs. He hugged his pillow even tighter and tried to tune out the nagging voice near the base of his skull telling him in no uncertain terms that this wasn't a good idea. Daniel Sullivan was not gay. He really liked women. He intended to marry one. Fine for Daniel. Only Crockett *was* gay—completely, irrevocably, and quite all right about it, thanks. He really liked men. He intended to marry one. He would have liked to marry Daniel Sullivan.

I'm going to get hurt, he thought, watching Daniel's big bent-over back, as he perched at the foot of the bed, tugging on his pants. I'm fuckin' *begging* to get hurt. Daniel walked into the bathroom, didn't bother closing the door: Crockett listened to the splash of water on water, the flush, then more water splashing into the washbasin. A few moments later Daniel emerged with the front of his hair wet, retrieved his shirt and shoes from the floor, and walked over to the bed where Crockett sat. He half knelt on the bed (one foot on the floor) and leaned in so close to Crockett their noses nearly met.

"Same time, same bus stop?" Daniel said. Crockett nodded. Daniel kissed Crockett's lips softly—once, then again—and whispered, "Later, sweetheart." And when Crockett's eyes opened, Daniel was gone. He listened to the sound of Daniel's footsteps, the door closing. He smiled. *Sweetheart,* yet. He slid back down into bed and covered his face with the pillow. Oh well, he thought. If I'm riding for a fall, at least I'll enjoy the ride.

Daniel simply didn't think about it. In a maneuver similar to *not* thinking about pink elephants, Daniel consciously *willed* himself not to think about the fact that he was in love with Crockett Miller, that he was in love with a man. And he was very much in love with Crockett; he knew it the moment he woke up next to Crockett that first morning after, and just lay there for several minutes, watching him sleep. To consider that feeling, let alone how good it had felt making love with Crockett, was to call into question his very self-identification. Daniel had decided years before that the basic difference between a gay man and one who wasn't, was that gay men fell in love with each other. Contrary to the old joke, "You are who you eat," Daniel believed something closer to "You are who you fall in love with."

The "Crockett thing," as Daniel quickly labeled the situation, would doubtless require some radical rethinking on Daniel's part, had he chosen to dwell on it: it was a circumstance that seemed to demand revision of Daniel's own definition of himself as a basically heterosexual man with vague bisexual leanings, or his definition of what was entailed in being gay, or maybe both. And for the immediate future at least, Daniel was highly disinclined toward involved inner dialogues, introspective philosophizing, or deep soul-searching with intent to restructure his own sense of sexual identity. For the time being, he just wanted to love Crockett. And let Crockett love him.

He was sure Crockett loved him, although he'd never exactly said so; he was probably more than a little confused. Hell, so was Daniel. It was a confusing situation—and precarious and fragile, and Daniel was afraid to jinx it. He only hoped Crockett would simply accept that Daniel cared for him, wanted him, and not complicate a complicated situation by asking himself, or Daniel, a lot of questions. Wouldn't gum up everything by *thinking* too much.

It just felt so good, loving Crockett. Daniel had no idea how long it would feel so good, but he saw no good reason not to sit back and enjoy the Crockett thing for as long as it lasted.

It lasted nearly a year.

CHAPTER 13

"WHY DO YOU WANT TO HAVE this test?" The man looked up from his clipboard and into Daniel's eyes. Daniel pushed back a pang of mild annoyance. This was the third time in twenty minutes he'd been asked that same question. One of the first things he'd encountered upon entering the clinic lobby was a television set playing a video tape (and playing and playing it, indefinitely) in which a matronly black woman in a lab coat encouraged the viewer to ask himself the question, "Why do you want to have this test?" A few minutes after sitting down (about halfway through his second viewing of the video), he was handed a clipboard with a questionnaire, of which question number one was "Why do you want to have this test?" And now, sitting in a tiny off-white room barely large enough for the tiny desk, two chairs, and two men it held, his pretest interviewer, a muscular young man of about Daniel's age wearing a very tight T-shirt and a waxed handlebar mustache, was asking him yet again, in an incongruously light, boyish voice, "Why do you want to have this test?" It struck Daniel as strange that, when they had an AIDS test available, these people should be so hesitant to administer it. They seemed to be all but forbidding people to be tested.

"I don't *want* to have this test," Daniel said, aware of the sarcastic edge creeping into his voice, "I sort of *need* to have it. See, a real good friend of mine is having symptoms, pre-AIDS symptoms, and—"

"I assume you've had sexual contact with this friend," Mustache interrupted.

"Yes."

"And are you experiencing any symptoms?"

"No. I'm not, but—"

"Then why test?" He leaned forward, elbows on knees.

"Because—" Daniel began, his tone a little louder than conversational: Mr. Mustache's gift for interruption was beginning to grate.

"Why not have safe sex, take good care of your body, go about your business?"

"Because my wife is six weeks pregnant, okay?" Daniel lifted his left hand up for the man to see. Mustache sat back in his chair. "I'm pretty sure I'm all right, but pretty sure isn't enough. Okay?"

"Oh," he said, averting his eyes from Daniel's. "I see." He made a mark on whatever paper it was he was playing with on the clipboard and said, "Okay. Why don't you take a seat in the waiting room and someone will call you in a few minutes."

Daniel stood up. "Gee," he said, his voice thick with sarcasm, "you mean you're gonna let me take it after all?"

"Whoa. Now, just hold on a minute," the man said, stopping Daniel where he stood. "Despite what you seem to think, *sir*"—he loaded the word with some sarcasm of his own—"we are not here to hassle you. Didn't you watch the video outside?"

"Four and a half times."

"Did you listen to it? We're talking about a disease with no cure, no vaccine, no nothing." The man's voice grew louder, his brow crimped with irritation. "Just lots and lots of sickness and death. And this one little pissant test that doesn't even test for the disease itself, for chrissakes. Just antibodies in the blood. That's the cold, ugly reality in the year of our Lord 1985, and we have a responsibility here: we can't just hand out this test to anybody who thinks they want to know. Because a lot of people discover afterwards that they didn't *really* want to know. A positive result can sound an awful lot like a death warrant. I know."

The silence hung in the air between them for a moment. "I'm sorry," Daniel said finally.

"Yeah." The mustache man turned his face away. "Take a seat outside." Daniel turned and opened the door. "Hey," the man called from behind. Daniel turned; the ends of the man's mustache were tilted upward in an attempt at a smile. "Good luck." Daniel smiled in return and said, "Thanks."

Crockett was seated just outside the door as Daniel emerged. He had decided to be tested, against his doctor's advice. "I have to know," he'd said to Daniel on the telephone, his voice strangely calm. "I have to know for sure." He looked up and said, "Did they try to talk you out of it?"

"Didn't they, though." Daniel sat in the chair next to Crockett's. "How about you?"

"Oh, we had a nice long chat. This very sweet little lesbian rattled off the top five reasons not to get tested, and I told her I wanted it anyway. And she argued some, and I told her I wanted it anyway. And then she said she strongly advised against it, and I said thanks, but I wanted it anyway." He shrugged. "Funny thing is: I'm ninety-nine percent sure of the outcome, and I'm still scared."

"Same here," Daniel said.

A very young man in a lab coat (with yet another clipboard) emerged from a nearby door and said, "DA thirty-one, please. DA thirty-one." Daniel's code number. When he'd first called the clinic, the voice on the other end asked for two letters and two digits, to be used as the only means of identification throughout the entire testing process, his guarantee of total anonymity. Daniel chose the first two letters of his name, and his age on his next birthday.

"Here," Daniel said, raising a finger. "Come on in," said the young man with a genuine-looking smile. Rising from his chair, Daniel turned to Crockett, smiled a smile he didn't particularly feel, and whispered, "It's showtime, folks." Crockett raised his crossed fingers.

"I'm sure you hear this all the time," the lab-coated young man said, wrapping a length of rubber tubing around Daniel's upper arm, "but you look a lot like Superman."

"You're right," Daniel said, suddenly aware of the tension in his jaw. "I hear it a lot." Daniel watched the veins in his arm bulge. He wasn't very comfortable around needles during the best of times, and this wasn't one of them. He was also a bit surprised to be faced with a male nurse who looked like a UCLA undergraduate dance major. The nurse, freckled and cute, with a lot of curly blond hair and a name tag that read Andy, was probably twenty-five, but he looked scarcely twenty-one.

"Okay," Andy the nurse announced in a voice like Monty Hall making a deal, "it's quiz time. Ready? Good. When is tongue wrestling not considered safe?"

"Tongue wrestling?"

"Deep kissing," he said, tapping Daniel's distended blood vessel with two fingers. "Tongue sushi is not considered safe when either participant's gums are bleeding. So no tongue wrestling for about half an hour after brushing your teeth, okay?"

"Okay," Daniel said blankly, quietly hoping nurse Andy would just *stick* him, already, and get it over with.

"Look!" Andy said, loudly and suddenly enough to make Daniel jump. "Up in the sky! It's a bird! It's a plane! It's—" By the time Daniel felt the little sting in his arm, Andy said, "It's all over." And he pushed a cotton ball into the crook of Daniel's arm, shoved Daniel's hand up to his shoulder, and said, "There now, that wasn't so terrible, was it?" He smiled with what seemed to be more than the requisite number of teeth. "No," Daniel said. "Not so terrible. Is that it?"

"That's it," Andy said, still smiling. As Daniel got up to leave, Andy touched him on his bent-up right elbow and said, "Hey."

"Yes?"

"So, DA thirty-one—are you, how you say, involved?"

"Yes," Daniel said, lifting his left hand and wiggling his fingers in Andy's face. "I am very much involved."

Andy shrugged. "Oh, well. Can't hang you for asking. See ya."

"See ya."

Crockett was still sitting outside the door when Daniel came out.

"You done it yet?" Daniel asked.

Crockett shook his head no, as Andy opened his door and said, "CM fifty-five please. CM fifty-five." Crockett stood up. "They're playing my song."

"Do you want me to wait for you?" Daniel asked.

"No, that's okay." Crockett walked one step forward, then

stopped and turned back to Daniel. "I mean yes," he said. "Please."

When Crockett was finished, and their tiny arm wounds sufficiently clotted to allow for driving, Daniel and Crockett walked together out to the parking lot. Daniel hooked his arm around Crockett's shoulders, and they walked that way a few steps before Daniel allowed his arm to drop.

"I guess I'll see you in two weeks," Daniel said. "If not sooner."

"Guess so," Crockett said, climbing into his ugly little car.

"Take care," Daniel said, knocking aimlessly on the car hood.

"You, too. Give my love to the little woman."

"You bet," Daniel said. Crockett started his car, and Daniel stepped back, turning toward his own car. He heard Crockett beep his horn as he pulled away down Santa Monica.

Daniel had barely pulled out of the clinic's parking lot before the nagging discomfort set in. He had lied to Maggie that morning: "I'm gonna go shoot a few baskets over at the high school with some of the partners," he said. He'd worn sweats and high-top Converse shoes to the clinic. He'd even gone so far as to enlist Harold Benjamin to back up his alibi.

"If the subject should ever come up," he'd said the day before, leaning over Harold's desk, his fist tight around a crystal paperweight, "we're playing basketball together tomorrow morning. Okay?"

"What on earth is a basketball?" Harold said.

"Very cute, Benjamin. Just cover me, all right?"

"My, my," Harold said, barely above a whisper, "married scarcely a year, and already embroiled in some tawdry little affair."

"Cute again, Harold."

"So are you going to tell me what this is about or what?"

"I'd really rather not," Daniel said. "Would you just do this for me, please?"

"Anything for you," Harold said, a smile on his face that made Daniel wonder if Harold actually thought he was having an affair. He briefly considered telling Harold the truth, but quickly decided against it. The fewer people who knew about this thing, the better.

Daniel pulled his car into the high school a few blocks from his house. He jogged over to the track, and immediately broke into a hard run. He ran lap after lap, until he'd worked up a good, steady sweat; until he was sure he'd come home smelling like a man who'd just played some serious b-ball, until a pain stabbed him like an ice pick in his left side and he had to stop. He fell back onto the crisp brown grass along the track, gulping air, embracing the slash of pain across his side like a monk embraces penance. Lying to Maggie, telling even a relatively small lie for what he truly believed was her own good, for the good of their marriage, pained Daniel more than the cramp in his side.

I'll never lie to her again, he thought, clutching his ribs. No matter what. Still, when he got home and Maggie asked, "So how was basketball?" Daniel said, "Fine. Great." Maggie, just back from the supermarket, stood in front of the open trunk of her car, which was filled with well-stuffed paper bags.

"You smell like a whole *team,*" she said, hefting a full, heavy bag of groceries out of the trunk and into the crook of Daniel's arm. "Did you win?"

"Nope," Daniel said. "I lost."

"Poor baby," Maggie said. She rose on tiptoe and kissed Daniel's lips, took a small bag from the trunk, then turned and headed for the house.

Daniel felt a residual pang in his side. He wondered if this was how he would feel if he were actually having an affair. As if the word *liar* were tattooed across his forehead. As if every word he spoke rang false as a tin bell. He hated the feeling. He wondered if perhaps he should have told Maggie about the Crockett thing from the very beginning, before he'd married her. But then again, why? He'd had other women before Maggie, and she had been with at least one other man: that guy in college—she'd mentioned him once or twice. Should he have read her a comprehensive list as part of the preparation for the wedding? How could he have possibly imagined that this horror, this goddamned disease would come in from out of the stage left wings, reducing Crockett's life to rubble, with the unspeakably ugly possibility of doing the same to his own?

He just wanted this waiting to be over. He wanted to crawl into bed, pull the blankets up over his head and just sleep for two weeks, and wake up to clinical proof that he was all right, that his wife and his unborn child would be all right. He wanted his life back to normal. He wanted his life back.

"Honey?" Maggie called from the back door, breaking into Daniel's thoughts. "You gonna bring those things in sometime today?"

And then he couldn't come.

Daniel had considered abstaining from sex ever since Crockett had dropped the bomb over a week before, but he could think of no way to suddenly stop making love with Maggie—or even to introduce condoms into their lovemaking, a course of action he'd also considered—without arousing his wife's suspicion, without having to lie, perhaps elaborately. The possibility that he might be infecting Maggie with AIDS every time he made love with her was beyond frightening, but Daniel did consider it a very remote possibility. Besides, he and Maggie had been making love, regularly and often, for over a year. Would another two weeks or so really make a difference?

Daniel's considered opinion had been no. Unable to consult Maggie on the subject, Daniel had decided on both their behalf that it would be business as usual—or at least the appearance of it—until he could get tested and receive the results of the test. For the few days between that fateful lunch date with Crockett and the morning he was tested, Daniel and Maggie had made love at least once each evening, and it was good, as it nearly always was. Then he went to the clinic in West Hollywood, and cute little nurse Andy drew blood from Daniel's arm. And that night, Daniel couldn't come.

It wasn't that Daniel was impotent. Indeed, he had barely slipped his arms around Maggie's waist and hugged her close before he was hard enough to cut glass. He just couldn't come. He thrust into Maggie until his arms buckled and his abdominal muscles cramped; until Maggie had come and come and come again and finally slapped wearily at his shoulders and begged him to stop. He used his hands; then Maggie used hers. Maggie used her lips and tongue, and while it wasn't exactly her forte—it made her jaw hurt—she did give it the old college try. And he couldn't come.

That first night, when Maggie finally kissed him good night, first below the waist, then above, and assured him it was probably just work-related stress and he'd be fine tomorrow, Daniel was reasonably sure he wouldn't be fine tomorrow. And he was right. He made love to Maggie, took pleasure in her pleasure, and when Maggie asked, "Did you?" he said, "Don't worry about it." A couple of nights later, it wasn't happening for Maggie, either. "What's wrong?" he asked, raw and tender and dripping with sweat. "Don't worry about it," Maggie said. The following night, Maggie had a little headache, and Daniel was tired.

The following night, he faked it. He thrust hard and deep, and made the sort of noise he seemed to remember making during orgasm. Afterward, when Maggie (who had been understandably reticent about the whole thing) stroked his back with her fingertips and asked, "Did you?" Daniel breathed in and out a couple of deep, sighing breaths and said, "Oh, yeah, babe. Oh, yeah." He waited for his aching, frustratingly malfunctional erection to subside, then turned over onto his back, and waited for sleep, praying silently that the dream would not come back.

The dream began the night after his orgasms stopped. It was always the same: Daniel was moving—half running, half flying—through a long, winding, maze-like corridor with no doors. He felt worried and frightened. He was looking for Maggie. He called out her name, as loudly as he could, but the sound of his voice seemed to stop inches from his lips and then evaporate. Still he ran, searched, and called.

And then the corridor stopped, and Crockett was there against the sudden wall, a ghastly spectre of Crockett. He was naked and emaciated, his eyes sunken, only the odd wisp of hair clinging to his flaking scalp, his face and body spotted with ugly purple sores. Daniel reached out one hand toward the waste that was his friend, while the rest of his body recoiled from the sight. He hid his eyes with his other arm, and cried out, his scream echoing back and forth off the walls of the dream.

He turned back and Crockett was gone, and in his place was Maggie: a skeletal, spotted figure bent into a corner, barely recognizable as Daniel's wife, but doubtlessly she. In her lap lay a baby. Little more than bone, curled and twisted into itself, barely alive, spotted with purple. Daniel stretched out his arms toward the hideous figures, and suddenly saw his own hands and arms, bony and gnarled, covered with sores.

Daniel's scream came from all around him, entered his body through every pore, then flew from his mouth, and he was screaming and screaming, and he was the scream.

That first time, he screamed loud enough and long enough to awaken Maggie before he woke up himself. And when he did awaken, she was already there, gently stroking his head with her soft, warm hand, her face close to his, whispering, cooing, as if to a small child, "Easy, honey. It's all right, honey. Maggie's here. It's all right." He lay trembling next to her for a few minutes, and then he slept again, a deep and seemingly dreamless sleep, for the rest of the night.

In the morning, as he kissed her awake on his way out to work, the first words Maggie spoke upon opening her eyes were "Are you okay, honey?"

"Of course," Daniel said. "Why?"

"You had some nightmare last night. You woke up screaming. Don't you remember?"

"No," he said. But he did remember it, completely and vividly. When the dream did not return that night, Daniel thought he was rid of it; but it came back the next night—the same dream, start to finish, as perfect as a rerun. It was like a living thing, intelligent and cruel. It seemed to be toying with him, awakening him in a cold sweat one night, then leaving him alone the next, coming back the next night, then skipping two. After that first night, Daniel did not scream aloud: he'd awaken from the dream, shaken to his very bone marrow, short of breath, his heart pounding in his ears, half surprised to find his wife, healthy and beautiful, next to him in bed. But at least he didn't awaken Maggie anymore.

Predictably, Daniel's disposition suffered. He quickly grew short-tempered and irritable, given to uncharacteristic Jekyll-and-Hyde mood swings; and even though intensely aware of the changes in his personality, he felt increasingly helpless to control them. He snapped at his secretary over the temperature of his coffee, then all but crawled to her desk minutes later to apologize. Harold Benjamin paid a friendly visit to Daniel's office one morning, obviously in the mood for a chat, only to be met by a fire-spitting ogre wearing Daniel's clothes.

"Yo, Daniel," Harold called, rapping on the doorjamb.

"What?" Daniel barked, glancing up from his desk only briefly.

"Nothing," Harold said, sounding retreat. "Forget it." Remorse hit fast and hard, and Harold was only a few steps down the hall before Daniel called out, "Harold! Wait up!" Harold stepped slowly back toward Daniel's doorway.

"You gonna bite off the rest of my head now?" he said, walking in and closing the door behind him.

"I'm sorry, buddy," Daniel said. "Really. I'm just . . . I don't know . . ."

"Hey, dude," Harold said, "stop me right away if this is none of my fuckin' business, but, um . . ." He leaned his fists against the desktop. "Frankly, my dear, I think you're losin' it."

Daniel dropped his head into his hands. "No shit."

"Everything all right at home?" Harold winced, obviously pained even to ask such a question. He tapped his finger against the edge of the picture frame propped on the desktop, drawing Daniel's attention to the wedding photo it held.

"Fine," Daniel barely whispered.

"You sure? This wouldn't have anything to do with last Saturday's basketball game, would it?"

"What?" Daniel's basketball alibi had slipped his mind.

"Seriously, man: you getting some on the side?"

Daniel's back stiffened. "No! Absolutely not!"

"Okay, okay," Harold raised his hands in defense. "I'm just askin'. What the hell is it, then?"

"I can't," Daniel said wearily. "I just can't talk about it."

"Okay, fine," Harold said, backing up toward the door. "If you change your mind, you know where my cell is." He turned to go.

"Harold!" Daniel stretched out his right hand toward his friend: suddenly he needed human contact. Harold approached, and grasped Daniel's hand. "Thanks, buddy," Daniel said.

The following morning, Daniel shook Maggie awake,

shouting, "Where are the fucking clean handkerchiefs? Is it too damn much to ask that I have a fucking clean handkerchief?"

Maggie sat up in bed, tousled and sleepy-eyed. She took a long, bosom-lifting breath and, in a husky but deliberately calm voice, she said, "Daniel, what is happening here?"

"What?" Maggie's quiet had punctured Daniel's bluster like a hatpin in a toy balloon: suddenly he felt quite small and ridiculous.

"Daniel," Maggie said, combing back her hair with the fingers of both hands, "this is not about handkerchiefs. Do you honestly suppose I haven't noticed? Your moods. Your nightmares. Your"—she looked away—"sexual problem. What *is* this? Is it me, Daniel? Is it us?"

"Oh, Maggie!" Daniel crumpled onto the bed in his best gray suit, shoes and all, and took Maggie into his arms, kissing her slightly sour mouth, her face, her hair. "No, sweetheart," he said. "Not you. Never you." The tears came before he realized it. "I'm so sorry, baby," he said through small, staccato sobs. "I'm so sorry."

"Honey," Maggie crooned, stroking down a little cowlick near the top of Daniel's head. "What is it, then? What is it?"

"It's—it's," Daniel stammered, half wanting to tell her, tell her everything, "it's work, you know . . . pressure . . . stress . . ."

"Honey, if this is what your job does to you, maybe you should think about doing something else. Really. You know I'll still hang around even if you decided to sell shoes door to door." She lifted Daniel's head and looked into his reddened eyes. "This can't go on, Daniel."

"I'll be all right," he said, rising up on his arms. He sat up and wiped at his eyes with the heels of his hands. "Soon. It'll all be all right soon." He hoped to God he was right.

* * *

Daniel's eyes flew open at six o'clock the Saturday morning of his return appointment at the clinic. The sun was already up, warming the side of his face where the light filtered in through the drapes. Dozens of little birds seemed to be bickering in the trees outside the windows. Maggie slept, warm and silent, on her side in a semifetal curl next to Daniel. He realized immediately that there was no chance of his going back to sleep—his mind was buzzing like an electric shaver—so he climbed out of bed and into his bathrobe. He started the Mr. Coffee, then rescued the *Times* from the front flower bed where the paperboy had lobbed it. He took a seat in the breakfast nook, drank cup after cup of decaf and read the newspaper, word for word, page by page, losing himself in other people's troubles with surprising ease. Only now and then—every three or four pages—it came back: the crushing, smothering feeling in his guts, the apprehension, the small but unspeakable fear; and he had to take a long, deep breath, a sip of decaf, and wait for it to pass.

A tiny ad in the middle of the Westside section caught his eye: large white boldface print against solid black, it read simply "AIDS Hotline," with a phone number beneath, the last four digits of which spelled out AIDS. Daniel stared at the big white words and numbers for over a minute, until they seemed to lose all meaning, until his vision began to blur.

"You're up awfully early." Maggie was there, seemingly out of thin air, with a cup of decaf and a sleepy smile. Her voice startled Daniel, made him jump. He closed the newspaper hurriedly, for no rational reason, his hand slamming with a dull noise against the table. Maggie walked around the table to Daniel, bent, and kissed his lips. Daniel found her musky morning smell strangely comforting. He felt the urge to bury his face in the curve of her neck, and hold her in his arms until it hurt. "You want some eggs?" she asked, heading toward the refrigerator.

"No, thanks," Daniel said. "I'm not really hungry."

"Me neither," she said. "But you'll need your strength if you're gonna play basketball."

Daniel felt himself wince at the reminder of his lie. "No basketball today," he said. "I just have to run a few errands. Go to the hardware store." Daniel was glad when Maggie didn't ask what he was going to buy at the hardware store, because he wouldn't have known what to say.

"You know what I think you should do today?" Maggie said, gesturing with an empty egg carton.

"What?" Daniel looked at his wife and felt a smile lifting his lips: in an ancient robe and slippers with little clown faces on the toes, hair uncombed, no makeup—she was beautiful. He ached with love.

"Relax," she said. "Mellow out. It would seem obvious that you don't relax enough." She punctuated the statement with a little head nod, then turned to crack eggs into a bowl.

"Yes, Mommy," Daniel said.

Crockett was already sitting in the waiting room when Daniel arrived at the clinic. Though they hadn't seen each other in two weeks, they had spoken on the phone three or four times. Daniel had told Crockett, and only Crockett, about his trouble in bed, and about the dream.

Crockett looked up, smiled at Daniel, and said, "Hi."

"How you doing?" Daniel asked, squeezing Crockett's shoulder.

Crockett shrugged. "All right, I guess. You?"

"I've had better weeks than the last two." He sat down next to Crockett, whose stiff posture (back ruler-straight, hands clutching his knees) and widened eyes bespoke anxiety at least matching Daniel's own. Daniel reached over and slid his palm over the back of Crockett's hand. Crockett turned his hand over until their palms met, and they sat together, holding hands as they had not done in nearly six years, until a young man with round tortoiseshell glasses and a clipboard emerged from one of the rooms across from them, and called Daniel's number.

The sound of Daniel's heartbeat nearly deafened him as he sat across from the guy with the glasses. A voice from somewhere deep in his skull kept repeating "Oh please God please God please." The man extended his hand and said, "May I see your slip, please?" Daniel pulled his wallet from his right hip pocket and fished out the small blue-and-white paper bearing the name of the clinic and Daniel's code, and little else: he'd had to show it upon entering the clinic—he realized he should have kept it out. The man quickly checked the slip against the papers on his clipboard, then handed it back to Daniel, who tucked it back into his wallet, his hands trembling as if palsied.

"What do you expect the result to be?" the man asked in a calm, even tone. Daniel felt as if all his entrails were surging upward toward his throat; he knew if he had eaten anything that morning, he would lose it now, all over himself, the tiny beige room, the guy with the glasses. He closed his eyes, waited a moment for his guts to settle. He drew in a very large breath through his mouth and used all of it to speak the word: "Negative."

"You're right," the man said. "It's negative." Daniel felt a large shiver shoot up through his body. He wanted to jump up and shout. He thought he might burst into tears. The glasses man said something.

Daniel said, "What?"

"I said, Do you have any questions?"

"Fuck no," Daniel said, a big smile on his face. He started to get up, then plopped back down into the chair. "May I go now?"

"If you don't mind," the man said, a little smile on his lips, "I have to do my spiel." Daniel fought to sit still: he was antsy as a five-year-old. "Now, if you've had unsafe sex within the last six months, you should come back and be tested again in about six months. And, of course, safe sex *only*." The man leaned well forward on the word "only." "Use a condom—always, always, always—I can't stress that enough. Safe sex is the only means we now have for stopping the spread of this disease." He paused, smiled at Daniel again. "Okay, now."

Daniel sprang up from his chair, took the man's right hand in his own, and gave it a vigorous pumping. "Thank you," he said through a wide grin.

Crockett was waiting outside the door, just as Daniel had left him. "You done?" Daniel asked.

"Uh-huh," Crockett said. He got up from his chair, and Daniel set the brisk pace as they walked through the waiting room and out the double doors. Once in the parking lot, Crockett stopped. He looked up at Daniel's smiling face and said, "Negative?"

Daniel nodded. "Yeah. Jesus, what a relief!" He gave his whole body a vigorous shake. "You?" Crockett's face had already told him everything, but he asked anyway.

"Positive," Crockett said. "Of course." He squinted in the bright sunlight, patted down his pockets in search of his sunglasses, which he was not carrying.

Daniel's smile fell slightly but refused to go away. Because he wanted so much to comfort his friend, and so that Crockett wouldn't see him smiling, Daniel took Crockett by the shoulders and pulled him into a hug. "Jesus, Crockett," he said. "I'm sorry."

Crockett said, "Yeah, me too," into the front of Daniel's polo shirt.

"You want some company?" Daniel asked, letting go of Crockett. "We could get a cup of coffee, some breakfast."

Crockett shook his head. "No. Thanks."

"You sure?" Daniel grabbed a handful of Crockett's shoulder.

"I'm sure," Crockett said. "I'm okay. S'not as if this was some big surprise, right? Go home."

"All right," Daniel said. "You know where I am if you need me."

"Thanks." Crockett turned toward his car, then stopped abruptly and turned back to Daniel. "Oh, fuck, Daniel," he said, a strange half-smile on his face, "I'm glad you're okay. I'm happy for you, and Maggie, and the baby and everything. You know that, don't you?"

Daniel nodded. "I know."

"See ya," Crockett called over his shoulder. Daniel stood in the parking lot and watched Crockett climb into the Thing and start it. He waved in the direction of the exhaust as Crockett drove away. Then he got into his car, started the engine, and immediately flipped on the radio. Springsteen was dancing in the dark as Daniel pulled out of the lot. Daniel smiled. He sang along with the radio, wiggling his lips against the car seat. He felt like dancing in the streets. He felt so full of energy and life, he could have parked the car on Santa Monica Boulevard and sprinted home.

He couldn't wait to get home. Suddenly, he was starved. And horny as hell.

CHAPTER 14

SHE WASN'T SURE WHAT IT WAS, but seeing the word *clinic* along the top of the little blue-and-white slip of paper made Maggie's breath catch. Daniel was in the dining room, replacing the old, unspeakably ugly chandelier that had come with the house, with a new fixture they had picked out together over a month before at a Lamps R Us parking lot sale. Maggie had been in the kitchen, preparing to make teriyaki marinade from her mother's recipe, when she'd discovered they were nearly out of soy sauce. A minor setback: a quick jaunt to the 7-11 was a small price to pay for teriyaki chicken. Now, in the bedroom, rummaging through her purse, Maggie realized she had exactly fifty-seven cents to her name.

"Honey," she called toward the dining room, over the sound of Joan Armatrading singing "Gimme love, with affection." "Honey, do you have any cash?" Which was her way of letting Daniel know she was about to dip into his wallet. Not that he would mind, of course, or forbid her to do it—she was his *wife,* after all. Just that she wouldn't want it to seem, even to herself, as if she were doing anything surreptitious, sneaky, Lucy Ricardo snoopish.

"I think so!" Daniel yelled. "Look in my wallet."

Maggie pulled a couple of singles, then removed a five, just in case she spotted a magazine she wanted at the 7-11. And then she saw the little flash of blue, incongruous among all that green. She removed it out of idle curiosity, read it over quickly, then stared at the slip for a long moment, looking for more than the scant information—just an address and some inscrutable letters and digits—the little piece of paper had to offer. Daniel hadn't mentioned going to any sort of clinic. Maggie felt her stomach lurch: Was there something the matter with Daniel? Something he was keeping from her? She knew herself well enough to know she wouldn't rest until she found out what this slip of paper meant, what this clinic—

Then it came to her, like a light switched on: not *a* clinic, she thought. *The* Clinic. She'd read about it—the clinic adjacent to the Gay Center, where they did confidential—

She dropped Daniel's wallet onto the dresser; bills fluttered to the floor. "Daniel," she called, hurrying toward the dining room.

Daniel was standing on the second rung of a small stepladder; he had the new light fixture cupped into the palm of one hand and was lifting it toward the wire-spewing hole in the ceiling where the old one had been. "Back so soon?" he said, turning toward Maggie's voice. First he noticed the strange, slightly panicked look on her face, and then the slip of paper in her hand. Suddenly, he felt very, very tired. He thought, Fuck. I can't believe I didn't throw it away. I should have thrown the goddamned thing away. In the relief and excitement of being confirmed free of AIDS infection, Daniel had simply forgotten about the little paper: it had remained tucked among the bills in his wallet for an entire week—Daniel hadn't even noticed it the few times over the past seven days when he'd removed money.

"Honey," Maggie said, "what is this?" Her voice sounded strangely high and unpleasant, even to her own ears.

Daniel lowered the fixture onto the towel-protected dining table and climbed slowly down from the stepladder. He had decided the moment he saw the slip in Maggie's hand that he wouldn't lie to her. He had lied enough. Maggie loved him, and if she had any clue how much he loved her, she would have to understand. She'd have to. He took a long breath, and used most of it to say, "It's from the clinic, over in West Hollywood, where they do"—he needed another breath—"AIDS testing."

"I know where it's from, Daniel, I'm just wondering what's it doing in your wallet." Maggie realized her voice sounded just this side of hysterical. Calm down, Maggie, she told herself. Calm down.

Daniel was trembling as if chilled, and he couldn't seem to stop it. He grabbed on to the ladder in an attempt to steady himself. "Come and sit down, Maggie," he said. Dread washed over Maggie like ice-cold water. "Oh, my God, Daniel," she said, approaching the table. Thoughts tumbled through her mind in the few seconds it took for her to get to the table and into a chair. He's got it. He's infected. I'm infected, and the baby, too. We're all going to die. She sat facing Daniel, her hands clasped tight around each other on the tabletop. "Tell me," she said. "Just tell me."

Daniel wrapped his hands around Maggie's. He looked into her eyes deeply, as if trying to find her soul, and said, "Tell me you love me, Maggie." She curled her fingers around his and squeezed so tightly it hurt them both. "Of *course* I love you, honey," she said, "just please tell me what's going on!" She was rapidly approaching what felt like some sort of stress threshold: she was afraid she might scream.

"Have you been tested for AIDS?" she asked.

Daniel nodded. "Yes. Three weeks ago."

"What on earth for?" Maggie demanded, her voice rising rapidly to a squeal. She knew as well as anyone the high-risk groups for AIDS infection, and she had been working under the assumption that her husband was in none of them.

"Because Crockett," Daniel said, "Crockett's infected. He's beginning to show symptoms."

Relief and sadness fought for space inside Maggie. "Oh, my God," she whispered, "not Crockett. I knew something wasn't right with him; I knew it. Poor baby." Then she slapped Daniel's hand and said, "Doggone-it, honey, that's no reason for you to run off and get tested." She punctuated her speech by tapping her fingertip on the back of Daniel's hand: "AIDS is only transmittable through blood transfusions and sex. For heaven's sake, honey, I thought you knew that much."

Daniel pressed his hands into the tabletop, still trying in vain to control his trembling. He stared down at Maggie's hands on top of his, then slid his hands out from under Maggie's. He crossed his arms over his chest, tucking his hands into his armpits. He said, "I do know that, Maggie."

Maggie felt nausea like a finger tickling the inside of her stomach. She closed her eyes, took a deep breath, and waited for it to pass. She stretched out her fingers, flattening her palms into the tabletop. "What do you mean?" she said. Oh God, she thought: he'd had a blood transfusion from Crockett, years ago.

"I've had—" Daniel began, then started again: "I've made love with Crockett."

She kept her eyes closed for a few seconds, while that small disjointed sentence played back in her mind a few times: "I've had . . . I've made love with Crockett." When Maggie opened her eyes, Daniel was looking directly into her face: she quickly averted her eyes from his. To her own surprise, she felt no immediate urge to scream or lash out, just a low sort of rumbling deep inside, below an eerie surface calm. She thought, Is this how a bomb feels just before it explodes?

Daniel searched his wife's face for clues, but found none. There was a strange death-mask quality to the face that said, "You've made love with Crockett?"

"Yes," Daniel said.

Maggie rubbed her palms an inch or two forward and back on the table; she watched the tops of her hands for a long moment, as if fascinated with their movement, before she said, "Really? When?"

"It was a long time ago, Maggie." Daniel was beginning to worry: screaming, verbal abuse, tears he was ready for—not this vague calm. Another pause, while Maggie studied the tops of her hands for several long, drawn-out seconds. Then she looked directly into Daniel's face and said, "So are you gay, or what?" The light, conversational tone of Maggie's voice struck Daniel as odd: she might have been saying, "How was your day, honey?" "I like gay men," she said, "I really do; it just wasn't my intention to marry one, you know?" She began tapping her fingers, quick, soft taps on the tabletop. "So are you? Am I your cover or something or what?"

"No, Maggie. I'm not gay." Daniel wanted to touch her hands; both because he wanted to touch her, and also because he wanted to stop the tapping. He started to reach out, then decided against it, and shoved his hands back under his arms.

"You're not gay." Maggie was tapping a little harder now. "You just had sex with Crockett, right?"

Daniel almost smiled. "I guess I'm bisexual. I've never really thought of myself as that, but I guess I am."

"Uh-huh." Maggie was nodding her head quickly, absently, up and down. "Were you lovers? You and Crockett?"

"What?" Daniel had heard the question: he just wasn't sure how he wanted to answer it.

"I said, Were you lovers, goddammit!" Suddenly, Maggie was screaming, and Daniel realized he wasn't ready for it at all.

"Yeah," he said softly, "sort of."

"God *damn* it!" Maggie slammed hard on the tabletop with the heel of her right hand, with a loud, dull thud, rattling the light fixture. "Either you were lovers or you weren't lovers!" She was leaning forward across the table, her face twisted and ugly in a way Daniel would not have thought possible.

"All right!" Daniel said, his teeth tightly clenched, his voice high and strained. "We were lovers, all right? All right? You happy now?" Then he was up and out of his chair, facing away from Maggie; his entire body trembling with a rush of adrenaline—he could have ripped walls apart with his hands.

"Happy?" Maggie shouted. "I suddenly find out my husband's been tested for AIDS, I suddenly find out my husband's bisexual, I suddenly find out my husband's had an affair with his best friend . . ." Her voice suddenly broke, and then her eyes stung with tears. "*Our* best friend, dammit," she said, as the tears came. "And here I'm making goddamn *teriyaki* sauce! Oh, I'm real happy, Daniel. I'm just happy as all hell." She threw up her hands, turned away from Daniel, and watched the tiny flowers on the wallpaper pattern blur with her tears.

Daniel turned back toward Maggie. He realized he hadn't been ready for tears, either: the sound of her ill-muffled sobs sliced through him like a serrated knife. He walked toward her slowly, haltingly, like a child just finding the use of his legs. "Maggie," he said, "please don't." The sight of her trembling back, looking so small, so very fragile, brought tears to Daniel's eyes. He'd never made Maggie cry before; he'd honestly hoped he never would. "Please, Maggie." He reached out his hand and touched her shoulder; she shook him off to the sound of a particularly loud sob. He moved in as close to her as he could without making skin contact, molding his body around hers.

"Maggie," he said, "it doesn't matter now. None of it matters."

"Maybe not to you," Maggie said, her voice wet and rough with crying.

"Maggie, I'm not infected. I'm fine. You're fine, the baby's fine."

"The *baby,*" she said, half growl, half hiss, as if she were carrying some sort of reptile inside her. She shrunk away from Daniel and turned to face him, her back against the wall, her face red and puffy, nose running. "That's what really matters to you, isn't it? The *baby*! Is that why you married me? Because Crockett couldn't give you children?"

Daniel shook his head slowly. "No, Maggie," he said. "No."

"Well, you know something?" She half crouched, like a

cornered cat. "If I could rip it out of me right now, I'd do it!" Daniel stepped back, saddened, nearly sickened.

"Oh, Maggie," he said, "you don't mean that."

"Maybe I do," she said, "and maybe I don't." In her heart she knew she didn't mean a word of it. She hurt—she wasn't exactly sure why she hurt, but she hurt. And she wanted to make sure Daniel hurt, too. Seeing by Daniel's expression that she had more than succeeded, she immediately felt wretched for having done it. She slid down the wall and into a sitting position on the floor, and wept loudly into her hands, not exactly sure what she was crying for.

Daniel dropped to his knees, approaching Maggie on all fours. He tugged a crumpled handkerchief from his pants pocket and held it out to her. Maggie snatched it from his hand and blew her nose, making a wet, flatulent sound. He barely heard her whisper, "Shit." He sat cross-legged on the floor across from her, watching her cry, crying softly himself. Seconds went by, feeling like days.

"Why didn't you tell me?" Maggie said, her voice a wet whisper.

"I honestly didn't think it mattered. It was over and done."

"Was it?" Maggie said, her voice rising again. "*Is* it, really?" It suddenly occurred to her to suspect and possibly resent all the time they spent in Crockett's company: was this Daniel's way of having it both ways?

"Yes, Maggie."

"And did it ever occur to you that maybe I might not want to marry a bisexual?"

"Maggie"—Daniel's voice took a pleading tone—"I married you intending to be faithful to you. And I am. I haven't touched anybody but you since we've been married—practically since we met. What does it matter what my, what my possibilities are?"

Maggie wasn't sure what it did matter, but for the particular heated moment, she was sure it did. "So you just made that choice for me," Maggie said. "How dare you? Just how fucking dare you?"

Daniel sniffed, wiped at his wet face with his arm. "Would it have changed your mind? If you'd known?"

Maggie shrugged. "I don't know." She thought about the Jamesons. Daniel knew them from his acting days, and Maggie had met them shortly after marrying Daniel, at a party full of actors and ex-actors where she'd felt more than a little out of place from the word go. Jonathan and Linda Jameson were both performers: he a pop-eyed young character actor, she a stand-up comedienne—jovial, jocular, and seemingly quite comfortable with the thirty-or-so excess pounds she carried. Attracted by Linda's effervescent personality, Maggie had engaged her in conversation. After a time, Linda searched around the crowded room and said, "Where is that husband of mine? Probably in a corner with his hand down some guy's Levi's, if I know him."

Maggie's mouth dropped open. Linda smiled, touched Maggie lightly on the shoulder.

"Oh, I'm sorry, hon," Linda said. "I assumed everybody knew about Jono and me." And without explanation, she set off in search of her husband.

She'd asked Daniel about the Jamesons on the way home. "Well," he said, "the long and short of it is that Jonathan's gay. Or at least he prefers men. From what I understand," he said, "he and Linda do make love, and they care about each other quite a lot." He shrugged. "Linda wanted a husband, and Jon wants to have children."

Maggie cringed. She found the idea utterly repulsive. How could a woman marry a man knowing he didn't desire her? Maggie knew she herself could never bear it.

"Is that fairly common?" Maggie asked. "Among actors, I mean."

"Well," Daniel said, "let's just say it's not uncommon."

Maggie shook her head. She pitied Linda Jameson, and any other woman in her position.

Now Maggie wondered, Am I Linda Jameson? The thought brought a sour taste to her mouth, as if she might throw up. She swallowed it back. A minute limped by in silence. Maggie lifted her head, thumping the back of it against the wall behind her. "Do you still love him?" she said.

Daniel rubbed at his face with both hands for a second or two before he answered, slowly and carefully. "I care about him very much. You don't love somebody and then just stop. *I* don't anyway." He paused, looked into his wife's reddened face. "But I'm not in love with him, Maggie. I'm in love with you." His breath caught: he felt tears stinging at his eyes again, but he blinked them back. "You *know* that."

"I don't know *what* I know," Maggie said, rising rather clumsily from the floor.

"Where are you going?" Daniel asked.

"To the fucking bathroom," Maggie said as she walked away. "Okay?" She slammed the bathroom door behind her, locked it, and immediately turned on the cold water in the washbasin full force. She wasn't sure who that woman was, staring back at her from the mirror, but she looked like hell. Maggie splashed her face with cold water again and again, also managing to wet her hair, the vanity top, the wall, and the front of her "Born in the U.S.A." T-shirt—a gift from Crockett.

Patting her face dry with a towel, she decided the cold water had done little or no good: her face always puffed up so badly when she cried and seemed to stay that way for hours. She sat down hard on the toilet lid.

Good God, she thought. What just happened out there? As close as she could figure, her entire value system had been blown to smithereens, and she had suddenly turned into that little girl in *The Exorcist,* swearing and screaming, spewing venom and pea soup. Maggie didn't know why Daniel's confession had upset her quite so much: she only knew it had, that it still did, and that it likely would continue to upset her for some time to come. Not that she didn't feel she had every right to be upset, because she did. As far as she was concerned, Daniel had lied to her, if only indirectly—a lie of omission—when he'd married her: and it was one very big lie. Every time she saw Crockett, whenever he spent time with her and Daniel, it was like a little lie, a tiny satellite from the big lie, a small dose of deceit.

Suddenly, a fast image flashed through her mind, like a few frames of stray film spliced into a movie: Daniel with Crockett in his arms, kissing him passionately. It made her stomach push up toward her throat; it made her want to cry again. It was followed by an ugly thought: Daniel and Crockett were still lovers, carrying on behind her back, every chance they got; having a romping good time, having a good laugh at her ignorance, at her expense. She shook her head violently from side to side, as if to dislodge the thought.

"Oh God, Maggie," she whispered, "you're really losing it." She felt so tired. She wanted to crawl into bed and sleep for the rest of the day, for a week or two, or for however long it was going to take for her to feel good about her life again. And even now, knee-deep in a sludge of very dark emotions, she was relatively sure that time would come. She was going to be all right. She and Daniel would be all right. In time.

She loved Daniel. And he was right, after all: she knew Daniel was in love with her. He'd never given her the smallest cause to doubt his love. Besides, she thought, you don't just *know* somebody loves you, like you know two and two make four. You feel it inside, like you feel sunshine on your skin. She felt Daniel's love, she knew it from deep within. And from the outside, she knew there was no way a man (even an ex-actor) could fake the way Daniel made love to her. No way. She was definitely not Linda Jameson.

Still, in her less secure moments (and she had her share), Maggie could encounter some trouble believing this beautiful, sweet man could really be in love with her—little Maggie with the big lips and wide rear end and no boobies. Much as she knew better, much as she tried not to, she tended to see any reasonably attractive woman as a vague threat. Now, she might well have to add all reasonably attractive men to that threat—an unsettling thought. Hey, she thought with a nasty little laugh, maybe he likes me *because* I have no boobies. Was Maggie Taylor the next best thing to a boy? A substitute Crockett with baby-making capabilities?

Crockett. Funny, sweet Crockett. Why shouldn't Daniel love him? Maggie loved him. Whatever other feelings the thought of Crockett brought to Maggie at the moment, she cared about him. And now he was ill. He could be dying a slow, ghastly death. Maggie hugged herself tight. Poor Crockett. And then she thought: Oh, my God—it could have been "Poor Daniel and Maggie," too. Much as she felt terrible for Crockett, she was so glad it wasn't Daniel, so glad it wasn't her. She remembered Daniel's behavior of two, three weeks before: the tension, the moodiness, the totally uncharacteristic difficulties in bed. That must have been when Daniel was waiting for the results of his AIDS test. Thank God it was negative, she thought. Of course, if Daniel hadn't been inclined to take boys to bed, AIDS would likely never have been an issue at all: not for him, not for her. The lying son of a bitch! She could feel herself getting worked up again; she could feel the urge to scream rising up from the bottoms of her feet. She took a deep breath and fought back the urge.

Oh, Maggie, she said to herself, what are we going to do? Well, she thought, I certainly can't sit here all day, much as I'd like to. She realized the last thing on earth she wanted to

152

see, for the moment at least, was Daniel. She stood up, checked herself in the mirror. She seemed a little less red, a bit less puffy. When she opened the door, Daniel was standing right outside. He looked at her strangely, reached out his hand as if to touch her, then didn't. She was glad he didn't.

"Are you all right?" he asked.

She shrugged, and tried to smile, not entirely succeeding. "Fine," she said. "Never better." Actually, she felt as if she were slowly shutting down, like an old computer. "If you had to go, you should have knocked."

"I was worried about you," he said. "It's been half an hour."

"Really? Time flies when you're having fun." She started toward the bedroom, barely able to lift her feet. "I'm going to bed."

"It's two in the afternoon," Daniel said.

"Is it?" she said, walking into the bedroom. She was about to close the door behind her, when a thought zapped into her mind. She turned to Daniel and asked, "When we make love, do you ever think of him?"

Daniel breathed an audible sigh, shook his head. "Never," he said.

Maggie just nodded. She shut the door behind her and climbed into bed with all her clothes on. She fell asleep almost immediately, deep and dreamless.

Daniel watched the door close, and stared blankly at it—like the lead actor in an amateur production of Ibsen—for a length of time he could not have estimated. He suddenly felt, if not lost exactly, then at least strangely dislocated. Maggie had closed herself off from him, physically and otherwise, leaving him with a feeling of aloneness infinitely deeper than the mere absence of her company. Leaving him without the one thing he needed more than anything else at that moment: some reassurance that, whatever setback they might be facing, whatever the hurt, whatever the confusion, her love for him was still intact; that they would come through this thing together, that they would be all right. As it was, Daniel wasn't sure he had a wife anymore.

He had been genuinely amazed at Maggie's reaction. Not that he would have thought, even in his most sugar-frosted fantasy, that Maggie would say, "Oh, fiddle-dee-dee, why should I be upset by such a trifle?" But the ugliness that had gushed from his wife's mouth—that she would actually threaten their unborn child—shocked and frightened him. He had sat on the dining-room floor for more than twenty minutes listening to Maggie run water in the bathroom, wondering what she might be doing, growing apprehensive when sounds of movement ceased. Would she, might she actually try to hurt the baby? He tried to remember if they had any sleeping tablets in the medicine chest. He never would have considered Maggie capable of rash, irresponsible behavior—especially against herself—but suddenly he wasn't sure of much of anything. As Maggie had said, he didn't quite know *what* he knew.

He touched the doorjamb softly, as he would have touched Maggie if she had allowed him to; then he caught himself at it, turned and walked away. In the dining room, the new light fixture sat to one side of the table where Daniel had left it: naked wires dangled from the ceiling. Daniel lifted the fixture up from the table, then put it back down. He walked into the kitchen, picked up the wall phone next to the stove, and punched Crockett's number.

"Hello?"

Daniel felt a tiny bit better just hearing Crockett's voice. "Crockett."

"Daniel, hi. How goes?"

"She found out," Daniel said, knocking absently on the wall

next to the phone with his fist. "She knows, everything. About the test, about us—you and me." He told Crockett everything he could remember from the moment he turned and saw that look on Maggie's face, the paper in her hand.

"It'll be all right," Crockett said.

Daniel laughed, a barely audible little laugh. "Promise?"

"She loves you, Daniel," Crockett said. "Give her some time. Be patient; as patient as you can." He paused a moment.

"Does she hate me?" he finally asked.

"I don't think she likes either of us very much right now. But she loves you too, you know."

"Really?"

"Of course," Daniel said. "You know that."

"What about you?"

Daniel very nearly smiled. "You know that, too," he said. "Thanks for listening. God knows you've got troubles of your own. It's just . . . there was nobody else I could call."

"Anytime, you big lug," Crockett said. "Anytime at all."

Hanging up the phone, Daniel suddenly thought of something Crockett once wrote, the last couple of lines from the first short story Crockett had allowed him to read—four, maybe five years before. He didn't remember the title of the story, or the plot, or any of the characters, but he'd never forgotten those last lines: "Sex, for all the (mostly needless) hoopla some people like to whip up about it, is really a very simple matter. Hot, wet skin on hot, wet skin—simple. Love, on the other hand, can be a poisonous bee sting from Hell."

Maggie stood in front of the bathroom mirror, brushing her hair with a good deal more than the necessary force. Her hair had grown out to the point where only the ends were still curly on top, and it required excessive amounts of styling mousse to keep the sides flat; and this morning, Maggie really didn't feel much like messing with mousse. Actually, it was about time she had it cut again, but she was in no mood to deal with that, either. She hated her hair. This morning, she hated just about everything.

Maggie had feigned sleep until Daniel left for work, kissing her softly on the cheek. In fact, she had hardly slept all night. It had been nearly seven o'clock the previous evening when Daniel finally shook her awake from her unusual five-hour nap, feeling groggy and disoriented in the warm half-dark of the bedroom.

"Don't you think you'd better get up and eat something?" Daniel said. She grunted something inconclusive. "I cooked some chicken," he said. She couldn't see his face, but she could make out his shadowy form, standing at least three feet from the bed. "I would have made teriyaki, but we don't have any soy sauce." He started out of the room, his footsteps noiseless against the rug; then he stopped in the doorway, his body silhouetted in the light from the hall, and asked, "Are you okay?"

"Sure," she said, not nearly meaning it.

They ate dinner by the light of the newly installed fixture, in silence. They sat in the den and pretended to watch "Murder, She Wrote" and then something else—she couldn't remember what: Maggie's state of mind was such that, had she been asked during a commercial break to describe the previous twenty minutes' action, she would have been clueless. She sat facing the television, across the big blue sofa from Daniel, while her mind reran that afternoon's scenes over and over. At ten o'clock, she felt Daniel shift his weight, then rise from the sofa.

"I'm going to bed," he said, keeping his back to her. "You coming?"

"Not just yet," Maggie said. "I'd been planning to watch…" She hadn't actually been planning to watch anything, and she was utterly unable to make anything up. Daniel didn't seem to require further explanation. He turned to her and said, "Well, good night, then." He bent to kiss her, and it was a physical effort for her not to turn away. He kissed her softly on the cheek, turned, and left the room.

Maggie sat with the television on, watching more mind images of that afternoon, now and then changing them, rewriting history—having herself say something a little wittier here, a bit more cruel there, than she actually had said. She relived emotions with each replay, trembling with rage or weeping in confusion. Once, twice, and again, she told herself to stop it. "This is nuts," she said to herself. "Crazy and masochistic." And she'd force herself to focus her attention on Madge the manicurist pushing dishwashing liquid on television. But within a minute or two, the images returned, and she was off again; she found the little blue-and-white slip again, she made up something new and ugly to say to Daniel—in one variation, she slapped his face again and again, tirelessly. Only once did she have herself pick up Daniel's wallet, open it, pull out two singles and a five-dollar bill, put the wallet down on the dresser, and walk away, none the wiser and contented as a Carnation cow. She tried it once, and decided she didn't believe it.

By the time she tired of this game, there was a rerun of a bad made-for-TV movie, and the digital clock on the VCR read 12:17 A.M. She had to go to bed and at least close her eyes: she had to work in the morning.

When she slid into bed next to Daniel (not touching him, not sure why), she was immediately aware of the fact that Daniel was not asleep. They lay on their backs for a few elongated minutes, listening to the sound of their collective breathing. Finally, Daniel whispered, "Maggie?" She briefly considered pretending to be asleep, but thought better of it—he'd never believe she'd fallen asleep that quickly. "Do you still love me?" he asked.

Oh, God, she thought, that he should even ask that. She felt tears. She would have thought she had cried herself dry. "Of course I do," she said, still lying flat on her back, still not touching him.

"Thank you," Daniel said, his voice almost a whisper. After a moment he said, "I'd like to make love."

The thought of it made her want to roll out of bed and run. "Oh, no, Daniel," she said. "Please. Not tonight."

A moment of quiet so still she could hear Daniel lick his lips before he said, "May I hold you, then?" Maggie slid over in bed toward Daniel, and wrapped herself along his side, tucked into his armpit, her head on his chest. One moment, the feeling of him, warm and solid next to her, was so familiar and sweet that she felt she could forgive anything, forget everything. And the next moment, it was all she could do not to tighten her hand into a fist and hit her husband in the relaxed muscles of his belly, just as hard as she could.

Her workday went quickly—they generally did—and, except for a threatening spasm of nausea during her first low-impact aerobics class, uneventfully. Maggie discovered to her relief that it was relatively easy to put her problems out of her mind for longer periods of time than she would have guessed. Shouting roomfuls of people through several consecutive hours of bend and stretch, over the incessant thump-thump-thump of her dance remix tapes left little energy for conscious thought of any kind. Only during her lunch break, bent over a chocolate protein shake in the employee lounge, absently turning the pages of the current *Muscle and Fitness* magazine, did Maggie allow herself to dwell on It: Daniel's confession of his affair with Crockett, the truly disturbing concept of being married to a bisexual, her sudden and unexpected confrontation with the *fact* of being married to a bisexual, and her own sloppy goulash of emotions in the face of both concept and fact—all this Maggie had already begun to think of as It. She wished she had never learned about It. She wished It didn't bother her so much. She wished she could snatch back the past twenty-four hours, along with her old happy life, a life without It.

Inevitably connected to It, though separate from It, was the horrible fact of Crockett's illness. He had the *real* It. She had not spoken to Crockett since learning of his sickness amid the ugliness of the previous afternoon. Drumming her fingertips on the opened pages of her magazine, Maggie considered calling him on the telephone, just to say she knew and she was sorry and she cared. But she found she couldn't bring herself to get up and make the call. As much as she cared about Crockett, as much as the thought of him wasting away, his own body collapsing in on him, made Maggie's heart ache, part of her was angry, meanly and irrationally angry at Crockett. She hated the feeling, but there it was: if he hadn't had an affair with Daniel, if they hadn't met all those years ago, if Crockett had never existed—

No, she thought. She couldn't call him now. Maybe tomorrow.

The end of her last class found Maggie with the sort of stomach flutters she usually experienced on her way to the dentist's office. She didn't want to go home. She caught sight of Theo leaving the building, and she hurried toward the front doors after her.

"Well," Maggie said as she caught up with Theo, "one down, four to go."

"Indeed," Theo said with a little smile. "You have a nice evening, little mommy," she said, turning away toward her car. Theo had been calling Maggie "little mommy" practically from the moment Maggie had first told her of her pregnancy. "Well," she'd said, "you were right." She was the first person

Maggie told at California Fitness, just before giving four weeks' notice to Earl.

"Hey," Maggie called, hoping she sounded passably casual, "you want to go over to Keeler's and have a drink?"

Theo stopped and turned back to Maggie, with a scrutinizing look on her face that immediately made Maggie feel exposed and a little foolish. Much as she wanted her sudden invitation to seem casual, as if she and Theo had drinks together at Keeler's two or three times a week, the fact was that they had entered the bar together exactly twice before, both times for impromptu birthday celebrations for co-workers, both times accompanied by several other California Fitness employees. After a brief pause, Theo said, "Why not?"

Keeler's Bar and Grill was located in the same business park as California Fitness, a scant hundred yards across the parking lot. A large, open room with a long polished oak bar and a few minuscule tables, a 1959-vintage Wurlitzer jukebox, a dance floor only slightly larger than a cocktail napkin, and a well-maintained collection of hanging plants, Keeler's was typical of the kind of place many young, single, relatively successful straight Caucasians frequented in hopes of meeting, charming, and eventually bedding young, single, relatively successful straight Caucasians of the opposite sex. In the years since Keeler's opened opposite California Fitness, the foot traffic had worn an all-but-visible trail between the two buildings. A steady stream of young urban professionals—most of whom would likely have cringed at the term "yuppie"—poured from California Fitness and into Keeler's in ones, pairs, and groups, generally packing the room to its mirrored walls by nine o'clock on any evening Monday through Saturday, and keeping it packed until last call. At six twenty-five on a Monday evening, Keeler's was nearly empty.

When Maggie and Theo entered, only one stool at the bar

was occupied. The woman seated in the corner nearest the front door smiled and nodded as they walked past. She looked about Maggie's age, or so Maggie supposed, and she was pretty in what Maggie thought of as an obvious sort of way, a *Playboy* magazine sort of pretty, complete with blond hair (probably lightened), a perky turned-up nose, and a bosom that Maggie would have bet was surgically enhanced (although, of course, she'd been wrong about Theo). She was wearing a red strapless minidress in what looked like leather, with matching red spike-heeled pumps. The dress fit her like a coat of suntan oil, and lent her tightly crossed legs the illusion of unnatural length. She looked fabulous.

She was the sort of beauty who could bring Maggie's insecurities galloping to the surface at the best of times, which this definitely was not. Maggie suddenly felt extremely dowdy in her Levis, old alligator shirt, and Nikes. Climbing onto a stool near the middle of the bar, Maggie leaned in to Theo and said in a catty half-whisper she hated even as it fell off her lips, "Check Jean Harlow in the corner."

"I saw," Theo whispered through barely opened lips.

"Do you suppose she dresses like that for work?" Maggie said.

"Frankly," Theo said, "yes."

Before Maggie had a chance to ask what she might have meant by that, a deep male voice said, "What can I get you ladies?" Maggie looked up into the face of the bartender, who tossed a couple of tiny napkins onto the bar in front of them, then tossed them each one straight, perfect smile. It was a boyishly handsome face, but with a burst of deep creases around the eyes that made Maggie wonder if the wearer of that face might be older (perhaps a good deal older) than he seemed at a glance. His white tuxedo shirt barely contained his softball-sized biceps and massive chest and shoulders. He looked like a football player. Or maybe he just lifted weights.

It occurred to Maggie that he was probably gay, though she wasn't sure why she thought that. He just seemed so . . . meticulous, or something.

"Well?" Theo turned to her. "It's your party."

"I guess I'll just have a white wine spritzer," Maggie said. She really would have preferred something with considerably more kick to it, something to anesthetize her a bit, to dull some of her mind's rough edges. But she also knew she probably shouldn't be drinking any alcohol, what with the baby.

"Make it two," Theo said.

"Comin' up," said the bartender, flashing another toothpaste-commercial smile.

"So," Theo said as the big guy stepped away, "you want to talk about it, or would you rather just drink quietly for a while?"

"Talk about what?" Maggie said, feeling transparent under Theo's look.

"About whatever it is that's got you sitting in a practically empty bar with me and the leather lady and Joe Montana, instead of going home to your husband."

Maggie felt herself blush. She glanced down at her hands, picked at a cuticle. She had nothing to say, no small talk to make. She hadn't wanted to go home, neither had she wanted to sit sipping wine spritzers by herself. She felt more than a little silly. "I really don't want to talk about it," she said. She looked up at Theo, who shrugged and said, "Suit yourself."

"Look," Maggie said, "I'm sorry I dragged you in here. Why don't you go on home."

"Nobody *drags* me anywhere," Theo said with a little gesture of her head. "Besides, I've already ordered."

The bartender returned, set drinks down on their napkins. Maggie plunged a hand into her purse, fishing for her wallet. "I'll get this," she said, her face halfway into the purse.

"Excuse me," the bartender said, his voice just above a

whisper, "but the lady at the end of the bar would like to buy your drinks."

Maggie looked up from her purse. The red-dress lady smiled, and lifted a half-empty glass of wine in Maggie's direction. Taken slightly aback, Maggie pulled her hand from her purse and lifted her glass and smiled in reply. Red Dress raised her glass again, a bit higher. Glancing back, Maggie saw Theo toast the woman across the room. Maggie sipped her drink and whispered over the rim of the glass, "Should we let her do that?" The bartender leaned in dramatically close and whispered, "Don't look now, but she already has." Then he smiled again.

"Please convey our thanks to the lady," Theo said.

"Will do," the bartender said, walking back toward Red Dress.

"Well," Maggie said, swiveling back toward Theo, "isn't *that* interesting."

"Oh?" Theo seemed decidedly nonchalant.

"I mean, have you ever had some woman you've never seen before suddenly up and buy you a drink?" Theo's calm left Maggie a little worried that she might have shown herself to be unsophisticated.

"Yes," Theo said evenly. Before Maggie had time to consider whether this was something that happened to Theo Davis two or three times a week, or in just what sort of situations this occurrence might present itself, a blue-velvet voice behind her said, "Evening, ladies." Maggie jumped in her skin, spun around quickly, and collided sharply at the shins with Ruby Red Dress herself.

"Oh!" Maggie impulsively touched the woman's knee, then yanked her hand back. She noticed the woman wasn't wearing stockings. She wondered if the woman was wearing underwear, or if perhaps there was nothing under the tight red leather at all. "I'm sorry," Maggie said in a breathy voice she hardly recognized. The woman smiled and said, "No problem." Maggie realized the woman was not so much naturally beautiful (she had no cheekbones to speak of, and her eyes— of a sparkling blue that may or may not have been enhanced by tinted contact lenses—were rather close-set), as very good with makeup. The thought immediately struck her as unduly catty.

The woman held out her right hand, the blood-red color of her long nails matching that of her dress and shoes, and said, "I'm Moira." Maggie hesitated for a quick moment, then took the woman's hand. "Myra?" The woman leaned in close, still holding Maggie's hand; her lips, red and wet-looking, slowly enunciated the name, "Moira."

"Moira," Maggie repeated, slowly retrieving her hand from Moira's firm, warm grip. "I'm Maggie." Moira leaned forward in front of Maggie and offered her hand to Theo, repeating, "Moira." Maggie glanced down into the deep cleavage in the front of Moira's dress: compared with her and Theo, Maggie felt sure she must have the smallest breasts on earth. Theo took Moira's hand and said, "Theodosia."

"Theodosia," Moira said. "Beautiful name."

"Thanks," Theo said as they finished their handshake. "Had it all my life. And thanks for the drink," she added.

"My pleasure," Moira said.

"Yes," Maggie said, feeling just slightly out of sync, "thanks for the drink."

"You ladies work at California Fitness?" Moira asked, re-crossing her long legs.

"Uh-huh," Maggie said. "We're instructors. Both of us." Scintillating conversation, Maggie, she thought to herself.

"I thought so," Moira said. "You both have these fantastic bodies."

Theo smiled, lifted her glass in another toast, and said, "I like you, you can stay." Moira smiled and toasted back.

"So what do you do—Moira?" Maggie pronounced the name carefully.

"I'm an actress," Moira said. "Model." She smiled. "Isn't that just *too* L.A.? I am an actress-slash-model." She laughed a deep, throaty laugh of the sort Maggie thought should belong to some smoky Lauren Bacall type. Like everything else about Moira, Maggie found it slightly disconcerting.

"Anything I might have seen?" Maggie asked.

"Mmm"—Moira puckered her lips—"probably not." Maggie was going to ask Moira what sort of things she'd appeared in, just in case she might have seen one by chance, when Moira said, "You know, Maggie: with a little work, you could be stunning."

"Who, me?" It struck her as an odd thing to say to someone you'd just met. "I like your dress" or "What beautiful earrings," okay; but "With a little work you could be stunning"? Maggie wasn't sure if it was a compliment or just what.

"Absolutely," Moira said, giving the back of Maggie's hand a little press with her fingertips. "You have perfect skin, you have great eyes. Is that your natural hair color?"

"Of course," Maggie said, as if she had never heard of Miss Clairol.

"Well, you have beautiful hair," Moira said, pushing gently at a stray lock of Maggie's hair with her fingers. "You just have to *do* something with it."

"It's . . . I'm sort of between haircuts at the moment," Maggie said.

"I'm pretty good with hair, myself," Moira said. "I'd just love to do your hair sometime. Maybe help you with your makeup a little bit." She touched Maggie's jaw with a fingertip; Maggie felt herself pull back a little. "I mean it, you could be stunning." She leaned to one side to address Theo. "As for you, Miss Theodosia"—she wagged a finger in Theo's direction—"there's absolutely nothing I could do for you. As far as your appearance, I mean," she added with a little smile.

"Lost cause, huh?" Theo said. Maggie suddenly noticed just how sexy Theo managed to look in a loose-fitting pink sweat-suit and running shoes.

"You know what I mean," Moira said with a look that struck Maggie as downright flirtatious. "You've got those incredible cheekbones, and your skin will *never* age—I hate black women for that. I mean, you just mention the word sunshine and we wrinkle, right Maggie?" She pressed Maggie's knee. "You couldn't get me out into bright sunshine with a *gun!*" She tapped Maggie's knee again on the word "gun." "And I'll bet you're older than you look," she said. "Tell the truth: you're—what? Thirty . . . five?"

Theo chuckled. "Honey, I'll *never* see that side of thirty-five again."

"Older?" Moira said. "You're kidding!" She bent forward, and spoke in a loud whisper. "Are you telling?"

"Not tonight," Theo said.

Moira smiled. "Theodosia," she said, rolling the name around her teeth, "we have ways of making you talk."

"I'll just bet you do," Theo answered. Moira laughed that Lauren Bacall laugh again. Maggie heard Theo laugh, too, and she smiled, deliberately. She had the feeling she was missing something between the lines of this little exchange.

When the laughter had subsided, Moira said, "You know, I live real close by. I've got a bottle of Mumm's in the fridge. Why don't you come on by, both of you. We could all kick our shoes off and"—she did a little shoulder shrug—"relax."

Maggie was at a loss. What was happening here?

"I'm sure we'd love to," Theo said, "but we're meeting some friends for dinner in just a few minutes."

"Oh," Moira said. Her lips puckered into a little pout.

"Well," she said, recovering her smile, "maybe another time."

"Another time," Theo said.

"Well," Moira began again. She swiveled away from them, slipped down off her stool, and started away. Her back turned, she raised her right hand and wiggled her fingers as she said, "Good night, ladies."

" 'Night, Moira," Theo called after her. Maggie managed a half-audible, " 'Night."

Moira finger-wiggled toward the bartender and said, "Later, Dino."

"Later, babe," he said. Moira lifted her matching red leather jacket from the coatrack near the door, pushed the door open, and was all but gone before Maggie called, "Hey, thanks for the drink." Maggie stared down into the pale gold liquid in her glass for a moment. She wondered if they had somehow hurt Moira's feelings. She wondered if she had mis-interpreted Moira, or if indeed there had been anything to misinterpret. She wondered if—no: it was just on her mind, what with Daniel and Crockett and It and everything. But then again . . .

"Theo," she said quietly, not wanting the bartender to hear, still looking deep into her wineglass and pointedly not looking at Theo, "do you think she—Moira, I mean—do you suppose she might have been, you know? Hitting? On us?"

"Frankly, yes," Theo said calmly.

"Forget I said that," Maggie said very quickly, practically before Theo's words were out of her mouth, shaking her head, "that was a rotten thing to say, I don't know why I said that, just forget it." Then she stopped, as Theo's "Frankly, yes" registered. "Really?" She turned to look at Theo. "You really think so?"

"Get real, Mommy," Theo said. " 'Why don't we all go

over to my place, have some champagne, and *relax?*' Come on, girl!''

"But this isn't a"—Maggie lowered her voice further—"lesbian bar.''

"What's your point?" Theo said.

Maggie turned back toward the bar, raised her glass to her lips, her hand shaking enough to spill wine had the glass been fuller. She asked in a tight little half-voice, "Has that ever happened to you before?"

"Yes," Theo said.

"Oh." Maggie set her glass down without drinking. She argued with herself for a second or two, then took a deep breath and plunged in: "Have you ever—" and then she couldn't finish. It was none of her business and, besides, she couldn't think of how to put it without running the risk of insult.

"*Relaxed* with a woman?" Theo finished for her. When she turned to face Theo again, Maggie found a look on her deep brown face she could only interpret as amused. "Yes, Maggie. Matter of fact, I have."

Maggie felt a familiar sense of betrayal rising up inside her—why didn't anybody *tell* her anything?—and fought it down as best she could before she said, "Why didn't you tell me?"

Theo shrugged. "It never came up in conversation, did it? If you'd asked me, 'Theo, do you by any chance sleep with women?' I'd've said Yeah."

"If . . ." Maggie hesitated a bit. "If I hadn't been here, would you have gone with her? With Moira?"

"There was a time when I would have," Theo said, seemingly holding back a big smile. "But Susannah wouldn't like it."

"Your . . . girlfriend?" Theo nodded. "Jesus," Maggie

whispered. They sat quietly for a minute; Maggie tapped on her soaked cocktail napkin with her fingertips. She weighed her next question, wondered if she should keep it to herself. Well, she thought, we've gone this far. Finally, she asked, "Did you love your husband?"

"Husbandzzzz," Theo said, holding up three fingers. "Three in all. Three husbands, but thank God only one child, from my second husband, the good-for-nothin' muthafucka, excuse my French. Number three was another good-for-nothin' muthafucka. The only good thing about him was that he didn't give me any kids." She took a sip of her drink, licked her lips. "The first one was just a kid himself. We were both just kids. He was a young thing and could not leave his mother. And, yes, I loved them all. And now I love Susannah." She gave a little laugh. "After three consecutive bums, I finally married a doctor."

Maggie started. She nearly gasped. Susannah? Of course, it hadn't occurred to her the first time Theo had mentioned that name—Susannah was a common enough name. "A doctor?" she said.

"Mmm-hmm." Theo nodded. "A gynecologist, no less. How's that for convenience?"

Maggie said nothing.

"Are you freaked?" Theo asked after a moment.

"No," Maggie said, not looking at Theo, "I'm fine." Of course, she was considerably short of fine. She was a good deal closer to freaked. It wasn't that Theo Davis was gay, not in and of itself, anyway. It was more the fact that all of a sudden *every*body seemed to be gay. Her gynecologist—and Maggie had no doubt that Theo's Susannah was also *her* Susannah: how many gynecologists named Susannah could there be? This red leather lady. Probably the bartender, with his biceps like softballs and his phosphorescent smile. And maybe even her own husband. "I'm just fine," she lied, and finished her wine in one long swallow.

It wasn't until she had let herself in the front door and found Daniel sitting in the big reddish-brown leather wingback armchair his parents had given them as a wedding present, still in his suit pants and dress shirt, his hands wrapped around what looked like a half-empty Scotch rocks, that Maggie realized she had forgotten to call Daniel and let him know she would be late getting home—a serious breach of her own rule. Daniel looked up and said quietly, "You're home."

"Hi, honey," Maggie said, walking toward the chair. "I'm so sorry," she said quickly, "I stopped for a drink with some of the girls from work, and I just plain forgot to call." Daniel set his drink down on the coffee table, and stood up just as Maggie reached him. He made no move toward her, his arms hung at his sides. She raised tentatively on tiptoe and softly kissed his lips.

"Sweetheart," Daniel whispered, slipping his arms around Maggie's back, "I'm so glad you're home. I worried," he said, hugging her close. Maggie rubbed the small of his back with her palms and wondered if she were about to make a mistake: it felt so good in his arms. "I started thinking maybe you'd been in an accident or something, and then I thought, Oh my God, maybe she's not coming home. I actually checked the closets," he said, kneading the back of her neck with his fingers. Maggie took a deep breath, and pushed gently away from Daniel. "We have to talk," she said.

"I didn't know what you'd planned for dinner," Daniel said. "We could go get something. We haven't been to Cutter's in a while."

"Honey," Maggie said, stepping back, "we have to talk."

"What?" Daniel said, looking suddenly very young, like a frightened boy. "What is it?"

"Let's sit down," Maggie said, all but falling back into the sofa. Daniel lowered himself back into the leather chair. Maggie leaned forward, then changed her mind, sitting as far back as she could. She had to close her eyes before she could say it: "I need to get away for a while." She opened her eyes to find Daniel sitting stiffly straight against the back of the chair, his hands gripping its cushioned arms, his face void of discernible expression.

"You need to get away from me," he said. It wasn't a question.

"I just need some time away," Maggie said. "To think, to sort out my feelings."

"To decide whether or not you want to spend the rest of your life with a fag?" Daniel said, his voice even, his facial expression unreadable.

"Please don't do this," Maggie said. There was some small doubt in her mind that she could go on as Daniel Sullivan's wife: this was, in fact, her primary reason for wanting to lay a few miles of physical distance between herself and Daniel. Having him throw it back at her in such unpleasant terms made her recoil.

"*You* don't do this, Maggie," Daniel said. "Don't run away from me. It'll be all right. We'll make it all right."

Maggie sighed deeply. "I just need a little time, Daniel."

"How much time?" Daniel pushed himself slightly forward in the chair.

"I don't know," Maggie said. "Not long, I don't think. Daniel." She leaned forward toward him and reached for his hand, which he quickly snatched away. "I'm not doing this to hurt you, Daniel," she said, slapping at the arm of the chair where Daniel's hand had been. "I swear I'm not. I just need some time away, that's all." She looked up into his face and waited until his eyes met hers. "I think you owe me that."

Daniel's body spasmed, as if he were about to leap from the

chair, or maybe hit her, or maybe both; but finally he remained in the chair. He looked away from her and asked, "Where will you go? To Anne's?"

Maggie nodded. "Yes."

This time he did get up out of the chair, and started out of the room toward the bathroom, or maybe the den. "Do what you think you have to," he said.

"Daniel!" she called. He kept walking. She wasn't sure what she would have said if he had turned around. Maybe "I'll be back soon." She was reasonably sure she would be. Probably "I love you." Of that much, at least, she was certain. She leaned back into the sofa and waited for a particularly vicious throb in her throat to subside. She had made her decision behind the wheel of her car, stopped at a red light on Ocean Park Boulevard shortly before arriving home, and she was determined to go through with it. Despite the fact that it made her feel like something out of an old television comedy, even though it felt like something Alice Kramden might do, something Wilma Flintstone might pull, Maggie Sullivan was going home to her mother.

CHAPTER 15

HE IS BEING PURSUED BY A BEAST, possibly The Beast. He cannot so much see it as sense it at his back, huge and hot. He can hear its unearthly growl and snarl, feel its humid breath along the back of his neck. Crockett runs and runs, screaming for help until his throat feels shredded, helpless tears coursing down his face, running and running until it seems the muscles of his legs might split and fall from his bones.

And then the wall, infinitely wide, impossibly high; and he has no choice but to face the beast. He turns, bares his fangs.

Crockett awoke sitting up in bed, his body damp with sweat, his breath coming in gasps. The sound of his own snarling seemed to reverberate through his bedroom. He glanced at the clock radio, its lighted numerals throwing a shaft of green glow across the dark room: it was 3:05 in the morning. Crockett lay back, shivering with cold and residual panic, feeling small and helpless and sorry for himself. He turned over on his side and reached his hand out, wishing for a warm, solid body to cuddle against until he could sleep again. Bryan, he thought, stroking the cool sheet with his palm. The sonofabitch. He tried to imagine Daniel in bed with him, but it didn't work. Just another man who left, he thought. They always leave.

He recognized Johnnie right away, even across the room, even though Johnnie's back was turned. He'd have known that back anywhere. Crockett had just entered the men's weight room at the Beverly Hills Sports Connection—so called despite its location, well within the West Hollywood city limits—for the first time in several weeks. He had awakened that morning before nine o'clock, feeling relatively strong (he vaguely remembered having had a bad dream), and decided an easy workout might do him some good. He spotted Johnnie next to the Nautilus multiexercise machine, waiting with what appeared to be rapidly diminishing patience while a very muscular and very bald man in a brief one-piece workout suit executed a long, slow, seemingly excruciating set of toe raises. If the thick-muscled back and bulging upper arms displayed by his red tank top were any indication, Johnnie looked better than ever—and he'd always looked good.

He watched Johnnie shift his weight from one foot to the

other, watched Johnnie's buttocks shift beneath gray Spandex tights. It was one of those behinds that only black men seemed to have: so high and protuberant as to skirt the bounds of good taste. It was one of Crockett's favorite behinds. Johnnie Ray Rousseau's was one of Crockett's favorite bodies.

Suddenly, Crockett remembered—that he could have forgotten, even momentarily, brought a bitter little smile to his lips: he'd have to tell Johnnie. Probably then and there, next to the Nautilus multiexercise machine. Besides, even without his unpleasant medical announcement, there was every possibility Johnnie might not be utterly thrilled to see him. It was Crockett, after all, who had broken off all communication after Johnnie moved back in with that bodybuilder—Kevin or Kurt or whatever his name was. "I hope we can be friends," Johnnie had said. "I really mean that." And he probably had meant it. But Crockett hadn't been in the market for another buddy.

He started across the room toward Johnnie, feeling his heartbeat pick up speed. He had hardly walked three steps before Johnnie turned around at the waist, as if Crockett had called out to him. He spotted Crockett immediately, turned completely around, and started toward him, a smile on his face so warm Crockett felt as if he were walking toward a fireplace.

"Mr. M," Johnnie said when they'd gotten close enough for Crockett to feel the humid warmth and smell the sweet musky odor of Johnnie's exerted body. "The Divine Mr. M." Crockett smiled. It was good to see Johnnie, he was pleased Johnnie was glad to see him. And nobody else had ever referred to him as "the Divine Mr. M." They leaned in simultaneously—it was like a reflex—then quickly caught themselves. Whatever might have taken place on a regular basis in the sauna, steam room, and hot tub—and there was plenty—men pointedly did not kiss hello in the weight rooms of the Beverly Hills Sports Connection. Crockett and Johnnie traded wide, if somewhat sheepish smiles and presented their right hands. Johnnie tugged the fingerless glove from his hand and clasped Crockett's hand tightly. He pulled Crockett slightly closer; his dark, almond-shaped eyes made contact with Crockett's.

"It's good to see you," Johnnie said.

"How are you, Johnnie?"

"How do I look?" Johnnie had not let go of Crockett's hand.

"You look great."

"Then that's how I am." Johnnie finally released Crockett's hand, but not his eyes. "You've lost some weight," he said.

"A little," Crockett said quickly.

"How are *you*, Crockett?"

"Fine."

"Fine?"

Was that some sort of challenge? Crockett wondered. Could it be he looked even worse than he thought? "Pretty much," Crockett said after an uncomfortable second or two. Tell him, Crockett thought. Tell him now.

"Okay." Johnnie crossed his arms over his chest, making his pecs bulge. "You're fine." He looked Crockett over for a moment, smiling an equivocal sort of half-smile.

"I've never seen you here before," Crockett said, less than comfortable under Johnnie's gaze, which seemed to look all the way into him, as if he'd read the whole story in Crockett's eyes and was waiting for his confession only as a formality.

"No, I usually work out at the Santa Monica Connection. But I was in the neighborhood, and I do so love the scenery here." Johnnie grinned and wiggled his eyebrows. "If you catch my drift." As if in illustration, a babyfaced blond man walked past them, his outrageous musculature accentuated by a pair of infinitesimal satin shorts and the tattered remains of a tank top.

"While we're on that subject," Crockett said, "when'd you get so fuckin' big?"

"It was kinda gradual," Johnnie said. "Had to try and keep up with Keith."

Crockett hoped he hadn't visibly flinched at the mention of Johnnie's lover. "You still with him?"

"Yep." Johnnie smiled, nodded.

"Good for you." Crockett hoped his "Good for you" hadn't sounded as patently false as it tasted on his tongue. Johnnie's smile turned down at one corner. "You still singing?" Crockett asked him, just to slice through Johnnie's somehow accusatory quiet, just to say something. He knew Johnnie was still singing. Scarcely a week passed when Johnnie Ray Rousseau's name didn't flag Crockett down from the Calendar section of the Sunday *Times*. Johnnie was appearing at Gio's or Carlos & Charlie's, even the Vine Street Bar & Grill, though always on weeknights, Wednesdays or Thursdays—the Carmen McRaes and Anita O'Days booked the weekends. And scarcely a week passed when Crockett didn't plan to go out and see Johnnie. He'd even made reservations on two or three occasions at one club or another. Once, he'd shaved, showered, dressed, and driven away, only to lose his nerve like the air in a punctured tire and turn back less than a block from the club where Johnnie's name was misspelled "Russo" on the tiny marquee.

"I'm singing tonight," Johnnie said, when a small but solidly muscled young woman elbowed meaningfully past them, bumping them both on her way to the hip-and-back machine, letting them know they were standing very much in the way. With a hand on Crockett's shoulder, Johnnie maneuvered them against the nearest mirrored wall. "I'm doing a nine o'clock set at At My Place," he said. "Can you come?"

"I—" Crockett searched frantically for an excuse that wouldn't sound glaringly false, a lie that wouldn't show itself for a lie. Come on, dammit! You're a writer, for chrissakes!

"I'll comp you," Johnnie said. "Just give the dude at the

door your name. You busy tonight?" Johnnie's eyes would not leave Crockett's alone. He could no more lie to Johnnie than flap his arms and fly.

"No," Crockett said.

"Will you come, then? Say you will."

"I—" Say, I'd love to, really, but the headlights on my car are both out and I have this horrible ingrown toenail.

"Say you will."

"I—" Sounds like a ball, but I simply must wash my hair and get to bed early tonight.

"Say you will."

"I will." Why fight? There was no way he could lie and make it stick. Besides, why the hell *not* go? Johnnie obviously wanted him to. And seeing him here, hot and half-naked, Crockett realized that—while he wasn't looking—much, perhaps most of the hurt had gone away. Like a sniffle you don't miss once it's cleared up.

"You wouldn't lie to me, Crockett," Johnnie said. "Wouldja? Whatever else you may think of me, I never lied to you."

They'd met at somebody's house at somebody's birthday party—Crockett no longer remembered whose house, whose birthday, or who was President at the time. What he did remember was standing near the heavy-laden hors d'oeuvres table, sucking on a light beer and watching this good-looking black guy on the other side of the room entertaining a small clutch of men with some story or other, told in a one-man-theater group of faces and voices and a nonstop flurry of flamboyant hand gestures. He was wearing pleated pants, saddle shoes, and a violet beret. As the only thing darker than a good base tan in the entire place, he would have stood out anyway. In that outfit, in a roomful of alligator shirts and 501s, he looked like a Hostess cupcake on a platter of bologna sandwiches. In a milieu whose pervading fashion sense was David Bowie by way of Jack Wrangler, this guy looked like somebody crossed Harry Belafonte with Cab Calloway. Judging by the faces and the audible laughter from his small audience, he looked like more fun than "Saturday Night Live."

Crockett was weighing the wisdom of ambling over to the black guy, catching the tail end of his anecdote—he wouldn't have minded catching the guy's tail end, period—and maybe introducing himself, when suddenly the guy turned toward him, made immediate, solid eye contact, and shot him a smile warm enough to melt butter. He strode over to Crockett, his walk somewhere between Bette Davis and Sammy Davis, offered his big brown hand, and said, "Hi. I'm Johnny Ray Rousseau."

Soon they were standing close together, making the kind of small talk people often make when they'd much rather be horizontal while immediate circumstances dictate that they remain vertical. They were grinning and giggling like two refugees from the Incurably Silly ward at Camarillo, when a slender young man with dark curly hair and more than a passing resemblance to a bush baby leaned over Johnnie's back.

"Hate to interrupt, honey," he said, "but it's time to go to work."

"Yassuh, boss," Johnnie said, and kissed Curly's full, ruddy lips. Was this Johnnie's lover? Crockett wondered. And, Get to what sort of work? The questions scarcely had time to cross Crockett's mind: Johnnie had him by the hand—"C'mon!"—leading him toward the baby grand piano in the living room, where Johnnie perched on one end of the piano bench next to Mr. Curlyhair Bushbabyface. It was the first of many times Crockett would hear Johnnie Ray Rousseau sing. Later that evening, when Johnnie Ray asked him home, it was the first time he'd ever slept with a black man.

They had been seeing each other for just over two months off and on, as Johnnie's schedule permitted, when Johnnie left for a two-month club and concert tour of Japan. Johnnie kept in touch through letters and exotic picture postcards, and they picked up just about where they'd left off when he returned. One evening, about three weeks into that second shift, following a dinner of Johnnie's homemade chicken enchiladas, Johnnie looked meaningfully into Crockett's eyes, took his hand, and said, "I have to tell you something." This is it, Crockett thought: the kiss-off.

"There's a man I lived with for a couple of years," Johnnie began, "years ago. We loved each other, but—well, it just didn't quite work out at the time." Johnnie paused, as if weighing his words. Just get it over with, Crockett wanted to say, but didn't. "Anyway, I saw him again the other day and—"

"You're going back to him," Crockett finished for him.

"If he'll have me," Johnnie said. "And I think he will. He's—" Johnnie laughed a little. "Well, corny as it sounds, he's the love of my life. I have to try again. I'm sorry." Johnnie reached to touch Crockett's hand, but Crockett pulled away.

"That's a song by Brenda Lee," he said, and got up to leave.

"I like you very much," Johnnie said, holding him by the arm. "You know I do. I hope we can be friends. I really mean that."

No: Johnnie hadn't lied. It had hurt like a red-hot sonofabitch, anyway, but at least he hadn't lied.

"I have something to tell you," Crockett said. He took half a step closer to Johnnie, rapped his knuckles nervously against the mirror.

"Oh?" Johnnie inclined his face toward Crockett's—their foreheads nearly touched.

"I tried to call you, on the phone," Crockett said. "You're not listed."

"I know. I was getting entirely too many wacko calls. If I'd thought you'd ever want to call me, I'd have given you the number."

"No, it's not that, it's just—" Crockett lowered his voice nearly to a whisper. "Do you know what ARC is?"

"Of course I do," Johnnie said. "You?"

Crockett nodded.

Johnnie reached out and squeezed Crockett's shoulder. "Oh, kid, I'm so sorry."

"I just thought you should know. You know, in case you wanted to get tested or something."

"I have been," Johnnie said. "Keith, too. Neither of us is . . . we're both fine."

"Oh. I'm glad."

"Jesus," Johnnie said after a moment, "I want to hug you so bad." But since they were standing in the men's weight room at the Beverly Hills Sports Connection, he squeezed Crockett's shoulder instead.

Crockett was leaning against the kitchen counter in pajama bottoms and bathrobe, his feet, in sweatsocks and thongs, shuffling slightly to Michael Jackson music from the stereo, as he stared down the microwave oven, waiting for his Stouffer's fettuccine Alfredo to cook. He didn't much like Stouffer's, but at least they didn't require a lot of energy to prepare. The clock on the microwave read 6:55—he was in no hurry, but he couldn't afford to dillydally either. He had just recently awakened from a two-hour nap: he'd still felt pretty good after working out, but he didn't want his energy running out before nine o'clock, and better safe than sorry. When the telephone rang, Crockett danced a kind of conga—one, two, three, BOOM!—all the way into the living room, singing along with Michael: "wannable star-tin' SOME-thin'." He picked up the phone and answered in a bad Mexican accent: "Jel-low?"

"Crockett?" It was Daniel. His voice sounded unusually soft and husky, but Crockett would know Daniel's voice in a crowd.

"Daniel. Hi."

"She's gone, Crockett," Daniel said, without so much as hello. "She's left me."

"What are you talking about?" Crockett folded to the floor, sitting cross-legged next to the phone table.

"Maggie," Daniel said. "She packed some things and went to her mother's."

"Oh, Daniel." Crockett rolled onto his back. "I'm so sorry." Daniel didn't answer. "Did she say anything?" Crockett asked.

"She needs some time away, she said."

"Then I'm sure that's all it is, Daniel. She'll be back."

"I wish I knew that," Daniel said.

"Daniel, she's your wife. She loves you. She'll come back."

"You didn't hear the things she said the other day. You didn't see her face. I don't know: maybe this is just too much for her. I don't know if I'd blame her."

"Jesus fuck, Daniel," Crockett said, "did she say she was never coming back?"

"No," Daniel admitted softly. "She said she didn't know how long."

"Daniel," Crockett said, surprising himself with his ongoing defense of Maggie, "give the girl a break. She's been thrown a serious curve here. She said she needs some time. So give her some time."

Crockett could hear Daniel sniff. Was the man crying? "Thanks, buddy," Daniel said, and sniffed again. "I'm sorry to dump all over you like this, as if you didn't have your own shit to deal with."

"Shucks," Crockett said. "T'warn't nothin'."

"How—" Daniel cleared his throat. "How are you feeling?"

"Pretty good today," Crockett said. "I even went to the gym."

"Good deal. Don't push yourself too hard, though."

"I won't."

After a moment, Daniel said, "What are you doing?"

"Right now?"

"No, later. This evening."

"I'm going—" Crockett hesitated: was Daniel going to ask to see him? And would he throw Johnnie over to sit with Daniel while he pined for his wife? "I'm going out in a little bit."

"Oh." A beat of silence. "Well, you take care, then. I'll talk to you soon, okay?"

"Okay. I love you," Crockett added.

"And I, you," Daniel said slowly. "Bye."

Crockett sat up, hung up the phone. "My, my," he said aloud, "doesn't life just twist and turn." Whatever Maggie might have been going through—and Crockett could only guess, since he hadn't spoken to Maggie since the beans had been spilled two days earlier—he could not believe she could leave Daniel permanently. How could anyone, having Daniel Sullivan, completely and legally, ever bear to leave him? He hoped for Daniel's sake that she returned to him soon. But then again, part of him hoped to God she never would.

Crockett perched on one of a row of high stools at the back of the club, near the soundboard. He would have felt odd sitting at one of the tables in the company of strangers. Johnnie was even better than he remembered: his voice, always warm and sweet as cocoa, seemed fuller and stronger, his stage demeanor more assured. He looked utterly at home behind the microphone, dressed in a loose-fitting zooty sort of suit, flanked by a thin, Roman-nosed young man at the piano and a tall, lanky longhair plucking at a stand-up bass.

Still, Crockett found he didn't enjoy Johnnie's music as much as he once had. Where Johnnie once sang more familiar songs—Beatles tunes, current Top Forty, the occasional novelty number like "Lydia the Tattooed Lady"—now he seemed to favor more pieces that just seemed to ramble on, melodically and lyrically, with little or no hook and sometimes no discernible chorus. A couple of songs were almost entirely composed of that wordless shooby-dooby stuff that Crockett had never really liked.

There was one song Johnnie sang that Crockett could really feel: he'd heard it before but could remember neither the singer nor the title of the song. A song about an enchanted boy, and the greatest thing you'll ever learn.

After the set, Crockett wasn't sure if he should go up to Johnnie, or wait for him, or just slide down off the stool and go home. He felt encouraged when Johnnie emerged from backstage, immediately caught his eye from across the room, and flashed a big smile. He watched Johnnie walk from table to table, smiling and talking, shaking hands or hugging or kissing various people: handsome men of about Crockett's age seated together in groups, other men paired with stylish women (one of whom actually wore a leopard-skin pillbox hat), one female couple. The overall look of the crowd reminded Crockett of a book of photographs he'd once seen of Paris in the 1930s.

He slid down from the stool as Johnnie approached. Johnnie leaned in to kiss him, and he turned his face so Johnnie's lips landed against his cheek. Johnnie slipped his arms around him and hugged him close and tight; and, all at once, he never wanted Johnnie to let go. A little moan escaped his throat when Johnnie released him and asked, "So what did you think?"

"Your voice is better than ever," Crockett said. Johnnie smiled his one-sided semismile.

"But you hated the new material."

"Oh, no," Crockett protested, feeling transparent as Scotch tape, "I didn't hate it."

"It's all right not to like it," Johnnie said. "Mingus isn't everybody's cuppa soup."

Crockett smiled weakly. "I really liked that one song: 'There was a boy . . .'"

" 'Nature Boy.' Everybody likes that one. I like it, too."

"What happened to your other piano player? Smallish, dark. Big, big eyes. Pookie or something?"

A cloud passed over Johnnie's eyes. "Snookie. Snookie Rothenberg. He's dead."

"Shit." It hit Crockett's stomach like a lead Life Saver.

"Yeah." Johnnie nodded. "Shit."

"AIDS?"

"Sort of. Snookie found out he had it; decided he'd rather die all at once than . . . you know. He'd never been sick in his whole life. So he killed himself. Swallowed most of a bottle of, um"—Johnnie laughed, almost a cough—"Sominex. Sominex, for God's sake!" He looked down at the floor. "After he was out cold, his body tried to . . . eject the stuff and he, um, choked to death on his own vomit. I found him, two days later. He'd left a suicide note, and a list of piano players for me." He lifted his face to look at Crockett again. "My best friend."

"Oh, Johnnie . . ." Crockett so wanted to comfort Johnnie somehow, but what could he say? Suddenly, Johnnie grasped him by the shoulders, his fingers digging painfully into Crockett's flesh, his face full of anger and hurt and who could say what else.

"Don't you ever try anything like that. Don't you even think it, you hear me? Just don't!"

"I won't, Johnnie."

"Promise me!"

"I promise." The look on Johnnie's face frightened Crockett: he'd have promised anything. Still, while he had no immediate plans involving lethal overdose, he could certainly understand the attraction a bottle of an over-the-counter sleeping aid might hold. "Johnnie, you're hurting me," he said finally. Johnnie let go of Crockett's shoulders, then tenderly rubbed the areas where he'd grabbed them. "I'm sorry, babe. A bit of heavy drama in the night." He took a deep breath, blew it out. "So." He tugged at the collar of Crockett's alligator shirt. "What shall we do now?"

"I don't know. I didn't know if . . ." Crockett hadn't been sure if Johnnie planned to devote his entire evening to him or not. "What do you want to do?"

"I want to take you home with me," Johnnie said.

Crockett's mouth dropped open. "What about your lover?"

"He's in Minnesota, for his grandmother's funeral," Johnnie said through a wide smile. "Sleazy enough for you? My lover's conveniently out of town, so come on-a my house. Believe me, it's a good deal more innocent than it sounds."

"Oh." Crockett said, a little disappointed.

"Look, we haven't seen each other in far too long. You came here, so obviously you want to see me, right? So we could stay here, or go to a bar someplace, but frankly the best place for us to really relax and talk is probably my house. It's close. And it's comfortable. And besides"—he reached over and palmed Crockett's cheek with an incredibly warm hand—"you look like you could use some hugs. How 'bout it?"

Just inside the door of his house, Johnnie turned to Crockett and leaned in for a kiss. Again, Crockett turned his face away.

"Hey," Johnnie said, "not even a kiss?"

"Johnnie, I've got—I've got ARC."

"Yes. You told me."

"Well, do you think it's wise to kiss me?"

"Yes," Johnnie said, "I do." He cupped Crockett's face in his hands and kissed him softly on the lips.

"Oh, Johnnie." Crockett slipped his arms around Johnnie's back, and they held each other close.

"Oh, Johnnie what?"

"Oh, Johnnie, hold me, hug me, make me feel better." Johnnie stroked the back of Crockett's head. "No problem." He took Crockett's hand and led him away from the door.

Standing next to the big four-poster bed, Crockett watched Johnnie undress. He looked away—he didn't want to be caught staring—his eyes resting on a framed photograph propped up on the muscular dark-wood dresser. A smiley, professional-looking portrait of Johnnie and his lover, a good-looking Nordic type with a short reddish beard and a thick neck. Crockett glanced away quickly. He tugged his own shirt over his head and said, "I'm celibate now, you know." Crockett had been seriously considering celibacy for a couple of weeks, but this was the first time he had expressed the idea aloud.

"Oh?" Johnnie shucked his baggy pants and boxer shorts in one motion, releasing his dick, which was already raising its head toward the ceiling. "A lot of guys are making that decision. Don't mind him." He indicated his slowly swaying penis. "He's a little bit unclear on the concept." Crockett shoved his pants down: his dick was unclear on the concept, too.

Lying against Johnnie's warm, hard body, his head pillowed against Johnnie's chest, Johnnie's hands stroking trails of warmth up and down his back, Crockett suddenly felt tears spilling from his eyes, puddling in the space between Johnnie's pecs.

"What's the matter, kiddo?"

"Nothing."

"You just make it a practice to cry all over a guy's chest."

"It's just that, it's so good: being with you, you holding me. I haven't felt this good in a while." That was part of it. What Crockett chose not to mention was that, for a few minutes, he had managed to forget just how scared he was. Afraid of the seemingly inevitable breakdown of his immune system, of the ever-encroaching incapacitating illness, of a death worthy of a Stephen King novel. Fear had come to be the overall theme of Crockett's existence.

"Don't be afraid," Johnnie whispered. "You're going to be all right."

Crockett laughed a little. "That a promise?"

"Yes."

"Your lips to God's ears, as my agent likes to say."

"Something like that," he said, wriggling out from under Crockett.

"Hey," Crockett protested, "where're you going?"

"Nowhere. Lie down on your belly."

"Why?" Crockett asked while doing as he was told.

"Because it's time for your enema," Johnnie said, crawling down toward the foot of the bed.

"What?"

"I'm going to give you a massage, okay? You're wound up like an old Timex."

"Oh my God, I haven't had a massage in years." Crockett settled in, more than willing to succumb to Johnnie's hands.

"Just give me a minute," Johnnie said. Crockett could hear Johnnie breathing deep and slow, then what sounded like blowing into his palms, then rubbing them briskly together. Then Johnnie's fingers kneaded deep into the muscles of Crockett's shoulders, reminding him just how tense he'd been. He moaned softly under Johnnie's touch. Whatever ointment or rub he had applied to his hands penetrated Crockett's skin with a deep, glowing warmth, like Vaseline made from lightning, like Ben-Gay from paradise.

"What's on your hands?" he asked, his words muffled against a pillow.

"Nothing," Johnnie replied through a slow exhalation.

"No, seriously." Johnnie stopped rubbing, leaned forward, and cupped a hand over Crockett's nose. There was nothing but warm skin.

"How do you do that?"

"Something a friend of mine taught me," Johnnie replied; then his hands were on Crockett's back.

"But what is it?"

Johnnie leaned hard against the small of Crockett's back, causing every vertebra to click, one after the other, like dominoes falling, pushing the breath out of him with a whoosh. All the tension in his body seemed to follow.

"Hush," Johnnie said. He began to hum softly as he stroked Crockett's back. Crockett slowly recognized the song he'd liked from Johnnie's show. The one about the enchanted boy, and the greatest thing you'll ever learn. To love, Crockett thought over Johnnie's humming. And be loved . . .

He awoke with a start. He realized almost instantly that he'd awakened himself; that he had been singing in his sleep. His eyes darted around the room, a room he had never seen in daylight, and for a quick moment he didn't know where he was. Then he remembered. He turned over to feel the sheets where Johnnie had, presumably, slept; they were no longer warm, though Crockett could smell Johnnie's hair on the pillow.

He sat up quickly, amazed at the clearness of his head; how alert, how unusually wide-awake he felt. He did a double take on the antique-looking windup alarm clock on the nightstand: it was a quarter to eight. Crockett could hardly remember the last time he was awake this early, feeling nearly this good. He slid out of bed and into his pants and shirt. Opening the bedroom door, he could hear music: Bobby Darin and Johnnie Ray Rousseau seemed to be singing a duet. He followed the sound to the kitchen, where the morning sun through a huge window lit pale yellow walls, and a portable tape deck on the counter played "Mack the Knife," and where Johnnie, backlit and beautiful in jeans and no shirt, sang along—"Look out-a Miss Lottie Len-YAH!"—while pouring steaming water from a kettle into a Japanese teapot, unleashing the scent of ginger.

"Good morning," Crockett said.

Johnnie turned, smiling. Was it his imagination, Crockett wondered, or did Johnnie look different this morning? Older. Younger. Something. "Good morning, yourself. How do you feel?"

"I feel good. I feel better than I have any right to. What did you do to me last night?"

"Why don't you sit down, have a little breakfast." He indicated a tiny breakfast nook just off the kitchen, a table set for two with cantaloupe halves and strawberries.

"Johnnie—"

"Sit!" Crockett obeyed. Johnnie opened a cabinet, removed a couple of mugs as he spoke. "Last night, the massage thing, was basically a small . . . well, healing."

"Healing," Crockett repeated dully. "Like a miracle?"

"No," Johnnie said slowly. "More like a . . . healing. Of the holistic variety."

"Then what are you telling me?" Crockett's voice was rising in pitch and volume. "Last time I saw you, you were a singer. Now you're some kind of, what, witch or something?"

"Oh, no: nothing nearly so Gothic."

"Well, what then?"

"Well, grasshopper," Johnnie said with a little smile, "it seems I have a small . . . gift. Call it spiritual, call it metaphysical, call it Ishmael. I prefer to think of it in terms of energy.

See, there are these energy centers at various points in the body, called chakras. Sickness, disease, illness is often the result of energy imbalances among the various chakras. What I did, after relaxing you with a good old-fashioned back rub, was basically to help clear and balance your chakras, freeing up those energy centers to assist your body's natural healing processes. So you feel better today than you did yesterday, when your chakras were totally out of balance. Does that make any sense at all?" He leaned back against the counter, coffee mugs dangling from a long middle finger.

"Fuck no." This was brand new material for Crockett—energy centers and chakras and shit. The only kind of healings he'd ever had any contact with before were told about in Sunday-school Bible stories or claimed by the sort of polyester-suited, Dynel-wigged Bible-wielding wonderworkers his parents liked to watch on television during rerun season. Now a black gay jazz vocalist, someone Crockett had *slept* with on more than one occasion for chrissakes, was futzing with tea and cantaloupe and talking about this small gift that made his hands radiate, and it hardly seemed coincidental that Crockett felt better than he had in weeks. Jesus, he thought—only in L.A. "May I ask you something?"

Johnnie poured fragrant tea into mugs. "Ask."

"Just what sort of things can you . . . heal?"

"You wanna know if I've cured any lepers lately?"

"You know what I'm asking, Johnnie."

"Yes, I guess I do." Johnnie carried two steaming mugs to the table, and placed one within Crockett's reach. "As I said, mine is a relatively small gift. I do know somebody who might be able to help you. She's the one who brought out my gift. She healed her own breast cancer with meditation and macrobiotics: she's got the hospital records and the tits to prove it. She works with pyramids, crystals, visualizations, the whole nine yards. Anyway, I really think you should see her."

"Who is she? How do I know—"

"—she's not a total charlatan? You can take my word for it. She cured my allergies, and as you may recall, they were legion." Crockett did remember Johnnie spending night after sleepless night, his head stuffed and throbbing with congestion that no drug could seem to dent. Still, hay fever wasn't AIDS. "Theo's a very good friend of mine. Actually, she's my aunt." Johnnie's almond-shaped eyes peered into Crockett's. "Even if she can't cure you, she might be able to help keep you a little stronger, help you fight it a little better. And even if she can't do a goddamn thing, what have you got now?"

"I don't know, Johnnie." It was all so new, so very strange.

"Look." Johnnie pulled a business card out of his hip pocket, pushed it across the table toward Crockett. "Take this. If you decide to see her, just call. Tell her you're my friend. It's up to you." He shrugged. "I'm through."

Crockett looked down at the card. It read: "Theodosia Davis. Holistic Healings. Gratis." And then a phone number. Crockett picked up the card and slipped it into his back pocket. "Thank you."

"So eat your breakfast," Johnnie said. "You'll grow up big and strong like your Uncle Johnnie." Crockett couldn't hold back a smile. Johnnie smiled back, and lifted his mug of ginger tea in a little toast. "Drink this," he said, "and you'll grow wings on your feet."

"Inhale deeply, to four . . ."

Crockett breathed in, filling his abdomen first, his back, finally his chest with air to a slow mental count of four.

". . . and exhale completely, to eight."

He lay back on his living-room rug in the position Theo called Savasana—legs apart, arms akimbo, palms facing the ceiling—surprised to feel his abdominal muscles (strong from years of exercise) flutter and spasm as he struggled to exhale slowly and evenly to the slow eight-count Theo had set.

"Bring your mind to focus only on your breath," she said. "Pay attention only to the sensation of the air as it enters and leaves the body through the nostrils."

The increased energy level he'd experienced had lasted for two days following Johnnie's "little healing," and it was with some ambivalence that Crockett had telephoned Theodosia Davis the evening before: he wasn't sure if he believed Johnnie's talk of chakras and meditations, but he knew he had nothing to lose by calling. The velvety voice that answered the phone had seemed somehow soothing in itself. "Lord," she'd said through a warm, throaty laugh, "I haven't heard from Johnnie in a coon's age. You need me to come out tonight?"

Crockett had assumed he'd have to make some kind of appointment and wait. "Um, how about tomorrow?" he said.

"How 'bout I come out tomorrow after work, about six-thirty? You're on my way home."

Arriving at Crockett's door in sweat pants and a leotard, Theo Davis was one of the most beautiful women Crockett had ever seen. He had almost no sense of women as sex objects, but Theo was beautiful like art—anyone with eyes could see it. She looked nothing like Crockett's idea of a mystic or witch or voodoo priestess. She looked like she might be an aerobics instructor or something. As he shook her hand and took in her big, white smile (so much like Johnnie's), he found himself staring at her breasts: because they were just short of outrageous, and because, as far as her reputation as a holistic healer, they represented her proof. Crockett and Theo sat on opposite ends of the living-room sofa and chatted for a few minutes. She asked about his symptoms, which he listed, and his religious beliefs, which he denied.

"I don't know what Johnnie Ray's told you," she said, kicking off her white Reeboks, "but you should understand from the get-go that I'm not a medical doctor and I'm not a witch doctor. What I deal in, mostly, is the strengthening of the body's immune system through the reduction of stress, which even the medical establishment is coming to acknowledge as a factor in the strength or weakness of the immune system. Also positive affirmations, and creative visualizations, in which we attempt to change the state of the body by changing the state of mind." She tucked her long legs up onto the sofa in an uncomfortable-looking cross-legged position he'd seen in pictures of Indian yogis. "I might also give you some nutritional advice if you want." She looked deep into Crockett's eyes. "I don't claim to work miracles, and I don't claim to have a cure. But I do think I can help you help yourself. Keep you stronger. Okay?"

Crockett shrugged. "Okay." Theo directed him down to the floor, where she performed a healing similar (or so Crockett supposed) to the one Johnnie had done. It left his body tingling, his mind clear, yet with an overall sensation of relaxation: he felt as if he could do anything at all, or nothing at all.

"How you doin'?" she said.

"Great," he said.

"I'd like to lead you in a relaxation exercise before we're through."

"Coals to Newcastle," Crockett said through a long, deep sigh.

"What to who?" Theo said.

"Nothing."

"Fine," she said, and instructed him to lie on his back. He never would have believed how difficult a proposition it could be to breathe, just breathe. Stray thoughts, disjointed images, snippets of music darted across his mind, falling over one another.

"When the mind wanders," Theo said softly, firmly, "just bring it back." He tried to concentrate on the breathing, actually to feel the air rustling the hairs in his nose, all the while controlling the intake and exhalation to Theo's four-eight count. This is impossible, he thought. He saw nothing relaxing about this exercise, yet he continued to breathe, concentrate, breathe.

All at once, it was as if his body were a helium balloon, lighter than air, expanding slowly and steadily beyond the limits of what he had known as his body, beyond the limits of what he had known as his living room. His long, slow breaths gave way to tiny pulsating breaths. He seemed to be floating and falling at the same time. He was exploding from his very center in slow motion, breaking apart into the smallest possible particles of himself, as if to merge with the air itself, with the atmosphere, with the—

His eyes darted open. He gasped a big breath and pushed himself up into a seated position, and the particles of himself fell instantly back into place. His arm muscles spasmed, his fingers trembled against the rug. He had the eerie, disconcerting feeling of having nearly fallen over . . . something, a precipice, a cliff, perhaps; of having nearly fallen into . . . something.

"Crockett?" Theo stepped down from the sofa and down onto her knees next to him. "Are you all right?" She touched his face softly with her warm fingertips.

"I don't know," he said. "I got scared all of a sudden. I felt as if I were about to, I don't know—leave. You know?"

Theo nodded. "You shouldn't be afraid of it," she said. "It's a good part of why we meditate at all."

"What is?"

"Leaving."

"Leaving?" he repeated.

Theo smiled. "Leaving the body," she said in much the same tone she might have used had she said "Leaving the room."

"Leaving the—" Crockett suddenly noticed Theo's shoes were back on. And she had *Rolling Stone* magazine in her left hand, her index finger between the pages.

"How long was I—?"

"About fifteen, twenty minutes," Theo said. She wasn't wearing a watch. "I was just thinking about leaving you there and going on home."

"Shit," Crockett said, mostly to himself. He would have guessed two, maybe three minutes.

He rose on shaky legs. "I need a glass of water," he said. "Can I get you anything?"

"Do you have any herb tea?" Theo asked.

"I can brew up some ginger root," Crockett said. After drinking ginger-root tea at Johnnie's, he had immediately bought a large, gnarled root and a tea ball: he'd had ginger-root tea every morning since.

"That would be nice," Theo said, following Crockett into the kitchen.

"How'd you get into this . . . line of work?" Crockett asked, filling the copper teakettle from the tap.

"The healings?" Theo leaned against the counter. "Well, I'd read about Louise Hay—she cured her own cancer of the uterus—in a yoga magazine, years before they found my cancer. And I was determined they weren't going to take my breast. My doctor told me to my face I was crazy, I was committing suicide." She made a little razzberry sound with her lips. "Doctors—all they know is drugs and the knife. That's their whole bag of tricks. Anyhow, I used meditations, affirmations, macrobiotic diet." A smile spread across her face. "I took that macrobiotics and *gone*," she said. "I made up a recipe for macrobiotic onion dip. Sautéed onions and umeboshi plums and tahini—a mess of trouble for something that tastes just like Lipton onion soup mix and sour cream."

Crockett scraped a chunk of ginger root across the grater

while Theo continued: "Anyhow, I did my meditations and my macrobiotics and everything, and"—she made a big shrugging motion—"the lump in my breast got smaller. I'd feel it every day, and at first I thought it was my imagination, but I'll be derned if it didn't shrink. It took almost two years before it felt like it was gone. But I went back to my doctor—old quack—and his mouth fell wide open. It was gone. No lump, no cancer, no nothing. Just Sam 'n' Dave."

"Sam and Dave?"

Theo pointed to her chest. "Sam 'n' Dave."

Crockett smiled. "But that doesn't explain why you're making house calls, and for free."

"Just giving some back. To God, or the Cosmic, whatever you want to call it. I couldn't take money for it. I teach aerobics for money."

"Really?" Crockett said.

"Really. Why?"

"That's just what I'd have guessed you did for a living."

"You'd have never guessed from the wardrobe, right?"

"Right." They shared a small laugh.

Crockett opened the cabinet nearest his head and took out a bag of Chips Ahoy. He opened the bag, pulled out a cookie, and held it out toward Theo. She shook her head and said, "No thanks." Then she went on: "You know, I have kind of a special interest in AIDS. My son tested antibody positive about six months ago. So a lot of my work lately has been trying to keep Walter Junior healthy."

"I'm sorry," Crockett said.

"How's your family handling this?" While Crockett considered his answer, Theo reached into the bag of cookies, pulled one out, and took a healthy bite.

"I don't really have a family," Crockett said. He packed shredded ginger into a large tea ball.

"How so?" Theo said, her fingers covering a mouthful of chocolate-chip cookie.

"I was adopted, for one thing. And I haven't spoken to my adopted parents in years. When they found out I was gay, they decided it might be better for their relationship with Jesus if we didn't see each other." Crockett still remembered the look on Agnes Miller's face when he told her, the things she'd shouted at him as he left her home for the last time: "Thank God you're not my child," she'd said. "Pervert! I didn't give birth to you, thank the Lord!"

"Well, that's truly fucked," Theo said, "excuse my French."

Crockett shrugged. "Funny thing is," he said, "much as it hurt—and it hurt—I can't say I blame them, really. It was just more than they could deal with. I mean, homosexuality goes against everything Ed and Agnes Miller have ever believed. I might as well have told them I worshiped Satan and ate newborn babies for lunch. They're not bad people or anything. It's just that they're—" Crockett's hands gestured at the air as if trying to catch the right words. "They're *hicks*. Ed and Agnes are just a couple of decent, God-fearing, four-square Southern Baptist hicks from a town in Arkansas so small you could spit from one end of it to the other. They can't help what they are any more than I can help what I am."

"It's *still* fucked," Theo said. "I come from a town in Louisiana where people *do* spit from one end to the other. It's no excuse."

"It doesn't matter," said Crockett. "It's not as if I miss them or anything. We were never close. It's just that . . ." He hung the tea ball on the inside lip of the teapot. "There's something about being sick that makes you wish you had a family, even if you never liked yours."

Theo reached over and squeezed his shoulder: he could feel the extraordinary warmth of her hand through his shirt. "What you don't have is relatives," she said. "And I got

enough of *them* to be able to tell you that relatives ain't neces-
sarily the same thing as family. Family is where you find it."

Crockett nodded absently, not sure what Theo meant, suddenly sobered by the reminder of just how alone he felt. The
teakettle whistled.

He was at the word processor, working on a love scene for
Sweet Seasons and having a pretty good time ("Through the
filmy fabric of her panties, his touch seared her skin, the
pleasure nearly unbearable . . ."). Crockett had awakened
early, feeling refreshed, and had spent an unusually produc-
tive morning: he had written nearly fifteen pages before noon.
Just how much the previous day's visit from Theo Davis had
to do with this resurgence of energy, Crockett didn't even care
to conjecture—he felt good and he wasn't arguing with it.

As usual, he worked with the radio on. He kept it at a
relatively low decibel level and he only half listened, but he
found the constant noise much more conducive to work than
a houseful of silence. He was leaned back in his secretarial
armchair, arms crossed, staring into the sea of green letters on
the screen, trying to think of a euphemism for the female
genitalia that he hadn't used in the past several pages, when
he thought he heard the name Rock Hudson. If he only half
listened to the music on the radio while he wrote, he generally
paid even less attention to the news. He got up and started
toward the nearest speaker, when the telephone rang. Someone—was it Doris Day?—was saying something about how
tragic it was, and Crockett thought, Oh no.

He half ran to pick up the telephone: "Hello?"

"Crockett?" It was Daniel. "How are you doing, buddy?"

"Pretty good," Crockett said, happy not to be lying. "Pretty
good."

"Really? Glad to hear it. I was just wondering if you'd heard
about Rock. Rock Hudson."

"I think it's on the radio now." Crockett cocked his head, trying to hear the radio.

"He died this morning," Daniel said.

"It's on the radio now," Crockett repeated.

"Oh. You want to go listen to it?"

"Can you hold on a minute?"

"Yeah. Yeah, go on."

Crockett set down the receiver and ran to turn up the volume on the stereo. There was a snatch of dialogue from one of the Rock and Doris movies, maybe *Pillow Talk*. Someone reading a statement from Elizabeth Taylor: "I love him, and he is tragically gone." Then the announcer: "Once again, Rock Hudson died in his sleep at his Beverly Hills home. His battle with the dreaded disease that killed him . . ." And then the Supremes, singing "Stop in the Name of Love."

"Shit." Crockett turned the volume back down, went to pick up the phone again. "Daniel?"

"Yeah?"

"I appreciate your calling."

"It's a bitch," Daniel said.

"Yeah." Crockett heard his own voice break before he noticed he was crying. "It's a bitch."

"Hey," Daniel said, "you okay?"

"Yeah." Crockett sniffed, dug into his pants pocket for a handkerchief, and found he wasn't carrying one.

"All right," Daniel said. "Talk to you soon, okay?"

" 'Kay." Crockett hung up the phone, and folded down onto the floor, sitting cross-legged next to the phone table. He cried out loud, though there was no one except himself to hear. He cried for Rock, and for himself. For all of them.

CHAPTER
16

DANIEL'S HEART POUNDED OVER the electronic purring in his ear. He tugged at the telephone cord while the ringing continued at the other end: twice . . . three times . . . four. Click. "Hello?"

"Anne, it's Daniel."

"Hello, Daniel. How are you, dear?"

"I'm okay. How are you?"

"Fine, dear. Hold on a moment." He heard the thump of the receiver being set down, and Anne's suddenly distant-sounding voice saying, "It's Daniel." After what seemed a long time, Maggie's voice said, "Hello, Daniel," with nearly the exact tonality and inflection of her mother's voice.

"Hi, sweetheart."

"How are you?" she asked.

"I'm okay," Daniel said, stretching the truth considerably. He was far from okay. His wife had been away for four days, and he was hurt and angry, and he wanted her back. He fully understood Maggie's being upset or confused, but as far as he was concerned the place to work things out was not at her mother's house, but at her own house, with him. "How are *you*?"

"Okay," she said. "Are you eating all right?"

"Yeah." He'd been living on pot pies for four days: not that Daniel couldn't cook—he could hold his own in the kitchen—

but he could think of few things more depressing than the thought of cooking for one. "When are you coming home, Maggie?" He hated having to ask this question, knowing that any answer other than "Right this minute, honey" would feel like a hacksaw through him.

"Soon," Maggie said.

"Soon," he repeated dully. It was exactly the answer she'd given the day before. And the day before that. He felt his grip tighten around the receiver until his forearm trembled. Had Maggie been within arm's reach, he felt he could actually have lashed out at her. Could she possibly be hurting this much? "Fine, Maggie," he said, his voice a tight whisper. He hung up the phone harder than he'd intended to. He hadn't even let go of the receiver before the phone rang.

"Yes?"

"Daniel? It's Crockett."

Daniel smiled. "Hey, Crocker."

"Is," Crockett began, then started again, "has she come back?"

"No," Daniel said tightly.

"I'm sorry."

"That's a song by Brenda Lee," Daniel said, "as a friend of mine once pointed out." He could hear Crockett's sputtering laugh.

"Yes, indeed," Crockett said, and then quickly added, "so what are you doing for dinner?"

"Nothing," Daniel said. Just the latest in a long line of pot pies.

"Well, that being the case," Crockett said, "how's about I come over in a little while, with dinner? Zat sound good?"

"That sounds *real* good," Daniel said. "Though, to tell you the truth, I don't know what kind of company I'll be."

"I'm sure I can handle it."

"Just giving you fair warning."

"I stand warned," Crockett said. "Half an hour?"

"Fine," Daniel said. "Great."

"See you then."

"See ya," Daniel said; but Crockett had already hung up.

Daniel had changed from the suit he'd worn to the office into jeans and a Loyola Law School sweatshirt, and was at the kitchen counter, pouring himself a generous Chivas rocks, when Crockett rang the doorbell. The first thing Daniel noticed upon opening the door was just how much Crockett had managed to carry up the stairs to the house: he held a flat glass baking dish in both hands, there was a bottle of wine under one arm, and a plastic shopping bag hanging from the other. The second thing he noticed was that Crockett was wearing the pale green cashmere sweater Daniel had given him the one Christmas they spent together. It was nearly the exact shade of Crockett's eyes, and soft as a baby's breathing. "I like soft things on you," he'd said as Crockett opened the Neiman-Marcus box. Daniel remembered stroking Crockett's chest, his hand outside the sweater, moving the fabric back and forth over Crockett's skin, listening to Crockett purr.

"Avon calling," Crockett said through a smile.

"Hey, dude," Daniel said, holding the screen door open to allow Crockett in. "Can I take something?" he said as the screen slapped shut behind Crockett.

"Nope," Crockett said, walking quickly toward the kitchen, "I can get to the kitchen all right."

"Suit yourself." Daniel followed Crockett into the kitchen. "What's in the pan?" he asked.

"None other than Crockett Miller's justly famous lasagne."

"I am a happy man," Daniel said. Crockett's lasagne counted among his favorite dishes. "I was just making myself a drink," he said. "Can I interest you in something?"

Crockett had set the baking dish and wine bottle down on the counter, and was pulling lettuce, tomatoes, and other salad fixings from the shopping bag. Daniel watched a mischievous look travel across Crockett's face: he could imagine some naughty little Crockettism forming in his mind and making its way toward his lips. Crockett's lips parted, then closed. He turned to the oven, his back to Daniel, and set it to 375. "Sparkling water," he said finally, "if you've got it."

"That's not what you were gonna say at first," Daniel said.

"Nope," Crockett admitted, turning around and leaning against the stove. "I was gonna come up with something cute, but all of a sudden it just didn't seem . . . appropriate."

"And just when did you up and get appropriate on me?" Daniel said. He tipped a half-empty ice tray into his palm, then dropped three cubes into a tumbler for Crockett's seltzer.

"Your wife is not here," Crockett said, "and I am *trying* to be good." Daniel hoped his expression did not change at the allusion to Maggie's absence, but he was reasonably sure it had. "I'm sorry," Crockett added quickly. "That was tacky." Daniel poured seltzer over the ice in Crockett's glass and stared into the bubbles as he said, "No biggie."

Crockett pulled out a cutting board, then opened and closed a couple of drawers. "What are you looking for?" Daniel asked.

"Big knife."

Daniel opened a drawer and removed a large knife. He held it toward Crockett, handle first. "Best one we've got," he said. "Careful: it's real sharp."

"Thanks." Crockett moved toward the sink; Daniel stepped out of his way. "Why don't you go watch the news," Crockett said, rinsing a head of romaine under the running water. "That's what you'd usually be doing about now, isn't it?"

"Don't you want my company?" It felt good to have another person in the house, and Daniel saw no good reason to leave the room.

Crockett looked down at a handful of lettuce. "You know I *always* want your company," he said.

"I promise to stay out of the way," Daniel said, stepping back to lean against a wall, well out of Crockett's path. "So what made you decide to do this?"

"I donno," Crockett said, "I just felt like it. I was having a good day."

"You look good," Daniel said.

"Thanks,". Crockett said, that mischievous look coming back. "You're not so bad yourself, sailor."

"No, I mean it," Daniel said. "You look different than the last time I saw you—last couple of times." There was, it seemed, something different about Crockett. Daniel couldn't put his finger on it—maybe it was his coloring, or maybe it was just Daniel's own imagination—but he could swear Crockett looked healthier. It was the only word he could think of: healthier. "Are you feeling better?" he asked. "You look like you are."

"Yes," Crockett said. "I am." He shook out a double handful of lettuce leaves into the sink, took a quick look around the kitchen, and said, "Colander."

"Umm." Daniel had to think a moment. "The cabinet just at your right foot."

Crockett retrieved the blue-enameled colander and deposited the rinsed lettuce into it, and the whole of it into the sink. Wiping his hands on a dish towel, he leaned against the counter. "Some days are better than others—I don't know why, really. Also"—his eyes glanced away, and he hesitated a moment—"also, I've started seeing this woman."

Daniel's eyebrows shot upward. "You? A woman?"

Crockett laughed. "No," he said, "not like that. She's a holistic healer." He looked at Daniel as if waiting for laughter or ridicule, as if daring Daniel to laugh or ridicule. Daniel had heard of AIDS patients turning to resources outside the medical establishment, and he had no sort of knee-jerk prejudice against any of them.

"Do you trust this woman?" he asked.

"I think so," Crockett replied. "Johnnie Ray Rousseau recommended her. Remember him?" Daniel nodded. He did remember, vaguely: a black singer Crockett had been friends with for a while, and then wasn't. "Well, Theo's his aunt."

"Isn't that a man's name?"

"Short for Theodosia."

"Oh."

"I don't know if it's helping or what, not yet. I don't even know if I believe in it myself." Crockett did a big shrug.

"Believe in what?"

"You know," Crockett said, his voice a little louder, "the whole thing. Call it spiritual, call it metaphysical." He shrugged again. "Call it Ishmael."

Daniel wasn't sure what Crockett meant. "It's worth a try, isn't it?" he said, for lack of anything better.

Crockett smiled. "You know something," he said, "I come here, absolutely laden with good food, and do I get as much as a hug? No!" He opened his arms wide. Daniel walked toward him, and wrapped his arms around Crockett's shoulders. Crockett held him around the waist, tucking his head just beneath Daniel's chin. Daniel held him close for a long moment, stroking his back, enjoying the feeling of the sweater on Crockett, and the feeling of Crockett beneath the sweater. He had all but forgotten just how good Crockett could feel in his arms. Almost before he knew it, he was beginning to grow hard. Crockett pulled away before Daniel could, stepping back quickly, an odd smile on his face.

"Well," he said, "I guess that's about enough of that." Daniel turned his back and adjusted himself, feeling embarrassed beyond all cause. "I think I'll go watch the news," he said, walking stiffly away.

"This is delicious," Daniel said through a mouthful of pasta. Maggie had cooked lasagne from Crockett's recipe on numerous occasions, but it had never tasted as good as Crockett's. He almost mentioned that fact to Crockett, but decided not to.

"I've been called a lot of things," Crockett said, "but *never* a slouch in the kitchen."

Daniel lifted his glass of wine, at least partially to help cover his grin. After nearly a week of solitary pot-pie dinners, it was good to look up from such a tasty meal to see Crockett smiling at him from across the table. "Thanks for doing this," he said, his voice echoing in the glass.

"Hey," Crockett said with a smile, "no charge."

"I mean it," Daniel said, setting down his glass. "I haven't felt this good since"—he stopped himself—"in days." He looked down into his plate.

"Are you angry with her?" Crockett asked.

Daniel looked up. Crockett had speared a piece of food with his fork and held it halfway between his plate and his mouth. Daniel paused a moment before he said, "Damn right I'm angry with her. Sometimes I feel like I could kill her. And the funny thing is, I'm not sure I've got any *right* to be angry." He pushed himself back in his chair. "And I'm hurt. And I don't know, maybe I have no right to feel like I feel, but I can't help it. Maybe it's my own fault, you know? I mean, maybe I should have told her." He leaned forward, propped his elbow on the table, set his face into his hand. "I don't know."

"No," Crockett said. "What good would it have done? You didn't know. You couldn't."

"Yeah," Daniel said, taking apathetic stabs at his dinner with his fork; suddenly he wasn't very hungry. He took another bite and listened to himself chew for a moment. When he looked up, Crockett was staring intently back at him.

"Daniel," he said softly, "she'll come back. You know she will."

"Yeah," Daniel repeated. "Thing is, I don't know if I'd blame her if she didn't."

"Oh, Daniel." Crockett shook his head. "Maggie loves you. I know what that feels like, you know. Believe me, she'll be back."

"Promise?" Daniel made his best attempt at a smile.

"Guaranteed," Crockett said. "Now, eat your goddamned dinner, or you get no dessert."

Daniel smiled, a real smile. Crockett still had that effect on him.

Crockett washed the dishes, over Daniel's vocal protest. Washing dishes was Daniel's job when Maggie cooked, and he had planned to rinse and stack them in the sink and wash them in the morning. "Besides," he said, "there really isn't that much."

"I won't hear of it," Crockett said, squeezing a long ribbon of Palmolive liquid into the sink and turning on the hot water full force. "It may be your house, but it's *my* dinner party."

"Well then, I'll dry," Daniel said.

"Deal," said Crockett.

Daniel was wiping down one of the two dinner plates when the question occurred to him. "Crocker?"

"Yeah?" Crockett was applying a copper pot scrubber and considerable elbow grease to the Pyrex dish he'd brought with him, now encrusted with baked-on cheese and pasta.

"Have you told your parents?"

Crockett neither looked up nor missed a stroke. "As you well know, my dear Daniel, I have no parents. I am an orphan boy."

Despite the obvious sore point, Daniel took a breath and pressed on. "Seriously, Crockett, don't you think they should know?"

Crockett stopped scrubbing and looked up and over at Daniel, his jaw set. "Daniel, they wouldn't give a fuck. Trust me on this one, okay? They'd just as soon I was dead. Really."

"You don't really believe that."

Crockett stood upright, propped his yellow-rubber-gloved hands against the edge of the sink, looking as if he might throw a wineglass across the room. "Daniel, dear," he said, so softly Daniel had to lean in to hear, "I realize you were raised by Ward and June Cleaver and that it is therefore beyond your comprehension that anyone's parents might have been less than perfect"—his voice rose steadily in volume— "but believe me when I tell you that Ed and Agnes don't give a flying fuck about me, they haven't for years. Now, may we please just drop it?" He bent over and resumed scrubbing, just a bit more vigorously than before.

"Hey," Daniel said, feeling a little foolish, "I'm sorry."

"F'get it," Crockett said to the Pyrex dish.

Between the two of them, they finished a pint of Häagen-Dazs chocolate-chocolate chip with hot fudge sauce during the first twenty minutes of "Miami Vice." During the commercial break, Crockett got up from the sofa and carried the bowls and spoons to the kitchen, while Daniel tried to ignore a commercial for fabric softener, starring a squeaky-voiced animated talking teddy bear. Daniel hated most commercials, but hated this one especially. He reached for the remote control and punched the mute button, silencing the creature. Crockett returned halfway through the teddy bear commercial. "God, I hate that fuckin' bear," he said, and sat down close to Daniel, tucking himself under Daniel's outstretched arm. "Do you mind?" Crockett said, almost a whisper. Daniel was surprised, but hardly displeased. It felt good to have him close. "No," he said, bending his arm around Crockett's shoulder. "I don't mind."

When the commercials ended, Daniel faced the television and stared into the screen, trying in vain to pay attention to "Miami Vice." But Crockett was warm and solid against his side, so close he could smell his buddy's hair. There was just enough swelling in Daniel's crotch to be distractingly uncomfortable, and memories kept getting in the way.

He remembered the first night he spent with Crockett in Daniel's double bed—the second night of *A Midsummer Night's Dream*. It was a giant step forward in comfort from Crockett's single, and they covered every inch of it that night as they covered every inch of one another. They spent most of the following day in bed as well. They slept at Daniel's that night, too. The next morning—Monday morning—Crockett shook Daniel awake a full hour earlier than he was used to.

"I'm sorry, Daniel," he said, "but I have to go home and then get to work."

"What the hell for?" Daniel said, feeling sleepy and grumpy and possibly another dwarf or two.

"Daniel," Crockett said gently, while stroking Daniel's disheveled temple with his fingers. "I haven't got any clean clothes." Daniel moaned softly, rolled over on top of Crockett, and did a little horizontal dance.

"You shouldn't wear clothes, anyway," he whispered into Crockett's ear. "You look better without 'em."

On the way to Crockett's apartment, Daniel said, "Why don't you move some things over to my place. Some clothes and stuff. Okay?" It seemed the logical thing. If he and Crockett were going to be spending nights together—and all the road signs seemed to point in that direction—and as long as he was chauffeuring Crockett around town, it only made sense to use Daniel's apartment as home base. It's not as if I've run off and bought a diamond ring or something, Daniel told himself as he cleared two bureau drawers and some closet space for Crockett's things. It's not as if we're *living* together in any real sense, he said to himself.

Crockett never officially moved in with Daniel: he kept the rent paid up on his own apartment a scant few miles from Daniel's, though he seldom saw it. Daniel drove him by every few days to pick up his mail, and maybe some other little odd or end of his life—his omelette pan, or his red high-top basketball shoes. Unofficially and off the record, Crockett slept in Daniel's bed every night for the entire six-week run of *A Midsummer Night's Dream.* He showered and shaved in Daniel's bathroom and was driven to work, then to the theater, then back to Daniel's apartment in Daniel's car by Daniel.

They spent their weekend days together, lolling in bed half the morning through, kissing and cuddling; finally tumbling out of bed to watch cartoons and eat Cap'n Crunch from the box. They fell into a mutually satisfactory division of chores: Daniel cleaned the well-used bathroom, Crockett did their combined laundry in the humid, mildewed basement. They jogged together through the streets of their neighborhood, did push-ups and sit-ups in Mar Vista Park. They lunched on Chinese food and took in cheap matinees at the Nuart on Saturday afternoons, and sat up late after the show, watching the last half-hour of "Saturday Night Live" until Daniel inevitably fell asleep on the sofa, head in Crockett's lap.

Their shared routine had become second nature to them both by the time *Dream* reached the end of its run (six weeks of critical indifference and half-empty houses), and Daniel— who had at first assumed that the end of the play would signal the end of their living arrangement and their relationship, or whatever it was—found, to his relative surprise, that he didn't want it to end. After putting in a brief appearance at the cast party, held at Gilbert LaTouche's apartment, Daniel took Crockett home—that is, to Daniel's—and to bed.

After they'd made love, and just as Daniel was falling asleep, Crockett said, "So where do we go from here?"

Daniel said, "Why don't we go to sleep."

Crockett paused a moment before he said, "What about tomorrow?"

"How about we worry about tomorrow," Daniel said, pulling Crockett close, "tomorrow." He didn't want any long discussions. He just wanted Crockett to stay. They lay together in a dense sort of silence, back to front, for a few minutes; then Crockett pierced the quiet with the words, "I love you, Daniel."

"I love you, too," Daniel said, pulling Crockett even tighter against him. Crockett had never said that to Daniel before. Daniel had never said it to anyone before.

The Monday after *Dream* closed, Daniel resumed the life of an actor between projects: he checked in with his commercial agent, picked up the trades, went to three utterly pointless cattle calls. Business as usual, except that he was still more or less living with a man in what almost anyone would term a gay relationship. And with the show finished, he couldn't even pretend to himself that he was involved in a run-of-the-play affair. It was back to real life, and in real life, Daniel Sullivan was in love with a man.

Crockett, having been cured of the acting bug with one play, continued his current word-processing job. He purchased a thick spiral notebook which within a couple of weeks had become his constant companion. He forever seemed to be scribbling something down. "I think I'd like to try some sort of writing," he said, though it would be years before he would offer Daniel any of his work to read. In the meanwhile, he took it upon himself to have dinner started, if not warm and waiting, when Daniel came home in the evenings.

By this point, Daniel had quietly stopped dating or even trying to date women. Being with Crockett had quickly come to feel as warm and comfortable as an old down ski jacket; and once he'd said "I love you," he found himself saying it often. It did not take Daniel long to realize the situation was leaning toward the indefinite—a year, two years, till death do us part—and that realization made Daniel nervous. If it had never been his intention to fall in love with a man, it was even less his intention to marry one.

By the time he'd finally managed to tell Crockett it was over between them, he had tried to, had come close to doing it a dozen or more times over a period of months. He did love Crockett; he didn't want to hurt him, much as he knew he'd have to, sooner or later. And it certainly wasn't as if he didn't enjoy being with Crockett. This just wasn't the life he wanted to live. Actually, it was very close to the life he wanted; only he wanted it with a woman.

He arrived home from work, having rehearsed any number of speeches and scenes in the car, to find Crockett hunched over the dining table, writing in the latest in a series of notebooks. Crockett glanced up and said, "Hi, honey." He tilted his face upward, and Daniel kissed his lips. It occurred to Daniel that he was kissing Crockett hello and good-bye. "I'm sorry," Crockett said, "I haven't started dinner. I've just been so into this story." He pushed his chair back from the table and started to get up.

"Wait a minute," Daniel said. "I need to talk to you."

"Oh?" Crockett sat back down. "What's the matter?"

Daniel started to take a chair, then decided it might be better to stand. Unable to meet Crockett's eyes, he focused on a point just above his head. "I'm not quite sure how to say this," Daniel said.

"Well . . ." Crockett sat up straight in his chair, his hands gripping the edge of the table, as if bracing himself. "Why don't you just . . . say it."

"Listen"—Daniel touched Crockett's fingertips with his own—"you know how I feel, about you."

"I think I do," Crockett said.

"But," Daniel continued slowly, "you also know that, well, I'm not gay."

Crockett slipped his fingers out from under Daniel's. "You've been known to do a pretty good imitation of it," he said.

Daniel almost smiled. "Yeah. I know. What I meant was, you know I want to get married someday. I want to have kids."

Crockett nodded slowly. "So . . ."

"So, I think it would be the best thing, the best thing for me, if we could think about not being together. Anymore." He ran what he'd just said over in his mind, marveled at the clumsiness of it. He hoped he had put the point across: he didn't want to have to try again.

Crockett didn't say anything for a long moment. Daniel looked down: Crockett didn't seem to be crying. He'd been afraid Crockett might cry, but in fact his face seemed nearly expressionless. Finally, Crockett said, "All right." He stood up and faced Daniel. His expression remained calm, as was his voice when he asked, "Will you drive me back to my place?"

"Crockett, you don't have to go anywhere right now."

"Yes, I do. If you'll give me half an hour, I'll just gather my shit, and I'm outa here. Don't worry: I know exactly which things in here are mine. This won't take long at all." And he turned and walked quickly away.

"Crockett!" Suddenly, he wanted to take it all back. Maybe. But Crockett had gone into the bathroom and shut the door. He emerged after a few minutes and headed for the bedroom.

Daniel sat on the sofa and watched in silence as Crockett gathered his belongings on the floor near the front door. He was surprised how little there actually was. After what seemed a remarkably short time, Crockett stopped in front of him and said, "Would you please help me carry this stuff to the car?"

Twenty minutes later, Crockett's things were sitting inside a different door. Crockett stood next to them, across the threshold from Daniel.

"Well," Crockett said, wearing a look Daniel could not begin to read, "thanks for your help. Thanks for . . . for everything."

"Do you think you'll ever want to be . . . my friend?" It would not have surprised Daniel, of course, if Crockett never wanted to see him again, anywhere, ever—who could blame him? Still, selfishly, he did want Crockett's friendship, if he could possibly have it. Crockett shrugged and shook his head at the same time. "I don't know. Gimme some time."

Daniel nodded. He wanted to hug Crockett, but didn't know if he should even try: he leaned slightly forward, his arms sort of spasmed aimlessly once, and that was all. Finally, he said, "I'm sorry."

"That's a song by Brenda Lee," Crockett said, and slowly closed the door.

Daniel returned to an apartment that suddenly felt oppressively large, echoingly empty. It had taken less than ninety minutes to get Crockett Miller out of his life. It took less than ninety seconds to miss him like the devil.

"Lemme ask you something," Daniel said.

"We ate *all* the ice cream," Crockett said, without averting his eyes from the television. "Every bit of it."

"No, not that. It's just that—never mind."

"No, go on," Crockett said, scooting himself out from under Daniel's arm. "You've interrupted 'Miami Vice' in the middle of the big car chase, you've perfectly *ruined* the entire program for me now, so you might as well ask."

"I'm sorry.

"Daniel, I was kidding." Crockett wrapped his fingers around Daniel's thumb and gave it a squeeze. "What is it?"

"Do you—" He looked away from Crockett's eyes, toward the television, and started again. "Do you resent me, the way I ended our—our relationship? Just boom, just like that?"

Crockett let go of Daniel's hand, dropped his hands into his lap, paused a moment before saying, "Jesus fuck, Daniel. What the fuck made you come up with a thing like that? Now? Right in the middle of 'Miami fuckin' Vice'?"

"I'm sorry," Daniel repeated. "I was just sitting here thinking about it. About us."

Crockett grabbed the remote and clicked the television off. Then he got up from the sofa and sat on the floor, his back against the TV stand, and looked up at Daniel. The sad smile on his face made Daniel ache: he looked down at his hands. Crockett didn't say anything for a few seconds, not until Daniel raised his face and looked at him again. "No, Daniel," he finally said. "I never resented you. I never hated you. Jesus, how could I?"

"I hurt you," Daniel said.

"Of course it hurt. It hurt like a motherfucker. But then again"—he shrugged his shoulders—"it's not as if we were married or something, right? I mean," he said, looking up at the ceiling like a schoolboy looking for the answer to an arithmetic problem, "I knew it couldn't last. From the beginning. Hell, you're not gay. You never said you were. 'I like women,' you said. 'I intend to marry one.' And so you have. So no matter how good it was, in bed—and it was real good—"

Daniel failed to keep back a smile.

"And no matter how many times you said you loved me—and I believe you meant it—"

"You know I did," Daniel said. "You know I do," he nearly whispered.

"I never let myself forget: sooner or later, you would want, would need, whatever it is that draws a man to a woman—pussy, children, I don't know. Sooner or later, you'd say, 'That's it, game's over.' I always knew I was loving on borrowed time." Crockett laughed a percussive little bark of a laugh. " 'Loving on borrowed time,' " he repeated. "Spoken like a romance writer."

Daniel patted the side of his thigh. "Come back." Crockett crawled back onto the sofa next to him. Daniel wrapped his arm around Crockett's neck and stroked his chest. "I'm sorry," Daniel said.

"That's a—you-know-what," Crockett said.

Daniel smiled sadly. "Yeah," he said. "I know."

"Eight-nine-eight, what city?"

"Um, Irvine." Daniel tapped a nervous finger against the telephone. His heart, his guts told him he was doing the right thing, but his head kept saying if Crockett didn't want to tell his own parents, then it was none of *his* damned business. Crockett had been on his mind almost constantly from the moment he'd awakened that morning: when he wasn't thinking of Maggie, wondering if today would be the day she'd come home, he was thinking of Crockett. Perhaps he'd dreamed of Crockett, but he didn't remember. More likely it was just having spent time alone with Crockett the night before, sitting and holding him, finally talking about their breakup so many years after the fact. He had come close to asking Crockett to stay the night with him, to sleep next to him; but it hadn't seemed appropriate, to use Crockett's term. Not that he'd had any intention of having sex with Crockett—there were far too many reasons why that would have been the worst of ideas. But even without sex, Crockett sleeping on

Maggie's side of the bed smelled of infidelity. Besides, would it have been fair to Crockett to ask him to stay because Daniel felt lonely and a warm body next to him would have been nice? As it happened, Daniel had simply held Crockett in a lingering hug at the front door, kissing him rather clumsily on the side of the head, before thanking him for dinner for the fifth or sixth time and wishing him good night.

"Go ahead," said the operator. Daniel paused. "Hello, go ahead please," said the operator.

"Um, Miller, Ed. Edward." There are probably a couple hundred Ed Millers in Irvine, he thought. She's gonna ask me which one, on which street, and I don't have a clue. I should mind my own business, he thought.

"Thank you, please hold for that number." Click. And the computerized fembot voice read off seven disjointed-sounding numbers. She was almost finished before Daniel thought to pick up the pen and write. The voice repeated the number, and Daniel scribbled it down. He held the button down and punched 1, 7 14, then the number, his heart beating faster than usual. The receiver purred into his ear once, twice; then someone picked up.

"Hello?" A woman, older.

"Um." He could still hang up. It might not even be the right one.

"Hello?" the woman repeated.

"Hello," Daniel said in a surprisingly loud blast of breath. "Is—is this Agnes Miller?"

"Yes." Her voice had the slow upward lilt many women develop in their fifties and beyond. "Who am I speaking with, please?"

"You don't know me, ma'am," Daniel said, suddenly feeling very young. "My name is Daniel Sullivan. I'm a friend of Crockett's."

There was a pause on the other end that worried Daniel a little. Was she going to hang up?

"Did he give you this number?" she asked, her voice tightened a bit.

"No, ma'am: I called four-one-one."

"I see," she said. "And what can I do for you?"

Strange, Daniel thought. Not so much as, How is he? "You are Crockett's mother, aren't you?"

"We adopted him," she said. "Why are you calling, please?"

This was a major mistake, he thought. But he was in it now. "Mrs. Miller," he said, "do you know what AIDS is?"

"Yes." Her voice had gone quieter. "Of course."

"Mrs. Miller, Crockett is infected with the AIDS virus. He hasn't got AIDS itself, not yet anyway, but he isn't well, either, he's—" Daniel was at a loss for a good one-word description of Crockett's condition. He considered hanging up right then: he'd said what he'd called to say—now she knew. Mrs. Miller didn't say anything for a moment, but Daniel could hear her breathe slowly in and out a couple of times. Finally, she said, "Well, I guess it's his own fault, isn't it? I don't mean to be harsh, but it is, isn't it? You're probably that way, too," she added. "Aren't you? Homosexual."

"No," Daniel said quickly, "I'm married."

"And you're a friend of his?" As if the thought of a married man being friends with a homosexual was more than she could imagine.

"I don't think you understand," Daniel said. "Crockett could die."

"Well," she said after a few seconds, "then I guess it's God's will."

Daniel felt as if he'd been shoved in the stomach. "He's your son," he said.

Nothing, for several seconds. And then she hung up.

Daniel replaced the receiver slowly, his hand trembling. He lifted it quickly back to his ear, and punched Anne Taylor's number quickly, in one spasmodic motion, and listened as the telephone rang, again and again.

CHAPTER 17

SHE WAS STARING AT THE PICtures again. Maggie had found herself drawn to the photographs set atop her mother's spinet piano at least once each day for the six days since she'd packed a suitcase and come to Anne's small Woodland Hills home, seeking temporary asylum from her husband. And from herself. She had telephoned Anne from the kitchen.

"Mama," she said, her voice trembling despite all her effort to steady it, "I need a big favor."

"What is it, dear?" came her mother's familiar, sweet, mellow voice. "Are you all right?"

"I'm okay, Mama," Maggie said. "I just need to stay with you for a while. A few days, maybe a week. No questions asked."

"Oh, Maggie," Anne said. "You and Daniel? It's not about the baby, is it?"

"Please, Mama," Maggie said, sounding, she thought, a bit too much like a whining child. "No questions."

"All right," Anne said after a moment. "No questions."

Maggie hadn't returned to work since the Monday following the day she had termed Black Sunday, the Monday of white wine spritzers with Theo and Moira the actress-slash-model, the Monday she decided she had to get away. She had called California Fitness on Tuesday morning and informed Earl as calmly as she could that she wasn't coming back. "I've got more than enough sick leave and vacation time," she said. "I'll be in sometime this week to pick up my check." Earl said, "Goddammit, Maggie," and then she hung up. She might have gone back and spent the remainder of her time teaching low-impact and stretch classes, but the drive into Santa Monica from the Valley, an hour or more each way on the freeway, was more than she wanted to deal with. Most things were more than she wanted to deal with.

Maggie wrestled her attention back to the book on the piano's music stand, its spine cracked open to "Maple Leaf Rag." The trio section was giving her fits, as it always had. Maggie had hardly touched a piano keyboard since her senior year in high school, when, at the prelims of the all-district music festival competition, she had frozen: sitting at the grand piano, her mind had drawn a sudden, complete, and inexplicable blank. She would likely have been unable to remember her own name, let alone "Wedding Day at Troldhaugen." She had burst into tears at the keyboard, crying all the way home in Anne's car, continuing to weep uncontrollably for the better part of two days. Now, Maggie had been playing every day for the past week, forcing herself through the frustration of once-intelligent fingers gone stupid, until she could stumble through some of the simpler pieces in her old *Collected Rags* book.

When she wasn't playing the piano, Maggie watched television: Bugs Bunny cartoons, game shows, and soaps during the day, two or three carefully selected hours of prime time in the evenings. She had also cooked dinner for herself and her mother each day. Her daily bouts with nausea had all but disappeared, had been replaced by a nearly constant appetite. It was all she could do not to eat her way through the cupboards every day, but she still cared too much about her appearance to allow herself to drown her sorrows in food.

She got up from the piano bench and went into the kitchen. She opened the oven—a Fifties-vintage built-in with a round window like a porthole—releasing a burst of garlic-heavy aroma. A roasting leg of lamb sputtered and hissed. Stuffed with sausage and studded with slivers of garlic, it was one of Anne's favorite dishes, and one of Maggie's. She hadn't cooked it in over a year: Daniel didn't like lamb. Maggie poked the roast with a fork, just to watch the juice trickle from the deep brown sinews, then closed the oven and returned to the piano. She sat on the bench, settling into the permanent indentation her behind had made in the cushion over years of practice. She launched into the pesky trio section of "Maple Leaf," but stopped after a few measures and reached for the smaller of the two photographs standing on top of the piano.

The silver frame was engraved along the bottom: "Jimmy & Margaret—Easter 1964." Maggie looked at the tall, handsome man with short dark hair and a square-cut jaw, wearing a dark square-cut suit—the picture was in black and white, but in Maggie's memories the suit was blue—with thin lapels and a narrow necktie. His striking good looks were apparent even from the distance necessary to include the little girl in the picture—Margaret Elizabeth Taylor, five years old, her tiny left hand hidden in her daddy's big right.

Maggie studied the tiny image of herself more than twenty years earlier. She had some trouble finding herself in that little girl with the riot of blond curls, wearing a white dress, short and impossibly fluffy with petticoats, white patent-leather shoes, and a matching purse, which, as Maggie remembered, contained a large crumpled wad of white tissue paper and a dime. The little girl's face, though pretty in a dimply, button-nosed five-year-old sort of way, was round and plump as a dumpling, her knees no more than dimpled depressions in stumpy legs. Maggie liked to joke in college that at five years old she had looked like Dom De Luise starring in *The Shirley Temple Story*.

Her own appearance notwithstanding, and this was hardly her finest hour, physique-wise, this was one of Maggie's favorite photographs. It was, in fact, the only existing picture of Maggie with her father.

Jimmy Taylor had been an actor. By Easter Sunday 1964, he had been a working actor for eight years, having appeared in more than fifty films, by Anne's count. At sixteen, he collided with James Dean in a school hall in *Rebel Without a Cause*. At eighteen, he sat at a table on a soda-shop set and smiled enthusiastically at Sal Mineo in *Rock, Pretty Baby*. It was that same year, 1958, during the shooting of *High School Jungle*, that he met Anne Myers. "He was the handsomest boy I'd ever seen," Anne had told Maggie more than once—she'd recounted her romance with Jimmy Taylor whenever Maggie asked; and she'd asked often, especially during her teenage years. "So tall; dark, but with those blue, blue eyes. And that smile. He could melt an entire soundstage full of girls with one smile. He was better-looking than John Derek, Tony Curtis, the lot of them," she said. Photographs of Jimmy Taylor—both professional publicity shots and snaps like the one in Maggie's hand—upheld Anne's claim.

Anne's part in *High School Jungle* was called "4th Girl" in the closing credits. She had three lines of dialogue ("Two of which were 'Crazy, man!'" Annie admitted with a laugh) to Jimmy's two lines (both of which were "Crazy, man!"). It was Anne's first screen role, and her last. Within six months of meeting Jimmy Taylor, she was Mrs. Jimmy Taylor. Within ten months of that, she was Margaret Elizabeth Taylor's mother.

Jimmy continued to work in pictures: small parts in B movies, even smaller parts in the occasional first-rate production—

a career composed of an ever-growing string of near misses. He was a serious contender for Peter Van Daan in *The Diary of Anne Frank,* but lost out to Richard Beymer, with whom he later crossed paths when he was chosen to play one of the Jets in the film version of *West Side Story,* only to sprain an ankle so severely in dance rehearsals that he had to be replaced. In eight years, Jimmy Taylor had never starred in a picture, had never even been billed. If he'd been female, Jimmy would have been termed a perennial starlet, perpetually poised on the brink of success. "Still and all, he hardly ever doubted he'd make it, sooner or later," Anne said. "It's like a sickness with actors; but to be an actor, you have to have it."

Maggie stroked the glass over her father's image with her fingertip. She remembered her father with surprising clarity, considering her age at the time of his death. Maggie was almost six years old when Jimmy Taylor was killed, thrown and severely trampled by a snake-panicked horse while filming a bit role on "Gunsmoke"—his first job in television—on location in Bakersfield. He was twenty-four years old. Maggie still remembered the way his eyes crinkled at the corners when he smiled, and the sound of his deep, husky voice as he hugged her in his arms and said, "How's the prettiest little girl in the world?" She remembered the way he smelled early in the morning when she'd crawl into bed between him and her mother: a warm, sweet-and-sour sleepy smell.

She did not attend her father's funeral, but she remembered the day of it clearly, distinctly, the way Daniel claimed to remember the day President Kennedy was shot. She remembered the black dress her mother wore, and the way her face looked as she said, "Daddy won't be coming home to us anymore. He's gone to Heaven to live with God and all His angels, and he'll live there forever." Crying never occurred to Maggie—not only because death is not a concept easily grasped by a five-year-old child, but because her father's frequent absences had become a fact of life early on: such was the life of an actor's child. Now, at least, she knew where he was. That night, and every night for years, following her "Now I lay me down to sleep," Maggie said good night to her daddy.

The physical resemblance between Jimmy Taylor and Daniel Sullivan had not occurred to Maggie until the first time she'd brought Daniel to meet Anne. The look on her mother's face as she greeted Daniel with a handshake, the shadow that darted across her eyes, the shiver at the corners of her smile made Maggie afraid there was something about the man she loved and planned to marry that made her mother immediately uncomfortable. The moment Daniel walked out of earshot, Anne grasped Maggie by the arm. Maggie was surprised and initially worried to find her mother blinking back tears. "He reminds me so much of Jimmy," she said. And then, as if Maggie might be wondering Jimmy who, she added, "Your father." It was then that Maggie had first looked upon the pictures on Anne's piano with new interest. Daniel, noticing the pictures himself, had smiled broadly and motioned Maggie over. "Sweetheart, is this your mom and dad? Looks kinda like you and me, doesn't it?"

Maggie set the picture down and picked up the other: Anne and Jimmy on their wedding day—he in a dark suit indistinguishable from the one in the picture taken over five years later, she in a simple but flattering white suit and a small veiled hat, their shared joy evident from their wide smiles. Maggie stared into the glass-covered photograph, at the two good-looking young people: the pretty blond girl still recognizable in her mother, and the dark, handsome man Maggie never got a chance to know. Her vision blurred slightly from staring, and the couple suddenly looked so much like herself and Daniel that Maggie shivered.

What, she wondered, had her parents' sexual relationship been like? She tried to imagine the handsome couple in the picture, holding one another and kissing passionately, but the image that came to her mind looked too much like herself and her husband, and she shook it away, much as she had laid a third photograph—one of her and Daniel's wedding pictures—down on its front immediately upon entering Anne's house a week before.

Had her father been anything like the lover her husband was? Had he made sweet, naughty love to Anne? Had he left her wet and weak? Strange things to wonder about one's own father, Maggie knew; but she couldn't help wondering.

Had Jimmy Taylor ever considered making love with a man? It immediately struck her as a ridiculous, almost blasphemous notion. Of course, the thought of Daniel Sullivan making love with a man would have seemed easily as ridiculous a week ago. What might Anne have said or done, if suddenly she had been faced with the revelation that her husband had had sex with a man, a man she knew? It was such a different time, of course, twenty-five years ago. There had been no gay community, relatively few openly gay people. Would a young wife, even a former actress, have known that such people, such acts existed? Would she have divorced Jimmy immediately, run away; or proven the very model of the faithful, understanding wife, and pretended that nothing had changed?

What *has* changed? Maggie asked herself, about herself.

Maggie had come so close to confiding in her mother, but her initial conflicting feelings of anger, hurt, and—especially—shame, stopped her. The hurt and anger would have been easy enough to express, but the shame was more difficult to sort out, and nearly impossible to explain, since even she didn't quite understand it. Maggie felt as if she had failed somehow; that she should somehow have known that Daniel had this hidden homosexual side to himself. Furthermore, part of her felt—practically from the moment she had set foot inside her mother's house—that only a child would have left, for even a short time; that leaving Daniel stacked failure upon failure. That part of her nagged almost incessantly—while she cooked, while she watched television, and especially when Daniel called—that her place was back in her own house, with Daniel, working it out with him, for better or worse.

She would go back to Daniel: she'd been reasonably sure of that even as she'd packed her bag to leave, and she had had her mind fully made up before she had spent more than two days with Anne. She could have gone home days before, but a strange sort of pride kept her back. She had said she needed time away, and by golly she was going to stay away for a while—for two weeks, she'd decided—before she'd go home. It was the pride of a contrary, foot-stamping child, she realized, and it was an aspect of herself she didn't like very much; but there it was, nonetheless.

She liked her other reason for staying even less: the desire to hurt Daniel. And she knew he was hurting. She could tell by the sound of his voice on the telephone—he had called her every evening since the second day she'd been away—the voice that asked her "How are you?" every day, that never failed to ask "When are you coming home?" that offered a nearly inaudible "Okay, sweetheart" to her stock response, "Soon." She had genuinely enjoyed his hurt the first couple of evenings. Now, each day she found she enjoyed it less.

She missed Daniel. She loved him. And she knew Daniel loved her. She knew it in her head, her heart, her soul, and if there was some place deeper inside her than that, then she knew it there, too. Just how long it might take before she'd feel about him, feel about the two of them as she had before learning about him and Crockett; whether, in fact, she could ever feel exactly the same, she had no clue. But she knew she would go back to her husband and try to gather up the scraps of their marriage and stitch them back together. She had to. And in six more days, she would. In the meantime, she had "The Young and the Restless" and "Maple Leaf Rag."

She heard the soft click of the front door, and she quickly set the picture back down on the piano and struck a series of random chords on the piano. "Hello, Mama," she called. Although she generally thought of her mother as Anne, and referred to her in the third person as Anne, Maggie almost always addressed her mother as Mama. "Hi, honey," Anne called from the entryway. After a moment, she entered the room wearing a tan suit, briefcase clutched in one hand, an expression on her face that Maggie could only interpret as vaguely troubled.

Maggie started to rise from the piano bench just as Anne bent at the waist, and she intercepted Anne's kiss on the face from an odd half-squatting position. She plopped back down onto the bench. "Bad day?" she asked. She could only imagine that the life of a high-school English and drama teacher (even in a high school with a relatively low crime rate, such as Woodland Hills High) must be fraught with frustration.

"Not the best," Anne said, setting her briefcase down next to the piano bench.

"Well," Maggie said, "you'll be happy to know I've got a stuffed leg of lamb in the oven—that should make you feel a little better."

Anne smiled weakly. "Yes," she said. "Smells good." She just stood for a moment, staring somewhere past and over Maggie's head.

"You want to talk about it?" Maggie asked.

"Yes," Anne said with some finality. "I believe I do. Move over." She sat on the bench next to Maggie, facing the piano. She took in a long breath, and let it out.

"What is it, Mama?"

"I'm afraid you're not going to like this very much," she

began softly. "When you called me the other week, you asked to stay with me for a while, and I said okay. You said you didn't want to talk about why you wanted to stay with me for a while, and that was okay, too. You said not to ask you about it, and I promised you I wouldn't. Well"—she hit a piano key with her finger, sounding a clear E natural—"I'm not going to ask you why you're sitting here at my piano, seven weeks pregnant, cooking leg of lamb for me instead of your husband; but I *am* going to talk about it."

"Mama—" Anne was obviously upset, and Maggie only wanted to let her know the sermon she seemed to be building up to was unnecessary—that she had every intention of going home—before Anne got any more upset.

Anne raised her palm, but continued to look straight ahead. "Now just hush up and hear me out. I'm still your mother," she continued, "and it's still very much my prerogative to lecture you now and then, especially when you're back living in your old room."

"Okay, Mama." Anne seemed intent upon having her say; Maggie saw no good reason not to allow her that.

"I don't know what Daniel's done, or what you think he's done, and you don't want to tell me and that's fine. All I want to know is"—she turned to look at Maggie—"do you love him?"

"Yes," Maggie said. "Of course I do."

Anne nodded, turning again to face the piano. "And do you feel he loves you?"

"Yes."

"Then what are you doing here?" Anne said, her voice suddenly twice as loud as a few seconds before. She turned to Maggie, her lower lip trembling as if she might cry.

"Mama—" Maggie leaned forward, intending to put her arms around her mother, but Anne raised her hand again as if in defense. "I'm sorry," she said, turning away again. "I shouldn't have raised my voice. It's only that, if there's *love* there, Maggie—" She hit another piano key and let the note ring and die. "I just don't want to see you fuck it up!"

"Mama!" Maggie's eyes rounded, and she couldn't hold back a smile. She could hardly believe her mother had used the F-word.

"I'm sorry," Anne said, "again."

"Mama," Maggie said, reaching over to stroke her mother's wool-jacketed shoulder, "you don't have to—"

"Yes, I do," Anne said. "Don't worry, I'm almost finished. Now, you know you can stay here as long as you think you need to. Just try not to wait until maybe he's not sure he wants you back. Whatever he's done . . ." She reached up and retrieved her wedding picture from the top of the piano. "It's been twenty years," she said, seeming to speak as much to the photograph as to Maggie, "more than that. There's never been anybody else, in all that time." She tilted her head toward Maggie. "Did you know that?" Maggie nodded: she had always assumed so. "I wanted to. I tried for a while." She sniffed wetly. "After all these years, there's nothing I wouldn't do—" She sniffed a little breath. "Maggie, I'd sell my soul to have him back." Anne's entire body trembled, and she clutched the picture to her suddenly heaving breast.

"Oh, Mama—" Maggie wrapped her arms around her mother's shoulders, realizing for the first time just how small those shoulders were; and she held Anne close, rocking her softly while she cried.

Just after dinner, Maggie was bent over the kitchen sink, scouring the roasting pan with a ragged old Chore Boy pot scrubber, when she felt the warm wetness between her legs. She glanced down at the front of her jeans, assuming she had splashed hot water onto herself with her vigorous scrubbing. Then the pain hit, unlike anything she had ever felt before, as if her insides were trying to eject themselves forcibly from her body. It knocked her to her knees, clutching her abdomen, her pink-rubber-gloved hands smearing her front with soap and grease and tiny bits of lamb crust. She gasped a breath and attempted to cry out, just as the pain slammed into her again and she doubled over, toppling down into a fetal position. "Mama!" she called out, her breath short, her voice raspy and all but inaudible. She sucked in a long breath and screamed with all the strength she could gather: "Mama!"

When her eyes opened to see Daniel's face, she wasn't sure if she could believe what she saw. They had given her something for the pain, something that had reduced the agony in her lower abdomen to a dull, constant throb, and that had also put her almost immediately to sleep. She had no idea how long she had been sleeping, no sense of how much time had elapsed between feeling that first wetness, the initial pain, and this opening of her eyes in a narrow hospital bed. Her memory of that time was disjunct and unclear: Anne coming into the kitchen after what seemed like years, finding her crumpled to the floor, and calling her name out. Anne all but carrying her to the car. Pain as her mother drove her to Valley Hospital, every bump in the road like being bashed against a brick wall. Pain as she was lifted onto a gurney. Lights and shadows, flashes of faces and sounds of shouting voices, white jackets and green ones, and the ceiling light fixtures blurring past, and Anne's voice saying, "Don't worry, baby, you're going to be all right."

Now, presumably awake, Maggie felt as if her head were made of cotton, her brain seemed to have slipped into low gear, her fingers and toes tingled strangely, and her vision was blurred and fuzzy. And the pain. She reached out one incredibly heavy hand toward what might easily have been some sort of hallucination induced by the painkiller, allowing a fifty-fifty chance that the image might dissipate and disappear, or that her hand might pass through what seemed so much like Daniel. When Daniel's hand touched hers, his fingers wrapping around her own, and she felt him, warm flesh and solid bone, she felt the tears collect immediately in her eyes. The noise that came from her was like that of a small wounded animal as her face folded into itself and squeezed out tears, like the juicing of a lemon.

"Oh, Daniel," she gargled through a throat full of tears and phlegm. She squeezed her husband's hand, and felt more than saw him lean over the bed rail, felt his free hand, his skin soft and cool against her forehead, stroking down to her cheek.

"Sweetheart," he whispered close to her ear, "don't." He kissed the side of her head, her cheek, her damp eyelid. "Please don't."

"I—" she hiccuped. "I lost the—the baby." Of this much, at least, she was sadly sure.

"I know," Daniel said, stroking her temple, so close they needed only whisper. Maggie clenched her teeth, holding back a wail that seemed to come from the red rawness of her womb, allowing only a high hum to escape a throat she only now realized was sore. Tears leaked from beneath her tightly closed eyelids as if they might never stop. "No, Maggie," Daniel said. "It's okay, it's okay."

"I lost the *baby*, Daniel," she repeated. Didn't he understand?

"I know, sweetheart," he whispered, softly stroking her temple. "I know."

"I didn't mean to!" The wail had escaped as she remembered what she'd said to Daniel that day—God, it seemed like years ago. He had to believe she hadn't meant that, couldn't have meant that. "I didn't mean to."

"Jesus, Maggie." She heard Daniel's voice crack. "I know that. Don't you think I know that?"

Maggie didn't answer. She cried, humming deep in her throat, not caring about the tears falling into her ears, dampening her hair and her pillow, not caring about her running nose.

"Please don't, Maggie," Daniel pleaded, holding both her hands in his. "We'll do it again. Don't worry: the doctor says there'll be no problem. We'll do it again. I'll be back to take you home tomorrow, and we'll—we'll throw away your diaphragm and we'll just—" She heard Daniel sniff, then turn away and cough. She opened her eyes again, and through a warped window of tears she saw the tears falling down Daniel's face, the trembling of his lips. "We're gonna be okay, Maggie," he said. He let go of one of her hands; she watched him reach into his jeans pockets, front then hip. "Shit," he whispered, and reached up to blot his wet face on the sleeve of his shirt. He sniffed and said again, "We're gonna be okay."

Maggie nodded. She needed to believe that.

CHAPTER 18

"IT'S FUNNY," CROCKETT SAID. "I feel good today. Really good. I feel like I'm in the best shape of my life." His eyes looked away for a few seconds, then back again. "It's hard to believe that . . . within a year, two years . . . I could be dead." Then the reporter was back on, a young woman with long brown hair and that tight-jawed sort of speech that so many TV news reporters seemed to have learned in some school somewhere, wrapping up the story: "As with other experimental AIDS treatments . . ."

Daniel turned to say something to Maggie, curled up next to him on the sofa, tucked beneath his arm—Crockett Miller on the seven o'clock news was certainly worthy of some comment—but he looked at her, staring straight into the television screen, her face a blank, seeming to look right *through* Tom Brokaw, and decided against it. Maggie hadn't seen Crockett, or even spoken of him, in nearly a month, since the day after she returned from the hospital. That first day back together had been quiet and tense, as if Maggie had been away for years instead of weeks. There had been no discussions, no apologies—how many times can two people say "I'm sorry"? Daniel had not even suggested that they make love: Susannah had warned Daniel that Maggie might be sore and tender for a while, and he certainly had no desire to cause her pain. All he wanted was to hold her, to feel her close to him. When he held and kissed her that night, he was pleased when she did not resist him, but responded to his kisses, trading caresses with him, hugging him tightly, finally stroking and sucking him to orgasm. It was more than he would have asked. He held her close, consciously keeping himself awake, listening to her breathing grow slower. When he was sure she was asleep, he whispered, "I love you so much, Maggie."

"I love you, too," she said. Daniel felt so full of love he might burst: Maggie was home.

Crockett called the following morning. Daniel had made breakfast, and he and Maggie were sitting in the breakfast nook with cups of coffee and the *Times*. Daniel got up to answer: "Hello?"

"Hi. It's Crockett."

"Hey, Crockett." Daniel looked over at Maggie, whose face had gone a disturbing blank, and whose mug-wielding hand had frozen halfway between the table and her lips. "Maggie's home."

"That's great," Crockett said. "So everything's pretty much all right?"

Daniel looked at Maggie again: her face and posture remained unchanged. "Pretty much," he said.

"Aw, great," Crockett said. "Can I talk to her?"

"Talk to her?" Daniel repeated for Maggie's ears. She shook her head slowly. Daniel nodded vigorously, mouthed an emphatic silent *yes* at Maggie, who closed her eyes and continued to shake her head no.

"Yes, Daniel," Crockett kicked into sarcasm mode, "talk to her. You know: hello, how are you. That sort of thing."

"You know, I think she's in the bathroom right now."

"Oh. Well, maybe I'll call back a little later."

"No," Daniel said, still looking at Maggie, who stared back into his eyes with what seemed an accusatory look. "How about I call you, okay?"

A small, uncomfortable pause. "Oh," Crockett finally said. "Okay. Well, look—tell her I said hello, and I'm glad she's back, and . . . call me, okay?"

"Okay, b—" He'd nearly called Crockett *baby.* "Okay, guy." Daniel hung up the phone, a long breath escaping with a sound like a punctured tire. Crockett had to know something was wrong. How could he not know? Maggie had finally managed to lift her coffee mug to her lips, and seemed to take a sip of record-breaking duration, most of her face hidden in the mouth of the mug, her eyes peering down into her coffee. "Maggie," Daniel said softly.

"I don't want to talk to him, okay?" Maggie said into her mug.

"Oh, Maggie . . ." Daniel leaned back against the wall, bumping the back of his head—once by accident and then again on purpose. Maggie set her mug down on the table, perhaps a bit harder than necessary. "Please don't 'Oh Maggie' me, Daniel," she said calmly. "I just don't want to talk to him. I would think you could understand that."

"Yeah," Daniel said flatly, crossing his arms tightly over his chest. "So how long, Maggie?"

"How long what?" she said, looking down into her coffee.

"You don't want to talk to Crockett today? For a week? Forever? What?" He realized he was raising his voice.

"I don't know!" Suddenly, Maggie was shouting too. "I just don't know, all right?" She lowered her head down into her hands, and spoke to the tabletop. "I'm being a bitch. I know I'm being this terrible, awful bitch, but I just don't want to talk to him. I don't want to see him." She looked up. "I don't want him in this house."

"I see." Daniel's throat hurt.

"I'm sorry," Maggie said, her voice a dark whisper. "I know what you must think of me right now. I know you . . . care about him. But I'm your wife."

Daniel nodded slowly. "My wife," he said, but no sound came. He looked down at the floor as if he'd dropped something, then back at Maggie, whose facial flaws suddenly seemed grossly magnified. The minute protrusion of her lower jaw, the slight downward slant of her nose—features that Daniel had always looked upon as endearing imperfections—all at once made Maggie's face ugly, like a fairy-tale witch. Daniel blinked quickly, bringing Maggie's face back into proper focus. "I would not have believed you could be this way," he said, his voice just above a whisper.

"Do you think I *enjoy* being like this?" Maggie said, leaning forward against the table. "Do you suppose I like feeling this way?"

"I don't know," said Daniel. "Do you?"

"No," Maggie said, lowering her voice. "No, I don't. But I can't help how I feel."

"Maggie." Daniel approached the table, rested his fingers

along the top of it. He could hear a desperate whine creep into his voice. "Sweetheart, I know you're hurt. But how do you think Crockett's going to feel if you just—just cut him off like this?"

Maggie studied her coffee in silence for a moment, then said, "I just need a little time, that's all."

"Time?" Daniel shouted, slapping his palm against the tabletop. Maggie's head rocked back; she looked up at her husband, his eyes narrowed, lips pulled back in anger and frustration. "Dammit, Maggie, that's the one thing Crockett hasn't got. Where the hell is your mind, lady? We're talking about a guy who's *sick* here. He's got AIDS, remember? AIDS? He could die while we're all waiting for you to get your shit together."

Maggie made a swatting motion with her hand, as if there were a fly in the room. "Oh, he's got ARC, mister expert," she said. "Not AIDS. ARC! He may never get AIDS. He could bury us all."

Daniel stood silent, every muscle in his body tense, breathing like a long-distance runner. He could not properly answer Maggie's assertion: she knew so much more about the disease than he did, and was probably right. "Well, I'm certainly going to talk to him," he said finally. "And I'm going to see him. You might as well know that."

Maggie shrugged her shoulders, lifted her mug of coffee, and calmly said, "Suit yourself."

He didn't call Crockett until the next morning, from work: he hadn't wanted to call when Maggie might overhear.

"So," Crockett said, immediately following Daniel's hello, "she hates my fuckin' guts all of a sudden, is that it? Or is she afraid I'm gonna try to steal you away or what?"

"I don't know, buddy," Daniel said, suddenly very aware of not having shut his office door. "She just—I think we just have to give her some time, you know?"

"I know that," Crockett said. "I told *you* that. And it's not like I don't understand how she must feel. I'm not entirely without sensitivity. But fuck, Daniel: I haven't done anything to her."

"I know," Daniel said. He couldn't defend Maggie. He didn't want to try.

"Well, you know something else? I thought we were friends. You tell her that. And you tell her she's not the only person in the world who hurts."

"I tried, buddy," Daniel said. He didn't much like the position in which he found himself: standing in the middle of no-man's land in a war between his wife and his best friend.

"You did?" Crockett's voice softened a bit. "Well, maybe you should tell her again. I mean, I know she's hurt and I'm sure she's confused and I can understand things being a little strained between us for a while, but fuckin'-A, Daniel—"

"Crockett," Daniel said as quietly as he could and still hope to be heard, "she lost the baby."

A small silence before Crockett said, "What?"

"She miscarried, Friday night. So she's a little—a little bit sore. Literally and figuratively. Okay?"

"Oh, shit, Daniel. I'm so fuckin' sorry. I swear to God."

"Yeah," Daniel said. "Me, too." He swallowed, his throat feeling that soreness again, and said, "Look: I'll be in touch. We'll have lunch soon, okay?"

"Sure," Crockett said. "Talk to you."

Daniel had kept in touch. He had spoken with Crockett on the telephone at least once, usually twice, per week, checking in on his health and trading a little small talk—always calling from the office. Maggie had not so much as mentioned Crockett Miller's name in four weeks, while Daniel made a point of talking about him to Maggie.

"Had lunch with Crockett today," Daniel would say. "He's looking pretty good." And Maggie would stare at the television screen as if thoroughly engrossed in a beer commercial. Or simply say, "That's good," and then let it drop.

Maggie had been back nearly three weeks when Daniel said over dinner, "I talked to Crockett. He sends his love." Maggie did not look up from her plate, but she said, "Tell him I said hello."

Now it was November already, mid-November, and Daniel could feel the end of 1985 slipping through his fingers. There was homemade chili on the stove, cornbread in the oven, and Crockett was on television. He had never mentioned signing up for any experimental AIDS drug programs, so Daniel was almost as surprised to see Crockett on television as he would have been to look up and see himself on the seven o'clock news. He had been viewing the story carefully, as he had viewed and read everything that came to his attention about AIDS for several weeks, with the desire to hear and understand everything, as if his striving to learn everything he could about this thing that had attacked Crockett might, in and of itself, somehow help him—in the same way he liked to imagine his thousand-dollar pledge to AIDS Project Los Angeles was a direct contribution to Crockett's healing. He'd watched the woman doctor pressing a stethoscope here and there along a blond man's bare back, and it did occur to him that from the back, the man looked like Crockett; when suddenly there was Crockett himself (now with his shirt on), speaking soberly but calmly about the possibility of being dead within two years.

He looked toward Maggie again: her face told him nothing. What, he wondered, was she thinking? What was she feeling? He refused to believe she could see what they had both watched and remain totally unmoved. One of those talking teddy bear commercials came on, and Daniel reflexively pressed the mute button on the remote before having to hear that obnoxious little voice. Just as the screen went silent, Mag-

gie slid out from under Daniel's arm, got up from the sofa, and
went to the kitchen, all without a word. She emerged from the
kitchen after a few seconds and headed to the bedroom. She
came out knotting the belt on her gray coat.

"Sweetheart," Daniel said when he saw her, "if you're cold
we can turn up the heat."

"Honey," Maggie said, her face still calm but her hands
tugging nervously at the ends of her coat belt, "I've got to go
out for a little while. There's something I've got to do—get."

"Do? Get?" What's going on? he thought. "Did you forget
something for dinner?"

"I won't be long," she said, rocking quickly from foot to
foot. "I promise. The chili's ready, and I've taken the cornbread out"—she was walking toward the door—"so if you get
hungry, just go ahead without me."

Daniel stood up and called after her: "Maggie?" But she
was out the door. He could have chased and caught up with
her, but then it occurred to him where she might be going.
He sat back down and watched Brokaw read the bad news,
with the sound off.

She pushed the doorbell. Then pushed it again and waited,
shifting her weight from foot to foot. He had to be home: his
car was parked out front, and Maggie could faintly hear music
coming from inside the apartment. She knocked on the door,
then waited for half a minute or so before ringing the bell
again. Maybe he'd seen her car in the street from the window.
Maybe he'd seen her coming up the stairs and just wasn't
answering the door. She rang the bell one more time, resolv-
ing to herself to turn and go if Crockett didn't answer. When
she heard Crockett's voice, seemingly from across the apartment, yelling "All right, goddammit, I'm coming!" she felt
both an adrenaline rush and a reflexive smile. "Keep your
fuckin' shirt on," Crockett called, closer to the door now; and

then the doorknob turned just slightly from side to side with a fast click-click-click.

"Fuck, shit, tits!" Crockett said, then called, "Just a minute!" Maggie's heart was beating fast as the key turned in the upper deadbolt, and then the door was open, and there was Crockett in a light blue hooded sweatshirt and jeans, looking at her through the screen door as if she'd fallen to earth from another galaxy.

After a long, hollow moment, Maggie renewed her smile and said as casually as she could, "Hello."

"Hi," Crockett said, not smiling.

"I was beginning to wonder if you were home," Maggie said. "I saw your car, but then you didn't answer the door."

"I was on the phone." He didn't ask her in or ask why she'd come or how she was doing: he simply stood and looked at her.

"May I come in?" Maggie said.

He seemed to take a few moments deciding whether or not he would let her in, before pushing the screen door open. "Sure." He stood aside and allowed her in. The place was filled with the familiar tomato-spicy aroma of Crockett's lasagne; there was music playing on the stereo—Maggie didn't recognize the singer—and she could see Crockett's word processor on the dining table, the screen lit up and covered with glowing green print.

"You've been working," Maggie observed, fighting off the encroaching silence.

"Uh-huh." Crockett nodded, then stood looking at her with a disturbingly blank expression. "I'm very busy."

"Crockett," Maggie said, a little desperately, "do you suppose we could possibly sit down?"

He gestured toward the sofa. "Sure. Sit."

Maggie, still in her coat—her chances for an extended visit looking slimmer by the minute—tucked herself into one corner of the sofa; Crockett sat in the opposite corner. Maggie cleared her throat and shifted in her seat. "I've been kind of an asshole," she said.

Crockett nodded, his expression unchanged. "I won't argue that," he said.

Maggie closed her eyes and took a long, audible breath. "You're not going to make this easy for me, are you?" She had hardly expected a red carpet and a glass of champagne, but he obviously wasn't going to give her an inch.

Crockett seemed to be holding back a little smile as he said, "Fuck no."

"I'm sorry, Crockett," she said, turning back to him. "I really am."

"You're sorry," Crockett said, making a face of mock astonishment. "Well, well, well well well. Maggie says she's sorry, and now everything's all better, right?"

"Dammit, you know I don't think that!"

"Of course you do. You cut me off, honey. One of my closest friends, allegedly. You don't talk to me, you don't see me, you don't want Daniel to see me. And now Maggie's feeling better about life, so we can all kiss and make up. Plus, you undoubtedly caught me on the news awhile ago and you thought, 'Oh, shit, the boy's gonna die, better make my peace.' So you come sashaying over here with a mouthful of I'm Sorry, and now I'm supposed to say, 'That's okay, Mags, I fully understand why you've been a fuckin' bitch to me for four solid weeks. Give us a kiss.'" Crockett's studied cool had shattered completely by this point—he was almost shouting. "Well, let me tell you something, girlie: I'm Sorry is a song by Brenda Lee. It doesn't make it all better. It doesn't mean jack shit. I'm Sorry doesn't change a fuckin' thing."

Maggie felt as if she'd been slapped hard across the face, two or three times; and she felt as if she'd deserved to be slapped. She felt tears coming, and she blinked them back, tried to will them back. "I know that, Crockett," she said, nodding agreement. "I'm Sorry doesn't change a thing. But, dammit, it's all I have." She blinked double time, fighting the cool sting in her eyes, but the tears came anyway. She reached out tentatively toward Crockett, then pulled her arm back. She opened her purse and rummaged inside for a handkerchief or Kleenex, but found none, there or in either of her coat pockets. She pushed at her wet eyes and cheeks with her hands and coat-sleeves.

"Oh, fuck, Maggie," Crockett said, reaching into his jeans pocket, "don't cry. I'm not worth shit when women start crying." He pulled a handkerchief from his pocket and held it out to her. Maggie hesitated. Should she accept a handkerchief, even a much needed one, from a man who'd just treated her to a vigorous verbal slapping? "It's all right," he said. "It's clean." Maggie's nose was starting to run. She took the handkerchief, blotting her cheeks, then blowing her nose loudly.

"I *am* sorry," she insisted into the fisted handkerchief. "I'm sorry I keep saying I'm sorry." She sniffled into the hanky. "What do you want from me?"

Crockett shrugged. "I don't fuckin' know," he said. "It's just that—" He sucked a couple of quick, hiccuppy breaths. "You hurt me so bad, Maggie." Crockett's mouth trembled, he made a wet coughing noise and clapped his hands over his face.

"I know," Maggie wimpered behind the handkerchief. There was a painful lump in her throat and another one to match in the center of her chest. She felt utterly helpless: she was crying and Crockett was crying, and all she could think of was to say she was sorry again. She started to offer Crockett his handkerchief back, then thought better of it. She tucked her legs up under her and crawled the length of the sofa toward Crockett—shoes, coat, and all. She reached out and wrapped her arms around Crockett's shoulders, managing a clumsy sort of hug: he with his hands still in front of his face, sniffing audibly, Maggie crouched and curled around him. Crockett slid his arms out from between their two bodies and put his arms around Maggie, and they held one another tight.

"I'm so sorry, Crockett," Maggie said—it just slipped out.

"I—I'm sorry, too," Crockett rasped, stroking up and down Maggie's hunched-over back. They let go of each other after a few moments; Crockett pulled his legs up onto the sofa and sat cross-legged, facing Maggie: his face was wet and mottled. He blotted his eyes on the sleeve of his sweatshirt, then looked at Maggie and said, "Anybody ever tell you you look like shit when you've been crying?"

Maggie laughed a damp, percussive laugh. "*You* should talk!"

Crockett smiled, sniffed, smiled again. "I love you, Maggie," he said. "Dja know that?" Maggie shook her head. She hadn't known that, and it was good to hear: she'd wanted to be loved by him. "I didn't either," Crockett said. "Not till recently. I knew I liked you, of course; but it was just over the past few weeks that I realized I loved you. 'Cause only somebody you love could make you hurt so bad. You know?"

Maggie nodded. "I know."

"I didn't want to," Crockett said. "Love you. I didn't even want to like you."

"I know," Maggie said.

"What do you mean, 'I know'?" asked Crockett, cocking his head to one side.

"I mean, I remember when we first met," said Maggie with a smile. "You were a major-league bitch to me."

Crockett laughed. "Oh, God," he said. "I was, wasn't I?"

"You certainly were," Maggie said, slapping Crockett playfully on the shin. "I'll never forget it: you sashayed into the room with this Bette Davis puff-puff attitude, and you said, 'And *you* must be the little woman.'" Crockett attempted to stifle a laugh behind his hands. "And Daniel," Maggie said through a cascade of giggles, "Daniel looked like he wanted to die right there. Or maybe kill you, and *then* die."

"Well, you know," Crockett said, "Daniel had been avoiding me for weeks. That's how it went with us. I could always tell if he was between girlfriends, 'cause it was 'Hey, Crockett, wanna grab a bite? Hey, Crockett, wanna take in a movie?' But if he was seeing somebody he was halfway serious about, I didn't hear from him so much. So I'm thinking, All right— who *is* the bitch? So I just dropped in, unannounced, hoping to find out. And there you were."

"Well, the funny thing was," Maggie said, smiling as she remembered, "Daniel was forever talking about you. Crockett said this and Crockett cooks a terrific that. And I thought it was just fine that he had this gay friend: I mean, I certainly didn't want to marry some homophobic jerk. And at the same time, he didn't seem to be in any big hurry for me to meet you. I remember thinking, How *odd.* And then you showed up that night, with this *at*titude, and I just didn't know what to think. But I remember thinking, He's really cute. And *really* weird."

Crockett's head rolled back in a big laugh. "And I tried so hard not to like you," he said. "But I just couldn't. You were just so sweet and funny. And then you complimented my chest."

"Your chest?" Maggie said.

"Don't you remember?" Crockett asked, leaning forward and pressing her knee. "You asked me if I lifted weights. No"—he corrected with a shake of his head—"you said, 'You must lift trucks or something,' and I said, 'Small Toyota trucks.' "

Maggie nodded. "That's right," she said. "And then I said, 'If you don't mind my saying so, you have a very nice chest.' "

"And I'd been knocking myself out trying to build my chest up for just months and months. How could I not love you?

And of course, we liked all the same foods, and all the same movies, and all the same singers. It was like suddenly finding my long-lost twin sister." He reached over and stroked Maggie's leg. "I didn't want to lose you," he said. "Excuse me." He got up from the sofa and headed toward the bedroom.

Maggie lowered her feet to the floor, sitting back in the sofa. She could hear Crockett from the bedroom, blowing his nose, sounding like a broken toy trumpet; and when he came back into the room, he clutched a handkerchief in one hand. "I'm glad you came," he said, sitting down next to Maggie. "My earlier behavior notwithstanding." He put his hand on Maggie's and rubbed the back of her hand with his palm. He watched their hands instead of Maggie's face as he said, "I was sor—saddened—about the baby."

Maggie was surprised to still feel a little throb in her belly at the mention of the baby. "I—" she stammered, not really knowing what to say. "It broke my heart," she finally said. "Losing the baby." Crockett squeezed her hand. "I tried so hard not to let it show too much, because I knew it broke Daniel's heart, too. He really wanted that baby." She sighed from her very toes.

"I hope it's not too sore of a subject."

"Oh, it's sore enough," she said, then added quickly, "I'm kidding. It's all right. My doctor says there's no reason why I shouldn't be able to get pregnant again and carry it full term. It's just a matter of time."

He gave her hand another squeeze. "Good," he said. "And you and the big guy—you're all right?"

Maggie paused a moment, then nodded. "We're all right," she said. "Things were a little tense there for a while. In the bedroom and elsewhere. But Daniel, he was so patient with me. Even when I was . . ." Maggie smiled. "Even when I was less than my usual delightful self," she said. "I think we're going to make it." Then she asked, her voice suddenly dropping to a whisper, "How are you, Crockett?" Crockett moved his hand from hers, placing both his hands in his lap. "Pretty good today," he said. "I'm feeling pretty strong; I'm working. Some days are better than others."

"I worry about you," Maggie said. "Even when I wasn't talking to you, I was thinking about you."

"Well, like I said to that reporter the other day, I feel good. I'm taking care of myself. I'm doing some holistic treatments with this lovely black woman—you probably know her, in fact: she works at California Fitness. Theodosia Davis?"

"You're kidding. Theo?" Well, Maggie thought, isn't Miss Theodosia just *full* of surprises?

"Uh-huh. She's doing a holistic healing thing on me. She's got me meditating, gives me nutritional advice. I haven't eaten meat in"—he rolled his eyes upward as he thought—"three weeks? And now my doctor's got me into this thymus experiment."

"The TV thing?"

"Right. See, the thymus gland—here—" He palmed his chest at the sternum. "They think it has a lot to do with the immune system. And this experimental drug is supposed to stimulate the thymus and strengthen the immune system. So, I'm driving down to Long Beach every morning for my shot. Every day for six weeks, then twice a week for six more, and I don't even know if I'm getting the real drug or not. I might be in the control group that's getting a placebo. Can you imagine going through this kind of hassle, and I could be shooting up sugar water every day. Although, frankly, I don't think it's the placebo, cause it hurts my arm like a sonofabitch." He shrugged. "I donno."

"Do you think it's doing any good?"

"Donno. It's too early to tell. I'm just taking it all a day at a time."

"Sounds a lot like life," Maggie said. She hesitated before

bringing up what might have been a touchy subject: "You look like you've lost some more weight."

"Actually," Crockett said, "my weight has pretty well stabilized." He smiled a characteristically mischievous smile and said, "Judging from those cheeks of yours, I'd say you've put *on* a few L-B's."

Maggie couldn't help smiling. "I have, and fuck you very much for noticing."

Crockett made a surprised face. " 'Fuck you very much'? Miss Maggie uses the F-word? Does this signal the end of civilization as we know it?"

She gave him a playful slap on the thigh, and let her hand rest where it landed. "Leave me alone," she said. "I haven't gone *near* a gym since I quit my job. Actually, I haven't done much of anything since I quit my job. I watch television, I cook, I watch television, I eat. I watch television." Crockett laughed, and Maggie smiled in reply. "I've got to get up off my ever-widening buns and look for a job. Except I don't know *what* I want to do. I'd like to write," she said. A little laugh, and then, "Except I have no talent. I know I'd like to do something with some creativity to it." She shrugged. "Daniel's being an angel, no pressure at all. In the meantime, I've put on five pounds, all of it on my face and hips. And every day I tell myself I'm gonna get to work on it, tomorrow."

"And are you going to?" Crockett asked.

Maggie nodded. "Tomorrow," they said together, and shared a laugh. When they'd finished, neither of them spoke for a moment. Maggie touched Crockett's hand softly with her fingers. "Look," she said, not looking at Crockett's face, "I don't mean to make excuses for my behavior—"

"Don't," Crockett said.

"But, when I lost the baby," Maggie continued, "I just went a little crazy. I needed to blame somebody. For the baby, for . . . everything." She finally turned to face Crockett, whose expression she could not read. "And you were elected." Maggie shrugged. "I was angry and hurt and confused." She looked down into her lap. "And," she said slowly, "I was jealous."

"Jealous?" Crockett said. "Of?"

"I don't know if I can explain this without sounding ridiculous," Maggie said.

"Has the fear of being ridiculous ever stopped you before?" Crockett said with one of his naughty-boy grins. Maggie pinched him hard on the thigh and said, "Does this hurt?"

"Ow!" Crockett pulled his leg away. "Yes!"

"Good," said Maggie. "What I was going to say," she resumed, "was that—" She paused, then started again. "One good thing about all this sitting around the house is that I've had plenty of time to think. That's what I thought I was going to do at my mother's, but I didn't. I've started writing a journal, and that's helped. Something about putting my thoughts down on paper."

"I know," Crockett said, still rubbing his thigh where Maggie had pinched.

"It was while writing in my journal that it came to me—out of nowhere, really—that what really bothered me about you and Daniel wasn't so much that Daniel might run away with you or some other man and leave me to face my thirties alone. Or the possibility that you were still carrying on together right under my nose. You aren't, are you?"

Crockett rolled his eyes. "No, Maggie," he said softly.

Maggie did a big wiping-sweat-from-the-brow motion, then smiled fleetingly, before her face grew serious again. "What really bugs me, I've decided, is this: you were in love with Daniel." She began counting out on the fingers of her left hand. "Daniel was in love with you. Daniel is in love with me, and it is not inconceivable—under other circumstances, of course—that I might fall in love with you. I mean"—she looked away—"I'm attracted to you. But *you* could never fall in love with *me*. Because you're, as you yourself once put it, queer through and through. So," Maggie said, making a summing-up gesture, palms up, "I was jealous. Not just because of Daniel, but because of you. I felt left out." Maggie sat well back in the sofa.

"Wow," said Crockett, interrupting a long period of silence. "As love triangles go, this is a pip."

Maggie smiled, nodded. "Yep," she said.

Crockett clasped Maggie's fingers in his hand. "Mags," he began, when the telephone rang, inches from Maggie's elbow. She gestured toward the phone with a questioning look. "Please," Crockett said. Maggie picked up the receiver and handed it to Crockett.

"H'lo?" He listened a moment, then smiled. "Hey, buddy." He looked right at Maggie, still smiling. "Maggie who? Oh, *that* Maggie." Obviously, it was Daniel. Crockett affected a deep, anchorman voice: "It's seven thirty-seven P.M. Do you know where your wife is?" He held the receiver a few inches from his face and said, "Mags, are you here for a Daniel Sullivan?"

Maggie did a big, showy shrug. "Oh, I suppose so." Crockett handed over the receiver. "Hi, honey," she said into the phone.

"Hello, sweetheart," Daniel said. "You might have told me."

"I know. I'm not sure why I didn't. How'd you know?"

"I didn't know," he said. "I hoped. Is everything okay?"

"I think it will be," Maggie said, her eyes on Crockett, who smiled in her direction.

"Good. You coming home? While we're still young, I mean."

Maggie smiled: that sounded like something she might have said. "In a few minutes," she said. "Have you eaten?"

"No. I'll wait."

"Okay, hon. I'll be home soon." She hung up the phone and said, "Gotta go."

"It's good to see you," Crockett said.

"Good to see you." Maggie stood up and reknotted her coat belt. "Listen," she said, "we're having my mom over for Thanksgiving. Daniel's cooking the turkey. It's not a big to-do or anything, just us. Will you come?"

"Oh, I'd love to," Crockett said, "but I've already got a date."

"Oh." Maggie was disappointed, but she certainly couldn't have expected him to be sitting around less than two weeks before Thanksgiving, just waiting for her to call. "Well, soon then. Okay?"

"Soon," Crockett said. He walked her to the door, his hand at the small of her back. "You drive carefully, now. And give my love to that husband of yours. What was his name again?"

Maggie stopped at the door and faced Crockett; took both his hands in hers. "May I ask you an extremely personal, possibly embarrassing question?"

"God, who could refuse an opening like that?" he said. "Ask."

"Well," she started; then started again. "About what I was saying before—" What she wanted to ask, more than anything, was whether Crockett Miller had ever entertained the smallest erotic, romantic, sexual thought concerning her. Whether he had ever fantasized about her, ever awakened from a hot, moist dream starring Maggie Sullivan. And she wanted him to say yes, indeed he had.

"About what?" Crockett asked.

And then she couldn't ask, just couldn't quite bring herself to do it. After all, Crockett was a gay man: by definition, he liked men, not women. Still, if he said, "Don't be silly, Mags, I never think of women that way," or, worse yet, humored her, spared her feelings, said, "Sure I do, honey," while his big green eyes registered a white lie and some friendly pity, she'd likely come away with her feelings good and hurt. "Nothing," she said. "Never mind."

"All right then," Crockett said. "Maybe next time. Nothing I like better than an extremely personal, possibly embarrassing question." He held his arms open. "Hug?" They leaned into each other's arms, swayed together like slow dancers. "Love you," Maggie said. "Love you," Crockett answered.

When they parted, Crockett said, "Now go home. But for God's sake don't let Daniel see you before you've splashed some cold water on that face, maybe put some makeup on. You look like you've been mugged and severely beaten."

Maggie made a face. "You really know how to make a girl feel good."

Crockett smiled, shrugged. "It's a gift." He opened the front door, held open the screen. He slapped Maggie on the fanny as she passed—she could barely feel it through her coat. "See you later," he called after her as she started down the steps. She waved backward over her shoulder as she walked out to her car, feeling better than she had in weeks.

CHAPTER 19

CROCKETT SWITCHED OFF THE word processor: he'd done enough for one day. Besides, he was hungry—which he considered a good sign. It had shaped up into quite an evening: first a surprise phone call from

Harold Benjamin, whom Crockett had not seen in nearly a year (and even then only casually, at the Sullivans' last Christmas party), then a visit from Mrs. Sullivan herself. Amazing what a little TV exposure can do. Harold had probably called mere seconds after Crockett's appearance on the news. Crockett had had no desire whatever to watch himself on television—he knew what he looked like, and he remembered what he'd said—but had set the VCR to record the broadcast with the set switched off. He had been typing furiously, pages from the completion of *Sweet Seasons* and eager to finish, when the phone rang.

"Crockett? This is Harold Benjamin. Do you remember me?"

"Harold," Crockett said, "of course I remember you. What in the world possessed you to call?" he asked, though he had a pretty good idea what had possessed Harold.

"I just saw you on the news," he said. "God, kid, I'm so sorry."

Crockett was touched by the audible crack in Harold's voice, but he thought it best not to let things get too heavy: "Jesus fuck, Harold," he said, "I'm not dead yet." By the silence on the line, he assumed his joke had fallen flat. "Harold? You there?"

"How are you, Crockett?" Harold said finally, in the same careful, slightly hushed tone of voice in which Daniel had taken to saying "How *are* you, Crockett?"—as if he were some sort of bomb that could explode at any moment.

"I'm okay," Crockett said.

"No, really," Harold countered.

"Really, Harold. I feel pretty good today."

"I'm glad," Harold said. "I'm real glad to hear that."

"Good," Crockett said. "I'm glad you're glad." He yanked impatiently on the telephone cord. Harold's obvious concern was all very nice, but this conversation was taking a slow bus to nowhere.

"Could I see you?" Harold said. "Are you free for lunch tomorrow?"

"Lunch?" What was this all of a sudden? Take-a-sick-homo-to-lunch week? Was Harold perhaps hoping for long talks about the nature of life and mortality over cobb salads? "Sure, I guess. I'm fond of lunch."

"Good," Harold said. "Good. One o'clock all right?"

"Sure. My schedule's pretty flexible."

"Old World?"

"Sure."

"On second thought," Harold said, "how about The Cellar. Less likely to run into my co-workers there."

"Fine."

"Tomorrow then."

"'Kay."

Seeing Maggie had been almost as big a surprise as hearing from Harold. He had all but given up on their ever being friends again. He'd called Maggie every possible variation on *bitch* many times over in the process of working through his anger and hurt. He had fantasized countless scenes of Maggie crawling—sometimes literally crawling—back to him, begging forgiveness and pledging eternal love and friendship, and himself turning the coldest of shoulders, sneering, "Fuck you, bitch. Who needs you?" He had at least half-wanted to do just that when Maggie actually did come, and had made what he knew even at the time was a halfhearted, halfassed attempt at it. But he couldn't make it stick. It had been too good to see Maggie, he'd been too glad she finally had come, finally ready to try to be a friend again.

He wasn't quite sure why he had refused Maggie's invitation to Thanksgiving dinner, why he had told her he had a date when in fact he had planned to spend the entire day alone. He'd watch the Macy's Parade on television in the morning, *Miracle on 34th Street* in the afternoon, cook a turkey half-breast for dinner, maybe work on some writing if he had the energy. He had to admit it constituted a clumsy stab at spiting Maggie, who would definitely not be spending Thanksgiving by herself; but somehow he couldn't have her thinking that without her benevolence he would have nothing better to do on Turkey Day than sit home alone, even if that were the case. He lowered a good-sized square of pasta onto a plate, long rubbery bands of cheese stretching from the spatula to the pan.

He had half a mind to call and reinvite himself over to the Sullivans'. "No," he said aloud, and twirled several warm cheese ribbons around a finger and popped the cheesy fingertip into his mouth. He'd see them soon. It was going to be all right.

Harold looks good, Crockett thought to himself. Better than he'd looked in years. Maybe better than he ever had. Crockett had spotted him sitting on one of the benches in front of the City National Bank building, legs crossed at the knees, hands folded in his lap, looking as if he might have been daydreaming or meditating. He turned as Crockett approached, lifted his aviator shades off his nose, and flashed that big toothy grin of his. Harold stood up as Crockett came closer, and it was at that point that Crockett noticed just how good Harold looked. He looked trimmer, seemed to be losing that everpresent spare tire of his, and above his buttondown collar his usual almost-double chin—it had never been a full-on double chin, just almost—was gone, leaving his jawline sharper and more defined. He looked younger. As he neared Harold, Crockett hoped the weight loss had been intentional.

"Crockett." Harold clasped Crockett's right hand warmly. "It's good to see you."

"Nice to see you, too," Crockett said. He had always liked Harold Benjamin, ever since the acting workshop and *A Midsummer Night's Dream,* all those years ago. At that point, Crockett had been under the brief impression that Harold was interested in him romantically. But Harold had made no move, and then Crockett met Daniel, and that was that. "You look good," Crockett added.

"So do you," Harold said, still holding Crockett's hand in his.

"No, I meant you look really good," Crockett said. He hoped Harold wasn't going to try to bullshit him, like someone talking to an obviously decrepit old person, shouting, "You look good, Grammaw! You got good color!"

"So did I," Harold said, finally relinquishing Crockett's hand. "Let's have lunch."

"Would you guys like a cocktail?" the waitress asked, seconds after they had sat down. She was tall and blond, and pretty in that way so many girls in L.A. were pretty. The room was crowded with blue-suited executive types, and dimly lit— Crockett could just make out the print on the menu.

"Not for me," Crockett said, scanning the menu, which hadn't changed much since the last time he'd had lunch at The Cellar, three or four years before.

"No," Harold said. "Thank you."

"You ready to order, or would you like a few minutes?"

"I'm ready," Crockett said, lowering his menu. He looked across the small table to Harold, who gestured for him to go ahead. "I'll have the seafood omelette, please."

Harold handed his menu up to the waitress. "Tuna salad, hold the hard-boiled eggs, no dressing, please."

"You want hot fudge and chopped nuts on that?" the waitress said with a wry smile Crockett found refreshingly incongruous with her Malibu Barbie looks.

"Very cute," Harold said, trying not to smile. "Does the act include bringing us some bread?"

"I'll see what I can do," she said.

"Diet?" Crockett said when the waitress had gone.

"Yes," Harold said, "and I hate it. We can't"—he suddenly dropped his voice to a whisper—"*fuck* anymore"—he raised his voice back to normal conversational volume—"and now I've given up food. I lie in bed at night, wondering what's left to live for."

"I'm sure you manage to think of something."

Harold smiled tightly; nodded. "Yeah. I do."

"So what brought this on? The dieting, I mean."

"I got tired of being fat," Harold said with a shrug.

"Harold, you've never been fat. I mean, not *fat* fat." He had always thought of Harold as stocky, just one of those men built wide, with a relatively low center of gravity.

"I've been fat," Harold said, "and I *am* fat. But I'm working on it. I've joined a gym," he said, rather as if he were confessing that he'd recently joined the D.A.R. "Me! And I go there, three times a week. I lift *weights,* for crying out loud."

"Why now?" Crockett asked.

"At this relatively advanced age?" Harold said.

"If you like." Crockett smiled. That was at least part of what he'd meant by "Why now?"

Harold shrugged. "Tell you the truth, I don't really know why now. I mean, part of it is having reached this relatively advanced age and just wanting to look as good as I can. I'm still looking for Mr. Right, or something similar. Though not with nearly the kind of fervor I used to. Also, I've been doing some . . . public speaking recently. And I feel more comfortable talking in front of large groups of people, the better I think I look."

"Really? What kind of speaking?"

"I'm doing some work, sort of in conjunction with APLA–AIDS Project Los Angeles. Speaking to groups, about various things." He lowered his voice again. "Safe sex, mostly. Condoms."

"You're kidding." Crockett found it difficult to imagine Harold Benjamin talking to a bunch of strangers about rubbers.

"No, really." Harold leaned in, speaking very softly, barely holding back a grin. "I'm really quite entertaining, especially when I pull the rubber over my head."

"You what?" Crockett said through a little laugh.

"You heard right," Harold said. "We've found that the most frequent excuse men give for not wanting to use rubbers is that they're just not big enough. Rubbers, I mean. See, all these faggots are so incredibly well hung that a condom is just too tight. So, I take out this condom"—he pantomimed pulling a tiny packet from his suit pocket—"remove it from its wrapping, and roll it down over my head, down to my upper lip."

"And it stretches all the way over your head?" Crockett chuckled at the imagined picture of Harold with a condom over his head.

"The good ones do. Some of the cheaper ones don't. We do *not* recommend those brands. If I'm feeling particularly festive, I'll blow up the rubber while it's on my head, like Howie Mandel does with the rubber gloves, you know?"

"I think I'd like to see that," Crockett said.

"Someday," Harold said. "If you're good." He smiled. "How are you doing, kid?"

There was that tone of voice again: Crockett was still surprised by the strange succotash of appreciation and resentment people's concern brought out in him.

"I'm okay," he said quietly, "today."

"You're not in full-blown," Harold said, leaving out the word AIDS.

"No," Crockett said. "I'm still symptomatic of ARC. I haven't been hit by any of the big ones," he said, knocking on the tabletop. "Is this wood? Some days, today for instance, I can hardly believe I'm even sick. Other days, it's a lot easier to believe."

"I'm not even infected," Harold said, though Crockett had not asked, would not have asked.

"Oh?"

"I got tested," he said. "Soon as I found out about the test, I got it. And I'm not infected."

The waitress strode past the table, depositing a basket of French bread and foil-wrapped butter pats. "I'll have your order up in just a minute," she announced over her shoulder.

"It's crazy," Harold continued, talking down into the tabletop. "I fucked around as much as anybody in the old days." He looked up at Crockett and said, "I went to a funeral last week. A man I lived with for about a week and a half back in seventy-something. He was thirty-two years old. Hell, I'm thirty-six." Harold paused for a moment, then began again. "I've got a buddy in New York who says he's lost nine friends already. Nine. But Bill was my first."

"I'm sorry," Crockett said. He wasn't sure he understood why Harold was telling him this. Maybe he hadn't told anyone and had to tell somebody. Maybe he'd already told anyone who'd sit still long enough. Crockett considered letting it drop—who was he all of a sudden to start giving out free advice?—but decided there was little to lose. "Harold," he said, "do I detect just a trace of guilt here? For being healthy, I mean."

Harold seemed to stare a hole into him for a moment. His face seemed to register anger: Crockett wondered if he'd overstepped himself, but then Harold's expression softened. He averted his eyes, lowered his face before he said, "Yes. Well, no"—he looked back into Crockett's face—"not guilt exactly. Maybe a little. Mostly, though, I just feel like I should . . . give something back. That's why the APLA work. Part of the reason, anyway."

"Give something back to whom?" Crockett asked. "God? The Fates? Your friend Bill?"

"I don't know," Harold said softly, shaking his head. "I don't know."

"Is that why you called me? Is this part of your work?" Lunch was lunch, and Harold was a nice enough guy, but Crockett had no desire to be used as salve for anyone's misplaced guilt—even Harold Benjamin's—over being one of the worried well.

"No," Harold said emphatically. He reached across the table and put his hand over Crockett's, just long enough for Crockett to feel the soft warmth of Harold's palm; then he pulled it back again. "No," he repeated. "I wanted to see you. The television thing just gave me a good excuse to call." He lowered his voice again to say, "I like you. I always have. You know, it never worked between you and me the way I hoped it would."

"What never worked?" Crockett asked.

The waitress was back. "Plate's hot," she said, setting Crockett's omelette in front of him. "Seafood omelette," she said as if it were a complete thought. "And"—she set down Harold's salad—"tuna salad, hold the eggs, hold the dressing. Anything else?"

Harold said, "No, thank you." Crockett shook his head.

The waitress called "Enjoy" over her shoulder as she left.

"May I ask you something?" Harold asked as soon as the waitress was out of earshot. As Crockett was afraid might happen, he was obviously changing the subject. "If it's none of my goddamned business, just feel free to say so."

"Ask."

Harold leaned forward again, nearly sliding his red paisley necktie into his tuna salad. "Remember back when we did *Midsummer Night's Dream* together, back in seventy-eight?"

"Of course I remember," Crockett said. "That wasn't so tough."

"I seem to remember you had quite a crush on Daniel Sullivan."

"Still do. I seem to recall you had one of your own."

"Yeah," Harold said through a smile. "Still do." He looked up at Crockett and started to say something, but didn't. He looked off somewhere beyond Crockett's left shoulder as he spoke. "Had one on you, too," he said. "Did you know that?"

"I thought maybe you did," Crockett said. "At first. But you never—"

"I know. I wasn't too swift about it, was I? Then you met Daniel, and—"

"Yeah, I know."

"Did you and Daniel Sullivan ever . . . did you ever make it with him?" He sat back abruptly and picked up his fork, suddenly very interested in the salad, spearing a tomato wedge. "Look," he said, still softly but very quickly, "forget I asked that, it's none of my business, I'm sorry." He shoved the tomato into his mouth and chewed animatedly, staring down into his salad plate as if *Gone With the Wind* were being shown in it.

Crockett nearly let the question pass, changed the subject: he had, after all, never told anyone about himself and Daniel. Not during the run of *A Midsummer Night's Dream,* when he'd wanted to grab every cast member, every techie, every passerby on the street and say "I love Daniel Sullivan and he loves me." Not after it was over. Not nobody, not no-how. Finally, it was because he had never told anyone before that he decided to tell Harold. Harold was stabbing at a chunk of tuna meat, and making quite a project of it. "Harold," Crockett said.

"What?" Harold said, not looking up from his salad.

"Yes."

Harold dropped his fork, which fell with a clinking sound against the edge of his plate, and looked up.

"Really?"

"We were lovers," Crockett said, his voice unintentionally coming out a whisper. "We were . . . in love . . . Daniel and I." He felt a smile tug at his lips. He was surprised just how good it felt to say it out loud. He added, "For a while."

"Jesus," Harold whispered. "When? During the play?"

Crockett nodded. "And afterwards."

"Jesus," Harold said again. "I knew it. I knew it at the time. The way you two looked at each other. Is he gay?"

Crockett shook his head. "I don't think so," he said. "He really likes women. He's married to one, as you've probably noticed."

"Jeeeesus," Harold said.

"Harold." Crockett reached over and touched Harold tentatively on the back of the hand. "You have to promise you won't tell Daniel I told you. I've never told anyone else. Please." He'd been called a lot of things, but never a blabbermouth.

"I won't," Harold said. "I wouldn't."

"As far as I know, only Daniel and you and I know. And Maggie."

Harold's eyes seemed to expand in his face. "Maggie knows?"

"It's a long story," Crockett said. He certainly didn't want to get into all *that,* right there in the restaurant.

Harold sighed, and sort of laughed and said, "Jesus."

It occurred to Crockett that he'd left his food untouched. He made some halfhearted jabs at his omelette with a knife and fork.

After a few moments, Harold asked, "Why'd you do the TV thing?"

"Why not? My doctor recommended me for the experiment, and I was at the clinic when the news people came to do the story. They asked me if I'd mind being on camera, and I said no I didn't mind. And so I just . . . did it. No big deal. I haven't even seen the thing myself. I taped it. I don't know why, but I just didn't care to see it." He put his fork down: he wasn't sure he even wanted the omelette at all. "I saw one of the little ads they were running for it, though. I wasn't even watching, really. I was writing. I had the tube on for background noise. And I looked up, and suddenly there I was: Crockett Miller has AIDS—film at eleven. Well, seven, actually. It was very strange." He remembered thinking how young and small the man on television looked. How could this man be dying?

"Anyway," Crockett continued, picking up his fork again, ready to make another try at the omelette, "it's not as if I have to worry about embarrassing my family or anything. As you may or may not recall, I have no family."

Harold shrugged. "Family is where you find it," he said, not even looking up.

Crockett smiled. "So I've heard," he said. He drove his fork into the omelette, cut off a good-sized piece of it, and managed to get it into his mouth. It tasted good, if a little cool.

"May I ask you another personal question?" Harold said, poking rhythmically into his salad.

"What the fuck?" Crockett said. "You're on a roll here."

"Seriously," Harold said.

"All right," Crockett said, setting his fork down carefully on the edge of his plate. "Seriously."

"Are you scared?"

"Of dying, you mean?"

"We can start with that," Harold said.

"I'm not afraid of death," Crockett said. "I mean, as far as I can tell, that's just nonexistence. I don't think the human mind is truly capable of grasping its own nonexistence—mine isn't, anyway. So I can't really be afraid of that. What I *am* afraid of is being sick. And being sick, alone. I mean, there's a good chance that sooner or later, I could get sick. Really sick. And when—if that happens, who's going to take care of me? You know?"

Crockett decided it was definitely time to pay some attention to his food. He looked down and took a good look at it. This wasn't something he particularly enjoyed talking about. If he'd known lunch with Harold Benjamin was going to entail discussing his deepest fears over a plate of rapidly cooling eggs, he might have stayed home with a peanut butter sandwich. He resolved to make one last go of the omelette. He picked up the fork and aimed it at the yellow crescent on the plate. He looked up quickly at the touch of Harold's fingers on his own.

Harold's hand, big and warm, cushioned like an old leather chair, curled around his own, and held it. Harold's eyes were warm as well, looking into Crockett's.

"I will," Harold said.

The little red light on the answering machine was blinking when he got home. He punched the button, then switched on the word processor while waiting for the rewind. He would likely finish *Sweet Seasons* before dinnertime, and he was eager to type the words "The End." He'd been so afraid he might never finish it, might never be able to even make a good start on any real writing; but for now things weren't looking quite as grim as that.

Beep. "What do you mean you have a date?" Daniel's voice. Crockett smiled at the sound of it. "Break it. Tell him you're not feeling up to it. Tell him you've decided to go straight. Bring the stud with you if you must, but you *be* here on Turkey Day, mister. About two. We both love you very much, but don't let that sway you."

Beep. "Hello? Is anybody there?" It caught him so off guard he nearly lost his balance. He hadn't heard her voice in years, yet he recognized it before she'd uttered four words. "Crockett," she said, "this is Agnes, your . . . your mom." A short pause, and then she said, "Lord, I hate these machines, I never know what to say. I don't know how long I have, so maybe I ought to hurry up." Crockett felt his throat swell. He leaned hard against the wall and wrapped his arms over his chest, hugging himself.

"A friend of yours called," she continued, "some weeks back." Daniel? he thought. Of course: who else? Crockett didn't know how he felt about that. He'd have to think about it later. "He told me about . . . he told me you weren't well, and . . . well, then we saw you on the television, your dad and me, and . . . I wanted you to know that I, I hope you have a good Thanksgiving, and that you'll . . ." There was a moment of quiet, just tape hiss; then Agnes said, "Lord, it's been so long." An audible breath, or maybe just something in the telephone line. "You can call if you want. I hope you're getting this, I probably ran out of tape a long time ago. I want you to know that we, I . . . I pray for you every day." Empty air, and then the dull percussion of hanging up.

The machine made the funny little *Star Wars* noise it made when it finished playing, and then began to rewind again. Crockett stood hugging himself, hearing if not exactly listening to the soft whir of the microcassette, allowing the tears to fall down his face and off his chin, dampening his shirt collar. The sound of Agnes's voice had brought childhood memories of this woman he'd called Mom for so many years tumbling over one another in his mind. The way she'd looked just back from the beauty shop, her hair in tight, waxy-looking curls around her head. The softness of her hands applying Bactine and a Band-Aid to his skinned knee, and the softness of her lips as she kissed the wound, making it all better. The sweet, cinnamon-heavy smell of her tiny mobile-home kitchen at Christmas time. For a few sweet-and-sour moments, he had not heard the voice of the woman who had called him pervert and abomination, but the woman who had called him Baby.

Crockett sniffed, then tugged out his handkerchief and blew his nose, wetly and noisily. "Well," he said aloud, dabbing at his damp face with the hanky, "that's about enough of that." He went to the bathroom to wash his face. He stared at himself in the bathroom mirror: his face was red, his eyes puffy. He looked like shit when he cried. He'd call the Sullivans right away. There was no good reason not to have Thanksgiving with them. Then he'd finish the goddamned romance, maybe even get it into the mail on Friday. He'd have Roz Shapiro and Cameo Romances off his back—for a while, anyway—and then, in a week or so, he'd get a good start on his real novel.

Maybe he'd call Agnes, sometime. Maybe not. He'd have to think about it. For the moment, he had work to do.